KT-162-829

CHRIS BECKETT

TOMORROW

~~OUR LOST ATLANTIS~~
~~HERE AND THERE~~
~~THE CAPTIVE GOD~~
~~THE DISTANT TOWER~~

CORVUS

Published in hardback in Great Britain in 2021 by Corvus, an imprint of Atlantic Books Ltd.

This paperback published in 2022.

Copyright © Chris Beckett, 2021

The moral right of Chris Beckett to be identified as the author of this work has been asserted by him in accordance with the Copyright, Designs and Patents Act of 1988.

All rights reserved. No part of this publication may be reproduced, stored in a retrieval system, or transmitted in any form or by any means, electronic, mechanical, photocopying, recording, or otherwise, without the prior permission of both the copyright owner and the above publisher of this book.

This novel is entirely a work of fiction. The names, characters and incidents portrayed in it are the work of the author's imagination. Any resemblance to actual persons, living or dead, events or localities, is entirely coincidental.

10 9 8 7 6 5 4 3 2 1

A CIP catalogue record for this book is available from the British Library.

Paperback ISBN: 978 1 78649 937 0
E-book ISBN: 978 1 78649 936 3

Printed and bound in Great Britain

Corvus
An imprint of Atlantic Books Ltd
Ormond House
26–27 Boswell Street
London
WC1N 3JZ

www.corvus-books.co.uk

For Maggie.

1 THE RIVER

Tomorrow I'm going to begin my novel. That's what I came here for. That's why I gave up my job and my apartment in the city. I was going to make up a story. There were going to be lots of imaginary people in it, and a beautiful wide green river – this river that's in front of me now, with its soft, cool, almost oily skin – and people would come in boats, like new cards dealt from a pack. It was going to be . . . But why am I saying 'was'? It *is* going to be like life, a microcosm of life, but more alive than actual life, so that people can read it and think to themselves, 'Of course, *this* is what life really is, and how wonderful this author must be to be able to see all that and communicate it to us.'

Tomorrow, then. Or if not tomorrow, then next week or, at the very latest, before the end of the month. I ought to get on with it, if only to avoid looking foolish when I return to the city empty-handed, but I have to admit that right now I find it hard to care about the opinion of my family and friends.

That's for another me to deal with. (The barriers we build between our present and future selves are important, I feel, just like the barriers we build between ourselves and others. Infinite empathy would be as bleak as no empathy at all.) And as to those imagined readers who are going to admire me . . . well . . . the truth is, isn't it, that I'm a fraud? What do *I* know about what life really is? What purpose is served by seeking the endorsement of people who don't know me, for an idea of myself that I know to be unreal?

But still. Tomorrow. Or next week, or certainly the week after, I'll make a start.

As the afternoon begins to cool and the swallows start to hunt over the water, I like to take a dip. It invigorates me. On my second day here I swam across to the opposite bank but the river is nearly half a kilometre wide, the current is challenging out in the middle and there were a few minutes there on the way back where I felt I'd lost control. So this evening I swim upriver. I watch the swallows on the way out and the bats in the dusk as the current carries me back. I turn round at a spot where a side channel flows in from a hot spring and there's a warm and steamy patch in the water.

When I return, I haul myself out by the big tree that grows right next to the cabin. Its leaves are the size of dinner plates, and its roots divide and divide again until they become strands as fine as human hair, bright red in colour, and spread out in the water to feed. I take a bottle of beer from the plastic crate I keep suspended in the river and sit on my veranda to watch the yellow moon as it rises from behind the trees on the far bank.

I have spent many hours on that veranda with its pleasant smell of river and sun-warmed wood. In fact, I've sometimes passed entire days there, just watching the water go by, the little dents and gradations on its surface, the bits of branch that drift down, the birds that cross from one side to the other, carrying nest materials or food. A few times a day, local people pass in their small boats, staring in at me, waiting for me to greet them before allowing themselves to wave or smile. Sometimes I smoke some weed – there's a plentiful supply in the overgrown plot behind my cabin – and from time to time I drink a beer, but most of the time I'm happy just to sit.

Because I *do* feel alive. This *is* what life is really like. This is what I so badly wanted to experience, even just in that extraordinarily remote, vicarious and fetishistic kind of way that consists of evoking it in my novel and then being told by others that I have created a vivid world for them. So why would I want to turn away from experiencing it directly, in order to stare at a white page and try to cover it with heavy, clumsy words? I imagine some gaunt starving man – why a man, though, and not a woman? – I imagine some gaunt starving woman laboriously writing out a fantasy for other people about a feast that would satisfy her hunger and theirs, while ignoring the large and delicious meal that's been laid out right in front of her.

That image makes me laugh.

There is no road to my wooden cabin. In these parts the river is the road. Today, Friday, as I do every Friday, I start up the outboard motor on my little boat and set off on the twelve-kilometre trip downriver to the modest-sized provincial seat. There's a kind of beach there where you can drag your boat out of the water. A tough-looking woman called Dido presides over the place with her three sons. She has one blind eye like a boiled egg. The other eye darts about, ensuring that nothing, however small, happens on her beach without her consent. She and her boys will watch over your boat for you for a small fee. I bought mine from her when I first arrived, fresh off the plane, unloading my cases and my box of provisions from the taxi, looking forward to seeing, for the very first time, my writing retreat up the river.

The town's main business is the onward shipment of products from the surrounding forest: latex, timber and certain minerals. Just downstream from Dido's beach the river turns sharply right to head east towards the sea, and there are docks with cranes to load and unload the barges that come up from the coast. The town has four banks, a produce market, a supermarket of sorts and (surprisingly) a fine, if modest-sized, cathedral in the Manueline style that would grace a much larger and more important city, and which makes me think, when I go inside, of a kind of coral, as if all of these elaborate columns and arches were the secretions of some sort of highly specialized polyp whose particular characteristic is that it quite naturally forms representations of . . . well . . . of something I vaguely feel I remember, as if from another life, or from that early period of childhood that everyone says they can't recall. (I think myself the truth is quite the opposite: we remember our experience of that time *so* well and *so* thoroughly that we just don't recognize it as a memory at all, but rather as the surface on to which all our subsequent experience is projected.)

A few streets from the cathedral there is a rather pleasant colonnaded promenade built more than two centuries later in the same pinkish, coral-like stone. Arranged in an elongated circuit like a Roman hippodrome, around a row of five fountains, the promenade was bequeathed to the city by a rubber millionaire who, having made himself rich by forcing indentured labourers to harvest latex for him for almost no pay at all, wished in his later years to be thought of as a good man, and so, along with a hospital and an orphanage, built this central meeting place that brings the whole town together. Some are inclined to sneer at the motives of a man like that. I am more cautious. We're all hypocrites. A common way of dealing with that is to loudly denounce the hypocrisy of others to distract attention from one's own, but isn't that hypocrisy squared?

In the middle of the central fountain stands a twice life-sized statue, not of the rubber millionaire, but of his friend, hunting partner and hero, the novelist Mago Barca, wearing what purports to be 'Carthaginian' armour, and staring boldly into the distance. The inscription below it comes from his novel, *Atlantis Rises*:

The Upper River is our nation's heart.
Master it, and we will master the world.

Large numbers of townspeople like to parade around this promenade in the cool of the evening wearing their best clothes. Others sit outside cafés watching them while small bats swoop and dive around the streetlamps. I have a friend called Amanda I sometimes meet here – we have a drink together, spend the night in her small apartment just up the road and return to the promenade in the morning to have breakfast in our favourite café – but today I buy what I need and, stopping only for a coffee and a pastry, return upriver at the end of the afternoon.

It's dark by the time I get back, but I keep a small blue light on the veranda to guide me to my mooring, its battery charged by sunlight during the day. When, after travelling for some while among dark, silent trees, I see it on the right-hand bank in the distance, a kind of happiness rises inside my heart that I feel I never experienced before I came here. This is what it feels like to come home.

It's only in the middle of the night that I worry about the precarity of my situation. Sometimes – and this was particularly the case in the first week or two – the thought that haunts me is that I'm all alone, and that at any point robbers, or guerrillas from any one of the dozen ragtag armies of the insurrection, or just impoverished locals with every reason to resent someone who has enough spare cash to take six months away from work, could arrive and do what they wanted with me. I lie and listen to the creaks and groans of my wooden cabin and the sound of the water, imagining small changes and odd silences, and piecing these together into very precise and specific images of enemies creeping towards me.

These days what haunts me more often when I wake at 2 a.m. is the thought that soon I'll have spent all my money, and then my time by the river will be over, and I'll have to return to the city and my old life, having not only failed to do anything constructive about building a new one, but having blown all the savings that I set aside for that purpose – and all of this will just be a small and shrinking memory, which, after a time, I will have to stop talking about to avoid boring people, but which I will idealize and fetishize for the rest of my life until nothing of the real experience is left, only a sense of a door, now beyond my reach, that I could have opened once but didn't. I'm already thirty-four, after all.

I can sometimes lie awake like this for several hours, appalled by my own lack of responsibility, yet in the morning

I shrug it all off without the slightest effort. For surely the matter is quite straightforward. If you have a choice between writing a novel and being a character in a novel, you've got to choose the latter, havent you?

A character in a novel. That's exactly what I feel like. Smiling to myself, I make a pot of coffee and carry it out to the veranda.

When she brings me my slops in the morning, Guinevere squats down beside my cage, her machine gun across her knees, and clears her throat. 'So, are you keeping well?' she asks gruffly.

It strikes me that, in spite of herself, she likes me, or at least finds my company more diverting than the very limited alternatives. (The truth is that my captors are almost as much prisoners as I am, forced to hide away underground in order to avoid detection by government helicopters. The only difference is, I am confined to a cage, and they have the slightly larger area of the cave floor in which to move.)

Yes, Guinevere likes me. She wouldn't admit it, even to herself, but she finds my company more congenial than that of her comrades. We certainly have more in common than either of us has with any of them. She talks, as I do, with the unmistakable accent of the educated professional classes of the capital. The rest of them are unschooled peasants, fighting not for a principle but for themselves.

'So you came upriver to find yourself and write a novel.'

'That was the plan.'

'How very middle class.'

'What do you mean by that?'

'This whole "find yourself" thing, this idea that there is something virtuous about expending surplus wealth on something so self-centred and indulgent. And then writing a book, no doubt celebrating that same self-indulgence for the benefit of others, while secretly hoping it will be a bestseller – you'll deny this, but I bet you were – so you can get rich and be famous and live even more comfortably on the back of a book about giving up comfort and wealth for the "authentic life". She offered those last two words as if with tweezers. 'That's the middle classes all over. You not only have to be more comfortable than ninety-five per cent of the people on Earth, you have to be self-righteous about it, too.'

I shrug. 'Whatever you say. I'm the one in the cage. You're the one with the gun.'

The cage is lined with chicken wire, nailed to a wooden frame. I can just stand up in it, though my head touches the wire above me, and I can just lie down. They've given me an old mattress, a blanket, a plastic bucket and a tin mug. Once or twice a day, they let me out to walk up and down the cave under supervision. There's no daylight, obviously. We're deep underground, and the only light comes from the gas lamp they keep burning all the time about ten metres away from me in the direction of the cave mouth, surrounded by their sleeping bags and cooking things. But I can tell when it's evening because the bats wake up further down the cave and come rustling by a few metres above my head as they set off for the world outside. A few hours later they return. About then my captors settle down and fall silent, except for the periodic changing of the guard at the cave mouth.

'You can say what you like to me,' Guinevere says. 'You know that perfectly well.'

'Okay, I will. I think you're every bit as middle class and self-indulgent as I am.'

As I intended, this riles her – it's the one bit of power I still have – but she doesn't want to show it. In the gaslight that comes from further up the cave, I can see the struggle in her face.

'Oh?' she says, with careful indifference. 'So how do you work that out? I've given up my family, my career, my rights as a free citizen, all for the struggle.'

'It must feel amazing to know that you are completely free of responsibility for any of the evils of the world.'

She studies my face through the chicken wire and, after several seconds – I can see the moment when it happens – she makes a decision to ignore my sarcasm. 'It feels good to be fighting for a better tomorrow, yes. You should try it sometime.'

'But can't you see that "fighting for a better tomorrow" is a performance for your own benefit, no more and no less than my "finding myself"? Your little group won't change the world. Come on, you know that. You must know that! Name me one guerrilla group like yours that didn't in the long run either disappear or become a criminal gang, or, in very rare cases, make itself into the government and sink into tyranny and corruption, like every other government.'

'Try saying that to Carlo.'

Carlo was the leader of their little group.

'Of course I wouldn't say it to Carlo. He'd get angry, and he might have me taken out and beaten.'

'Carlo has every reason to be angry. His family were thrown off their smallholding and left to starve. His father was killed by the police. He had to—'

'He had to look after his own younger siblings from the age of nine, and they had to pick up garbage in order to eat. Et cetera, et cetera. I know all that. He's told me at length, as if he was presenting his credentials, the proof that everything he says must be right and everything I say must be wrong, since I've never experienced poverty in my life, and the worst violence I've ever encountered up until now was when I was nine years old and a little boy called Roy, who was having problems at home, came up and punched me in the face.'

'The powerless see things that the powerful have the luxury of looking away from.'

'And yet Carlo wants power. I dare say if he's lucky he'll find a niche for himself. As a drug baron maybe. Or the ruler of his own little tinpot state. The absolute dictator of the People's Democratic Republic of the Upper River. I can just about imagine that. He'd have his own little harem of young girls from the villages that pay him tribute, his own little corrugated-iron throne room, young Jaco there as Minister of Defence on one side of him looking pretty in a fancy uniform, and shouty Rubia on the other as Minister of Foreign Affairs. That's what he wants, really, isn't it? Not a new tomorrow, just the power over others that he longed to have when he was small and helpless, and others had power over him.'

Guinevere regards me with an expression meant to indicate pity. 'You're very defended against the idea that it's possible to make the world a better place.'

But then Carlo growls something from over where the rest of them gather round their hissing lantern, and she moves away.

Next week I'll get down to it. There's plenty of time. It's not as if I'm short of material. All kinds of themes pass through my mind as I sit and watch the water, and many different settings suggest themselves: a coastal town far to the south, where the days are short in the winter and the clifftops are high and bare; a small city apartment whose sole dying tenant alternates between dreams from the past and present pain; a dark cave . . . I just don't feel ready to pick, from all these riches, the mere handful of items that I could make something with, and place them on an anvil, and beat them out of their natural shape in order to work them into the artificial form that we call a story. It would mean throwing away so much. You dream of building a mighty palace with towers and halls and courtyards, and you end up with a modest shed. I need to take my time with it, or I will be hamstrung by my own disappointment about everything I'm having to let go.

I have the same problem with life, to be perfectly honest. I find it hard to decide who to be.

I set off for a long midday swim and this time I explore that side channel upriver that comes down from a hot spring. Reeds and lilies rise from the bottom of the almost bath-warm water in which small, iridescent fish dart back and forth between green stems cross-hatched with sunlight. The trees on either bank frequently touch one another overhead to create the effect of a tunnel, along which small flying creatures hurry back and forth, gracefully dodging the vines and dangling roots that gorge themselves on the mineral-rich stream. It's hard work swimming upstream in warm water, so sometimes, when the water is very shallow, I stand up and wade. I suppose at some point it may become too hot to swim in, or too overgrown.

I reach a small lake. There is something primeval about it, surrounded by banks of primitive-looking white flowers and trees with huge flat leaves. Passing just a few metres away from me, a large pale creature sticks its smooth head from the water, exhales loudly and disappears again. At the far end of the lake a woman stands up to see what the noise was. Very tall, slim and athletic-looking, with a loose, somehow masculine way of standing, she's been sunning herself on the bank and is wearing a one-piece swimming costume. She spots me at about the same time as I spot her.

'Hello there,' I call out. 'I'm sorry to disturb your peace.'

'Hi. No worries.'

She relaxes, reassured, I dare say, by my accent being the same as hers. I certainly would have been in her place. Is it very prejudiced of me that I would be more frightened of a local person in such a context than I would of an educated person like myself from one of the coastal cities? I don't know. At least in part, it would simply be that I have more idea what to expect from my own kind. I sometimes visit the local village, two kilometres downstream from my cabin, and I like the people there. I like their friendliness. I like the way their kids are free to run about and have fun. I like their style and their capacity for just sitting and watching life go by in front of them. And of course, we descendants of settlers, or at least the more 'advanced' among us, now that our centuries-old conquest of the original inhabitants of our continent is secure and irreversible, and now that we ourselves no longer have other homelands to which we might notionally 'return', like to express reverence for the indigenous people of our country, their wisdom, their way of living in balance with nature, though in fact they're very alien to us and do things of which we'd strongly disapprove in any other context. For instance, they are extravagantly religious – on Good Friday, some of their young bloods simultaneously show off their manliness and their piety by having themselves crucified with real nails – they believe in witches, they preserve gender roles of a very old-fashioned kind, they set wire traps for animals which we'd deplore as barbaric if it were done by anyone but them, and they decorate their little huts, alongside lurid religious pictures, with magazine photographs of precisely the kind of trashy 'celebrities' that people like me deplore, though when I see the cut-out pictures through the open doors of the huts in my local village, I make an exception in their case and interpret these pin-ups as colourful examples of the inventive way in which these folk have taken things from 'our' world and repurposed them for their own.

She tells me her name – Amanda. I tell her mine. She has a cheerful, mobile face and a gruff, merry voice. I gather she's been working as a teacher for the past six months in a poor part of the provincial capital that has a high percentage of indigenous children. She had one of Dido's sons bring her up here in a boat, having read about the hot stream in a guidebook. He'll come back for her later.

'You hope,' I say, laughing.

She shrugs. 'He'll come. He doesn't get his money otherwise.'

We begin to talk. We learn that, back in the capital city, we lived in apartments separated by less than a kilometre, and that we have several acquaintances in common. We discover that her mother, like my father, was a distinguished academic – a sociologist, in fact – sufficiently eminent for me to have heard of her. (Amanda has heard of my dad, of course. Every educated person with a television has heard of him.) We are just beginning to find out also that we hold similar views on the government (it's terrible, it's *beyond* terrible, it's positively *embarrassing*!), politics (liberal-leftish), religion (firmly atheist), the insurrection (quite understandable in the circumstances, even if misguided), when, somewhat boldly, I place one finger on her lips and another on mine to make this chatter stop.

'Let's not bring the city here,' I say. 'Doesn't that defeat the point of coming so far? Let's leave all that behind. Look at those giant lilies over there, listen to the quietness. We could be in Eden.'

'You're very brave, living out here by yourself,' she says, after several seconds of silence. She herself lives near the cathedral in that town down the river, in the same street as the supermarket, in an apartment with electric power and running water, and connected to the internet so that she can keep in touch daily with her friends and family. 'I'm not sure I—'

I actually think *she's* very brave standing in front of a class of children every day, but discussing that would take us back to city-type chatter. 'Shhh,' I tell her. 'Look at the lake. Look how clear the water is, look how the trees enfold it and shield it. Nothing ever happens here. Not what the city would call "happening". Isn't that amazing? Really and truly, isn't this how you imagine Eden?'

She laughs and glances slyly at me. 'We should really be naked then, shouldn't we?'

'I suppose so.' A little thrown, I smile as if I thought she didn't really mean this. The idea *is* appealing, but it feels too complicated and ambiguous for me to want to pursue it.

'I'm not completely undefended,' I admit after a few seconds. 'I do have a gun back in my place. I take it out on to the veranda sometimes, so the local folk can see it when they're passing in their boats. I want word to get out that I have the means to protect myself.'

'Wow!' She is simultaneously shocked and impressed. 'Do you know how to use it?'

'My mother taught me. She used to shoot competitively at school. One of those posh girls' boarding schools, you know. They played lacrosse as well. They all had crushes on their PE teacher. Let's go further upstream. Perhaps we can find the source.'

And we half-swim, half-wade, until we reach a waterfall. She tells me that there's a small community somewhere up on the higher ground above this waterfall, the followers of a charismatic spiritual leader.

'Oh yes, I've heard of them. They come from the Northern Countries, right?'

'That's it. Apparently they possess the Holy Grail.'

She laughs at this preposterous claim – she has a warm and rather delightful chuckle – and so I laugh too, though I actually find it rather fascinating.

*

There are times when I come to and realize that my dreams are just dreams and that in fact I'm lying in a bed, three storeys above the ground, with many kilometres of concrete and stone all around me. There is a deep stillness here. I don't mean silence, for I can always hear the traffic in the wide and busy street below me – the impatient horns, the growl and rumble of trucks – and every three minutes, like an electric drill being forced through the dome of the sky, a jet plane passes overhead. But all that's taking place in another world where it's already tomorrow, and has nothing whatever to do with me or my apartment. A fly buzzing against the windowpane is an event in here; a drip falling into a coffee cup from the kitchen tap is a noteworthy occasion, like a voice crying out in a forest to remind you that you are not the only being in this world.

I have a frame I can use for walking, a commode and rails on some of the walls to help me move about. But I keep that to a minimum, since sitting up is a major exercise requiring several minutes of planning, preparation and internal pep talks between my brain and my limbs (as in, 'Come on now, legs, we can do this if we all pull together, we just need to believe in ourself . . .'). There are several women, most of them foreign, who take it in turns to come in the morning, the middle of the day and the evening to clean me up, leave me food and help me do whatever else I need to do, so I tend just to wait for them. I can tell when it's nearly time for the next visit because, about half an hour before, the pain starts to build up until, by the time they actually arrive, the ugly clamour of it is pretty much drowning out everything else, and I feel as if I'm trapped in a tiny prison cell, with walls of stone closing in. It's horrible if they're late for some reason, one of those things that is unbearable and yet must be borne. But when they do get here, the medicine they give me sorts everything out again almost instantly. It also makes me drowsy. As soon as they've gone I dive down gratefully into dreams and memories, like a fish released from a cruel hook back into the life-giving water.

There are places, deep down in the past, that are warm and safe. We had a big garden, for instance, around the house I grew up in, maintained for us by an indigenous man my parents were rather proud of, who we called Uncle Hector. Our house sat on the edge of the ridge above the city, and the garden was in two parts: the flat part on the top of the ridge, and the part that sloped down from the ridge towards the city. The flat side was artfully divided up by shrubs, flower beds, a pond and a little grove of ornamental bamboo, into several small, intimate lawns where you felt wonderfully cut off from the rest of the garden, never mind the house and the outside world. The sloping side, laid out by the same rather well-known designer, had a small spring, from which a stream wound back and forth across the steep gradient until it disappeared through a hole in the fence at the bottom. The stream passed among outcrops of rock and ferns and trees, which Uncle Hector kept to a manageable size, and there were huge brilliantly coloured flowers that were almost pornographic in the flagrant showiness of the invitation they offered to their pollinators, along with enormous white lilies with a strange bitter scent, and giant arum flowers with a purple spike surrounded by a sheath of green. At one point the stream divided for a stretch to create a tiny island, which, to me, was the most enchanted place of all, covered in large, velvety, deep red flowers.

I still remember the dangerous lusciousness of that red. How mysterious colour seemed back then – not just that particular red, but any colour, the more intense the better. I suppose when you've only been in existence a few years, you're still getting used to things like colour, you're still wondering what they really are. Now I'm back on the edge of existence again, I feel a certain connection with that state of mind.

I remember saying to Dad one day when I was still very small that I wished I could see a colour that wasn't red or blue or yellow or green, but another colour entirely. He said he was pretty sure that the people who made paints must have thought by now of every possible mixture. I told him I didn't mean a mixture like purple or orange, but an entirely new colour, as different from all the others as red is from green or from blue. He just laughed and said that was impossible because of wavelengths and rods and cones and so on, and drew one of his helpful diagrams, as if this was one of his popular-science programmes on TV. All of which was instructive, but I still felt that he'd refused to see the real point of what I was trying to say. Which was not very imaginative of him, actually, since some animals can see ultraviolet, and presumably they see it as something distinct from any other colour. But of course we'll never know what it looks like to them, and to my father this meant there was no point in even wondering about it. He could never see the point of questions that couldn't be answered, just as my mother couldn't see the point of things that served no useful purpose.

I'd still like to see that new colour, though. It would be like being born again and seeing, for the very first time, the deep, deep red of the flowers on my little island.

'So how is our hostage?' Carlo says.

I have been lying on my mattress, eyes closed and half-asleep, trying to find a way out of the dismal present, but now I jerk awake. Carlo hit me once, at the beginning, in that dreadful first couple of hours, when, after pleading and wheedling failed to work, I made the mistake of trying to argue with him. He would be intimidating even if he and his minions didn't have guns, and even if I wasn't penned in a cage. He has a certain knowingness that reminds me very much of the way the knowingness of sexually experienced people used to seem to me when I was still an anxious virgin, except that in this case the experience or lack of it is to do, not with sex, but with violence. This is a man who has been beaten and tortured, but he has also beaten others and – so I very much fear – tortured others, too. He has certainly killed. And it seems to me that his power within his little faction comes precisely from his willingness to take personal responsibility for killing and hurting people. Most people need permission for things like that. He is one of the minority of human beings who are quite prepared to give it.

'I'm all right,' I say. 'I appreciate the trouble you and your people take for me.'

He laughs. 'Like fuck you do.'

I'm actually not quite a person in his eyes. I'm the representative of an evil force. It is a common enough mistake, of course, to imagine that the line between good and evil passes neatly between 'us' and 'them', rather than winding back and forth untidily through all of us. God knows, it's a mistake made all the time by myself and my friends back in the capital, who (laughably, as it now seems to me) imagined ourselves to be on the good side of the line, simply because we were able to feel a degree of empathy for certain downtrodden groups, and took the trouble at regular intervals to express, on social media if nowhere else, our disapproval of those who didn't. So, yes, a common enough error, and not unique to Carlo at all. But still, it is frightening to be in the power of someone who places you firmly on the evil side.

'Not so pleasant to be the one who's a prisoner for a change, eh?' he says.

'Carlo, with all respect, I do understand your anger, I really do, but I've never held anyone prisoner in my life.'

'Of course you haven't. Because your lot delegate your violence to others and pretend not to know it's happening.'

'I'm not on the side of the government. I've never voted for that party. Nor have my parents. Nor, to my knowledge, have any of my friends. We all despise that lot.'

'I know. You vote for the "nice" party, the one that does the same thing as the government but with a sigh of regret, and with a few crumbs tossed towards the poor.'

'Actually, no, my parents vote for them, but I vote for—'

'I don't give a fuck who you vote for, my friend. What does it cost you to vote? Half an hour of your time, perhaps, to walk to the polling station and back once every four years. They even provide the pencil. What matters is that you lived a comfortable life on the backs of the rest of us, and knew it, and yet carried on anyway.'

'May I ask if you've set a ransom?'

'No.'

'Do you mean that you haven't set one, or that you haven't started negotiations?'

'You said, "May I ask if you've set a ransom?" and the answer to that question is no. I'd have thought that was clear enough for someone with your education. Aren't you supposed to be some kind of professor or something?'

'Well, not a professor, but—'

'I don't give a shit what your job is, my friend. The only

thing about you I give a shit about is that your dear pa is famous and rich.'

'He's not really *rich*. Unlike me, he *is* a professor. But that's all he is.'

'And how much does a professor earn?'

I tell him, estimating downwards as much as I dare. He laughs. 'And that isn't rich? *Seriously?* You honestly think that isn't rich? You do realize there are entire villages round here that see less money than that in a year? And don't tell me your dad doesn't rake in a whole lot more from his TV shows.'

I know, as a matter of fact, that my father earns considerably more from his many much-admired and frequently repeated documentary series and their spin-off books than he does from his university salary, but that seems to me irrelevant, so I don't go into it. 'Okay,' I say instead, 'but the *real* rich are the owning class. The billionaires, the oligarchs, the barons. I mean, I know my family is privileged, Carlo – I really do, and so do my parents – but we're still basically workers like you, we still work for pay.'

He affects to find this extremely funny, heaving with theatrical laughter.

'You're all the same. Just because you can point to someone even richer you think you are on the same side as the poor.'

I don't like plot, I think to myself, lighting a joint to have with my mid-morning coffee and drawing in the scalding smoke.

The green water flows by. Many thousands of tonnes of it, I suppose, pass my veranda in every second. I feel the drug entering my blood and spreading quickly through my brain.

Well, okay, obviously I *do* like plot in the sense that, back in the city, I often diverted myself with stories that set up puzzles or goals, and made you keep guessing what was going to happen until right at the very end. But this strikes me now as a rather empty pleasure, which arises from a need for neatness, a bit like completing a jigsaw puzzle, something that can also be fun, but no one would claim that doing a jigsaw of a picture is the best way of appreciating the picture itself.

I exhale. Actually, it's not like doing a jigsaw, I decide, and in my mind I'm moving pieces around and trying to fit them together. It's more like watching a jigsaw being done.

I inhale. Actually, no, it's nothing like doing jigsaws or watching jigsaws.

I exhale. It's like . . . What is it like? I don't know – and why does it have to be 'like' something, anyway? – but . . . well . . . my generation rightly distrusts the distinction my grandparents made between 'serious' novels and popular 'trash', yet there surely is still a distinction between stories that make you feel more alive and stories that just pass the time by tapping, like a fruit machine does, into your infantile need for resolution.

I inhale. The resinous smoke reminds me of incense in a church and makes me think of the elaborately carved columns and arches of that unexpectedly impressive cathedral that always puts me in mind of coral, a word that in turn evokes . . .

I breathe out. Some white object is floating down the river. On an impulse, I go inside to recover my pistol from its hiding place so I can take aim at whatever it is as it drifts past, some twenty metres out from the bank. I pull the trigger – bull's-eye! – I hit it on the very first shot. But a spurt of red shoots up and something pale half-emerges from the water, threshing violently, and briefly reveals eyes, a gaping mouth, and a single fin or flipper that reaches up as if appealing for help, before the whole thing sinks down again, leaving only a wine-dark stain.

Oh God, it was alive. I feel simultaneously sick and proud as I flip on the safety catch and return to my seat, caressing the warm gun in my hands. I relight my joint and inhale deeply with my eyes closed, not wishing to look at the river again until I'm quite sure that the pale thing will have drifted out of sight. What *are* those creatures? I mean, I know they're called naiads, but what actually *are* they? It looked like a small whale, but do you find whales in rivers, a thousand kilometres from the sea? I honestly don't know. And whales don't really have faces, do they, and that thing did, though I only glimpsed it, a big doughy lugubrious face, staring across at the small brown creature that had wounded it for no obvious reason at all. But perhaps I just imagined that.

I know very little about animals – my father taught so

many people about the natural world that it became almost a matter of pride for me to remain ignorant – but I can't help myself from wondering if such animals have partners that feel attached to them, or young that depend on them, and if so what kind of calamity my single foolish bullet may have brought about beneath the surface of the river, as if some clueless alien, simply on a whim, had descended to Earth and fired its ray gun at what it imagined to be a colourful piece of cloth, killing the beloved lone mother of six children who earns the money that feeds them and pays the rent for the little apartment they call home.

I exhale. Obviously there has to be some movement in a story, I think – there has to be something driving things forward – but my problem with the engine of plot is that it is nothing like what drives things forward in real life. A story driven by plot emphasizes intention and purpose *far* too much, when the way real life moves is more like this river, whose driving force is the weight of the water that has no choice but to run downhill towards the ocean by whatever route lies open in front of it. Human intentions and purposes are details, like the little patterns of waves and turbulence on the river's surface, and if you examined them closely enough, under (so to speak) a very powerful microscope, even they would turn out to be just more rivers flowing downhill to their own small seas.

And time doesn't work in the way a plot implies. Neatly tied-up strands at the end of a rich and complex book always seem to me an act of vandalism, like ending a symphony with *dum-diddlyumtum-tum-tum*. I don't want my book to have an ending in that sense. I want it to be like . . . What? I can't really say exactly, but into my mind comes the image of a stained-glass window, in which all the stages of a story are presented at the same time, each in its own little panel, so that we see (for instance), depicted in bright colours, the birth of the saint, her early life, her miracles, her persecution at the hands of a savage pagan king, her martyrdom on an iron wheel, her ascension to heaven – side by side and all at once, the saint helpfully identified for us in each panel by her distinctive green clothing, and each scene separated from the others, perhaps by organic forms such as branches or leaves, to show that, from the viewpoint of eternity, all of time is happening simultaneously in, as it were, adjacent clearings of a single forest, or the many rooms of a single building.

I inhale again. The fire crackles eagerly through the dried leaves. I caress the gun in my lap. It is undoubtedly my favourite possession. It's pleasingly heavy, it fits perfectly into my hand, and it gives me the truly magical power of being able to do great damage at a distance, almost instantaneously. I release the safety catch again and fire at random into the river, throwing up a column of water twenty metres away. Then I take one last drag on my joint and discard the butt.

I didn't sleep well last night, and the smoke and the heat have made me drowsy. As I close my eyes, with the gun still cradled in my lap, I remember once visiting the cathedral back in the city when the afternoon sun was throwing bands of colour across the flagstones – the big national cathedral, I mean, four times the size of the one in the town just down the river. I remember how, as I stood in the middle of the nave, my long dark shadow was a kind of absence, surrounded by patterns of blue and red light. And now, in my mind, the shadow becomes more and more indistinct until there is only light. (Can a shadow fade? Can you fade into light?) I'm asleep now and having an uncomfortable dream in which Amanda is calling out my name from her apartment in the town and somehow, although the whole point of being in this place is to be out of reach of other voices, I can hear her all this way up the river. And then I'm woken very suddenly by the shocking sound of booted human feet on the wooden steps that come up to the end of the veranda from the riverbank.

I jump up, my gun clattering on the wooden floor at the exact moment that I remember, too late, that it was on my lap.

I travel for five hours far above the ocean, having food and drink brought to me from time to time on a trolley rolled along a corridor with ten vertical kilometres of air beneath it, all at the expense of my employer and all so that I can deliver a paper – 'De-Sire: Towards a Nongendered Erotics' – at an international conference in a beautiful old university in a foreign country, and listen to the papers of others, and engage in formal and informal discussions over more drink and rather delicious food provided by the organizers and also paid for by my employer, along with other bright and interesting young people who are working on the same kind of topics as myself, but come from many countries in (I count them with satisfaction) no fewer than five different continents.

I know quite a few of the others from previous events in other countries. There are friends and allies of mine, and also rivals, such as the formidable Zoe of whom my friends and I privately like to make fun. But rivals are necessary, after all, to give your own position meaning, in much the same way that an opposing team is necessary in sport. And actually, just as two sporting teams both accept the rules of the game, my group and Zoe's don't disagree in terms of underlying principles. All the disagreement is about how those principles should correctly be applied in the case of the specific texts that our various papers discuss. In our polite way, we try to demonstrate that our opponents have failed to apply those principles correctly, thus raising questions about whether they understand them as well as we do or, much worse, whether they really subscribe to them in the way they claim. For instance, we might show that they have failed to recognize the 'problematic' nature of certain texts that they admire. Or we might, on the contrary, demonstrate that they have failed to understand that the material they themselves have identified as problematic is in fact quite the opposite and doesn't at all perpetrate the oppressive or discriminatory attitudes that, so they claim, are deeply 'inscribed' there, but rather 'subverts', 'disrupts' or 'interrogates' them, perhaps by using 'ludic' or 'coded' strategies that our rivals have taken at face value and so failed to recognize.

The undergraduates of the university are away at the moment because in this northern part of the world, rather exotically, it's the summer vacation, so we are being put up in their very charming quarters. In the evening, after the last paper has been delivered and we've all drunk a fair amount of red wine over a nice three-course meal, we split into groups and spread ourselves out, some inside the building, some outside, and a few heading off on expeditions into the beautiful old quarter of the city, in each case for the purposes of drinking and talking more. And now the conversation wanders from the subject of the conference itself and moves on to wider topics. We talk a fair amount about academic politics, and the many frustrating demands and constraints placed upon us (seemingly regardless of which country we come from) by short-sighted and politically compromised administrators that prevent us from doing what we would like to do, which of course would also be the best thing to do, both for our vitally important work and for society as a whole.

These problems are caused by capitalism. We all agree on that, even though I can't entirely avoid noticing that our actual political affiliations would suggest otherwise. I, for instance, give my support to a political party that considers itself considerably to the left of the centre-left party of which my parents are prominent members, but actually doesn't advocate dismantling capitalism or propose an alternative but rather demands higher taxes, improved public services and free tertiary education. But this evening's about solidarity, and, coming as we do from so many different parts of the world, we all find it reassuring to be in agreement that the very same force that oppresses the poor and endangers the planet is also the one that makes it difficult to obtain tenure and gives us too much teaching. This isn't the time for pedantic details.

In any case, I have other priorities. For all our fancy talk, we humans are animals, and my main preoccupation at the moment is the sweet pheromones drifting towards me from a particular scholar who I've met on two previous occasions, and who is now sitting no more than a metre and a half away from me on the opposite side of the table. Although we come from different continents, so there is very little scope for developing a relationship outside of these events – and perhaps, to be perfectly honest, *because* of that fact – we are definitely attracted to one another, glancing across at each other frequently with bright, smiling eyes as we sit among a larger group around a table in the college bar, and it seems to me entirely possible that we may share a bed tonight, if we can just negotiate a way through this situation that will allow us a little time to talk without the rest of them. One of the side benefits of a conference entitled 'Desire under Late Capitalism' is that such possibilities are constantly being discussed and rehearsed.

For long periods I'm alone in my cage, the only light coming from the constantly hissing gas lamp of my captors some metres away up the cavern. I lie on my mattress, slowly surveying the few things I can see and hear: the bumps and cracks on the ceiling far above me, just visible in the orange light; the dark hexagonal pattern of the chicken wire; the drip drip drip of water into a pool some way off down into the cave; the sharp whiff of bat shit; the rough backwoods accents of the guerrillas as they talk or horse around or quarrel over cards. The combination of tedium and fear and helplessness feels at times too much to bear, when I have no end date to aim at and no control over my own future, yet I have no choice but to bear it and have learnt that indulging my claustrophobia by banging on the wire or screaming will not be tolerated. I try to remember that, not so very long ago, I sat for hours and days quite happily in the small confines of my veranda with only a limited range of sights and sounds to occupy me and didn't feel constrained at all.

I have a pack of playing cards, a very cheap one, the kind with old-fashioned suits, rather than the modern international ones, and only forty-eight cards. I bought it in the sparse little shop in the village downriver from my cabin, and, because it happened to be in my pocket when they seized me, it's the one possession I still have with me, apart from the clothes I wear. When I feel that my sense of helplessness is in danger of getting out of control, and becoming a kind of panic, I use the cards to calm myself. Sometimes I play a game of patience, but more often I simply shuffle the cards, deal out a few of them, see what kind of stories they seem to tell, and then shuffle and deal again.

The Two of Coins, the Nine of Coins, the King of Swords, the Queen of Leaves.

The Three of Leaves, the Seven of Leaves, the Four of Leaves, the Ace of Swords.

The Prince of Coins, the King of Leaves, the Two of Swords, the Ace of Cups . . .

It's surprisingly soothing.

Guinevere doesn't come to talk to me these days, just brings me my food with a gruff 'here you are'. She sometimes accompanies me on my brief 'walks' a few metres up and down the cave, but there's always one of the others there too, and she makes a point of speaking to them and not to me. I wonder if I've offended her? I think it more likely that Carlo has told her to leave me alone, or perhaps just teased her about her obvious affinity with me. I can't very often make out the words they say to one another over there by their lamp, and I seldom hear Guinevere speak at all. When I do hear her, I notice, or think I do, that she is trying to adjust her speech to make it sound more like theirs.

None of them will tell me what's going on in the world outside. Sometimes I imagine a national effort to find me, the army and the police scouring the Upper River region with patrols and helicopters, daily reports on the TV, regular updates to the National Assembly from the Minister of National Security. The insurrection has had a steady trickle of victims of one kind or another, of course, and these are usually reported in the form of statistics, but I am, so to speak, one of the *real* people, one of the differentiated people, whose personal situation is assumed to be of national interest and importance when caught up in something like this. My famous parents would ensure that, as would my friends in the city, who all belong to a certain section of society that expects to be able to get the attention of the authorities, and has contacts of one kind or another in the political and administrative classes, and in the media.

It's interesting – or it would be interesting if I was in the mood to be 'interested' by things – the extent to which I take all this for granted. If someone my age had been kidnapped from that village just down the river from my cabin, I doubt it would have made the national news at all, and, even if it did, back in the city I certainly wouldn't have paid any attention to the story. My position back there was, as indeed I recall once writing in a social media post about a similar case, that 'there are millions of people in this country. If I were to be introduced to one of my compatriots every single minute of my life I still wouldn't meet them all. And every day, people are killed, exploited, abused. It's sentimental at best to focus on individual cases, and when the media focuses exclusively on the victims of the insurgents, it's something worse than that, something more cynical and deliberate. It's a way of deflecting attention from the structural injustices that caused the insurrection in the first place, and a way of erasing the many victims of a regime that refuses to provide sufficient hospitals for the poor, or make decent provision for those who can't work.'

Another possibility is that there is no search going on, and no media coverage, due to a deal that has been struck between my captors and my parents while negotiations are underway. I try to work out what kind of ransom my parents would be able to pay. Would it be enough? The guerrillas clearly hope to make a fair amount out of me, given the effort they are putting in to holding me prisoner. That said, though, I don't know if it's money they're after, or some other objective, like the release of one of their own from the government's prisons? If the latter, I hope my parents have been able to persuade the government to relax its often-stated policy of never giving in to terrorists. They are very well-connected, after all. My father is a national figure, and my mother used to go out with the Minister for Foreign Affairs during their university days: they still send each other Christmas cards.

But what I fear most is that my absence hasn't even been noticed. Perhaps the guerrillas haven't been able to decide how to handle this kidnapping. Perhaps they're arguing amongst themselves – Carlo often heads off to meetings elsewhere to discuss strategy – or waiting for the moment when this particular bargaining chip can be played to maximum effect. My friends and family know that I'm upriver by my own choice in a place with no connection to the phone network or the internet. It could be months before anyone misses me. I find that the hardest to bear: the idea that I'm trapped in the dark, and no one even knows I'm here.

Light falls on my face. Guinevere and Rubia are outside, Rubia carrying the gas lamp, Guinevere cradling a sub-machine gun.

'Time for your walk,' says Guinevere, and yes, she is definitely trying to suppress her metropolitan accent.

'Any news about my case?' I ask as I scramble to my feet.

Neither of them answers me. They open the two padlocks and let me out. Rubia lays down the lamp so she can fix the cuffs to my wrists and ankles. Then she picks up the lamp, and I begin to shuffle down the cave.

I say waterfall but it isn't a sheer drop, more a series of cascades coming down a rocky slope. And, although we are only wearing swimming things and our feet are bare, I suggest to Amanda that we climb beside it at least a bit of the way to see if we can reach the source. It's more of a scramble than a climb, in truth, and the warm brown rock is smooth and easy on the feet, its surface just rough enough to provide grip, with little patches of soft peaty soil from time to time where small plants have taken root, some with little white flowers like bells, some with crinkly yellow ones. In fifteen minutes we find the boiling pool where the water comes spitting and steaming out of the rock. It's a dramatic sight and a good viewpoint too – we're already high enough to see the river and the forest beyond it stretching all the way to the distant mountains in the west – but the pool itself is just too violent and deadly to be a restful place to stop, so we climb on to a flat ledge another thirty metres above it to rest and admire the view.

'I keep thinking about you in your cabin all by yourself,' she says. 'You must get lonely, surely?'

'There's a village a couple of kilometres downriver. I go there sometimes. You'll have passed it on your way up.'

'We passed a few huts.'

'Well, it barely *is* a village, but it has a tiny church made of corrugated iron, and a shop. You know the sort of thing: a few cans of sardines on one shelf, some bags of flour on another, a pile of out-of-date copies of various celeb magazines . . . And I go down to the town every week as well.'

'You'll have to come and see me next time.'

'Yeah. Sure. Of course.'

She glances across at me, clearly noticing my lack of enthusiasm, but she doesn't comment on it.

'And your book? You said you hadn't written a word?'

'Not a single word.'

'Oh well, I expect you're working on it in your subconscious.'

'God knows. I suppose my subconscious has its own agenda. Trouble is I'm not sure it's very interested in getting published.'

I gesture at the view in front of us, and the various rocks, flowering plants and wiry shrubs that are rather picturesquely arranged around us, as if this was a rockery in a garden. There is a cool breeze blowing up here, which is welcome after swimming and wading along a stream of hot water. 'I want to capture the whole of life,' I tell her. 'I know it sounds preposterous but it's true. And that's my problem, because really I can't hope to capture even a tiny part of it. I mean, look at that bush over there. Just that one bush. Words, drawings, even photographs . . . you couldn't capture it. There's no substitute for the thing itself. And even looking at it now, when it's right in front of us, we're not really taking it in.'

'What do you mean?'

'Well, shut your eyes. Tell me how much of it you can remember. How many stems has it got? What shapes do they form? How many flowers are there on each stem? How many petals on each flower?'

She consults her watch. She needs to be back in time to meet Dido's son Harold when he comes with the boat. 'A little further?' she suggests. 'I reckon I'm okay for another half-hour before I need to turn round.' And immediately she begins to climb quickly and confidently up the rock, as if some new of kind of gravity was drawing her upwards.

'Perhaps we'll find the Grail,' I say.

'No chance.' She speaks without pausing in her smooth ascent. 'Those people are a long way away. It must be a day's climb from here, just to get to the top of the—'

But now she stops to check out a red bird sitting on an outcrop fifty metres away, which she says is a pterosaur, unique to the Upper River area and actually not a bird at all.

'Looks like a bird to me,' I say.

She is visibly disconcerted. 'You really don't know about pterosaurs? I'm pretty sure your father did a whole series about them once!'

I laugh. Pterosaurs are the last surviving relic of another entire group of flying reptiles that have claws in their wings, and jaws with teeth. Really I know that perfectly well but I like to pretend ignorance of such things, because it always shocks people who know about my famous dad.

Amanda carries on, then suddenly yelps. 'Fuck. I've twisted my ankle.'

'Badly?'

'Not badly, I don't think.'

I catch up with her. She holds out her injured foot for my inspection. It strikes me, though quite possibly completely erroneously, that you can learn a lot about a person's history by the way they act after an injury. Amanda expects attention. I don't mean that she makes a fuss because she really doesn't, yet somehow it's clear that her expectation is that, in a situation of this kind, whoever is with her will jettison whatever else is occupying them in order to look after her. This provokes a brief twinge of sibling-type jealousy – how come she gets all this attention? – which I have to overcome before I can meet her perfectly reasonable expectations and look at her ankle.

'There's nothing to see yet. I guess you may get some swelling or bruising later. Does it hurt when I do this?'

'Ouch, yes. But it's not absolutely excruciating.'

'Do you reckon you can put any weight on it?'

'I think so, as long as I'm careful. And once we get down, we can pretty much float back to the lake, can't we? But we'd better head back now, if you don't mind, because I'm definitely going to be slow.'

'Of course. Let me know what I can do to help.'

'When we get back to the lake, would you mind waiting there with me? I feel a bit helpless like this, you know? We could drop you off at your cabin on the way back.'

I'm not completely happy with this plan. I can put up with the kids from the village, who come by in boats trying to sell me things – I sometimes even find them entertaining – but I don't really want other people seeing my cabin. But once again, it's a perfectly reasonable request.

'Of course,' I tell her. 'I wouldn't even think of leaving you alone.'

*

'So, am I really doing this? Am I really giving up all of that for the sake of this stupid book of mine, which I may never write?'

Wrapped up in my raincoat, I'm walking alone along the top of a high black cliff. Far below me, grey waves smash themselves on the black rocks to become a cold white foam that runs a few metres up the lead-coloured sand, before the grey sea sucks it back again.

The choice I've made seems crazy, even to me. What is so great about a book that, even if I do write it, and assuming it gets noticed at all, will soon grow old and be forgotten? It's not as if I believe in the idea of Art or Literature, in that hushed, trembling-voiced, capital-letter sense. I know that many people live perfectly rich and interesting lives without so much as opening a book. I know plenty of people who read voraciously but still lead mean and timid lives.

Seabirds, grey and white, wheel about below me, shrieking as they go back and forth from their colonies, and far away down there on the beach, lie hundreds of plump black seals.

It's not as if I haven't written books already. The memoir of my captivity made me quite famous for a while, and pretty rich, and I've written seven novels since, albeit with steadily diminishing sales. But none of them is the real book. They're all just things I turned out while I was waiting for the real book to come to me.

And yes, very probably, she's quite right and the real book will never come. But what she doesn't understand is that to give up on it, to stop even trying, would be like admitting that all there was in the world was . . . well . . . *this*.

What I mean by 'this' is represented for me just now by the line in the distance where the slate-coloured sea meets a sky whose greyness is so pale as to be almost white. Long rows of wind turbines are in the process of being assembled out there. (Towards the northern end of the array, some of them are already operational, racing round in the relentless wind, with little red lights blinking as a warning to ships and planes. Down at the southern end, they're still just white stumps.) But it's not the bleakness of this particular scene I really mean, for this place fits my mood in a way that some warm, jolly sunlit location wouldn't, and that, if not exactly comforting, is almost restful, in the way that it's sometimes restful to give up hope and just sink down to the bottom and lie there. What I mean by 'this' is the world itself, unadorned, without elaboration.

For a moment I feel a fear creeping over me that began in the Tower of the Grail, the fear of waking up and discovering that—

But let's not go there, eh? Let's at least not go there.

Anyway, I suppose she'd say that I've got it all wrong. My problem isn't getting that book out of myself, it's getting myself out of the book and into the world.

The seals laze on the beach below me as if this bitingly cold place was some sort of beach resort and they were sunning themselves in this thin and watery light.

'I'm not giving it up,' I mutter. 'It's the only handle I have on being me.'

I turn round and go back to the town, where I order a beer and some potato chips in a bare little bar with a grey linoleum floor and no ornamentation other than a framed and signed black-and-white picture of our president. Hated by all my friends back in the city, he is a local boy here and is much admired.

There's only one other customer, a slight but rather good-looking man, a few years younger than myself, so we strike up a conversation. I learn that he's called Ham, and it turns out he's read not only my bestselling memoir of my captivity, but also one of my novels. 'I could see it was good,' he says, 'but to be honest it wasn't really my thing. I much preferred the other book. That was great. I don't like make-believe, I guess. I prefer books set in real places, and I like them to have a good fast pace.' I think of giving him my usual answer – that books are *never* set in real places, least of all books with a good fast pace – but it sounds hollow in my head, and even rather obnoxious.

I learn that he's an engineer and works on those giant turbines. I confess to him I have absolutely no idea how you go about building a structure like that in the open sea. 'Writing books seems pretty trivial by comparison,' I tell him, not being falsely modest, but really meaning it.

'Are you kidding?' he says, God bless him. He has beautiful sad brown eyes. 'You could learn to do what I do in a few years, but never in a million years could I write a book.'

*

In the middle of the night, when the moonbeams slip through the cracks in my wooden walls and the insects rattle and hum along the riverbank, I think about my dad. Of all the people I know back in the city, he is the one I most dread going back to without having written my book. Because I know that if he had to spend six months in this cabin, he'd not only write a book, he'd draw and photograph each new animal he came across, he'd spend hours with botanical keys identifying every plant, and he'd learn the local indigenous language, with its incredibly complex grammar, which, so I have heard, has a different set of verb endings for each of thirteen noun classes, including 'long objects', 'springy objects', 'objects that resemble human genitals' and 'animals without wings that have high-pitched cries'. He would also involve himself in some way in the village school, create his own detailed map of the area, and set about building a boat, based on the local canoes, and using only the tools that would have been available here before the conquest. I don't like to think about telling him that I didn't so much as start the book that was supposed to be the whole reason for my interrupting my modest academic career, didn't keep a journal in any serious sense, didn't make anything more than the most superficial contact with the people in the local village, didn't even get round to discovering what kind of creature those naiads are, with their odd, sad, doughy faces, though I did manage to maim or kill one of them for no particular reason at all.

Tomorrow, I tell myself. Tomorrow I must start that novel. Yet I know quite well that when the morning comes, I'll toss aside these promises. I'll say to myself that the point of life is not to notch up achievements, but to live, to experience being alive, and that this will make sense to me, though now it just seems like an excuse for indiscipline and idleness.

My gun falls to the floor with a hollow clatter. So this is it, I'm thinking. This is how it happens. My peace is over and now the opposite of peace begins. However far you travel, wherever you go, and however you try to protect yourself, you can't escape the worm. Whatever the place, whether it's green and lush like this, or bleak and bare, whether it's full of people, or lonely and isolated, whether it's urban or rural, modern or traditional, rich or poor, the worm is always there in some form or another, gnawing away beneath the world, looking for its opportunity to sneak in.

I dive after the gun, and this means that when the stranger speaks I'm on all fours on the wooden boards of my veranda.

'Sorry, did I startle you? I called out to you from the boat, but you didn't seem to hear me.'

'Oh, hello, Amanda.' I scramble to my feet, trying to fold the gun out of sight with my hands, though really it's too big to hide.

She smiles. 'Yes, it's just me. I thought I'd come up and see you. I hired my own self-drive boat from Dido. Good God, is that your gun? Do you have it by you all the time?'

'No, I was just . . .' I decide not to tell her about the pale animal. She'd know all about those creatures (as any normal person would), would wonder at my ignorance, and be shocked by the irresponsibility and cruelty of what I've done. 'Just doing a bit of target shooting for fun and I dozed off. I smoked a bit of weed, as you may be able to tell.'

'Your eyes look pretty red.'

'It does that to you, I'm afraid. Not an attractive look. But, you know, I wasn't expecting visitors.'

She frowns, detecting a reproach. 'Well, I couldn't let you know I was coming, could I?' she observes mildly, and even humorously. 'I mean, obviously if I'm interrupting something important ...'

'You're not interrupting anything more than me taking a snooze. I'm sorry if I sounded unwelcoming. I've never had a visitor here before.'

'I thought you might like one. I mean, you've visited me a couple of times, after all.'

'You just startled me, that's all.' I'm trying my best, but I can't quite get the resentment out of my voice, even though I know I've nothing to resent. 'A combination of stoned paranoia and being fast asleep. I thought you might be a terrorist or something.'

I lay the gun on the rickety little folding table I have on the veranda for my cigarette papers and matches and playing cards.

She is slightly but not entirely mollified. 'Well, it's lucky you didn't shoot me, then.'

'The safety catch is on. No risk of that. Have a seat. It's nice to see you. I'll go and get another chair for myself. Can I get you a drink or something?'

'A coffee would be nice.'

'Okay. I should warn you I use river water, so there's a bit of an earthy taste, but it's all been boiled and strained.'

Inside my dim cabin, and out of her sight, I set the kettle to boil on the gas ring and spoon ground coffee into a stained metal jug. This is how it is, I'm thinking. You meet someone by chance, you spend a few hours together, you sleep over a couple of times at his or her flat, and – bam! – it turns out that, without meaning to at all, you have become a member of a two-person entity that has rules and expectations, and within which certain behaviours are permitted, and certain attitudes, even if not actually felt, must nevertheless be expressed and acted out in order to avoid causing offence. And this, in microcosm, is how society works, and why whole tribes of people will all claim to subscribe to certain values that they manifestly don't really follow, while others do exactly the same thing with an entirely different set of values, and also why it's often very difficult to speak out loud what you really think, or even to *know* what you really think, because of the lifelong accumulation of these compromises, and the internalization from infancy of the expectations of those around you, resulting from a need to be liked and not be left on your own, so it is often easier to deny some unalterable fact about your own self – and deny it even *to* your own self – than it is to go against what is generally agreed to be the consensus within your own particular group, although it may in fact just be what everyone thinks they have to say, and deep down they may all agree with you.

It's not that I don't like Amanda. And all she's doing now is what most people would do if they were living in a strange place and met a reasonably attractive person of their own age and background: establish a friendship, create a routine of get-togethers and shared activities, get to know one another, visit one another's homes, start to construct a common language. Actually, I like her very much. She's warm and funny and – or so I sense – kind and loyal, and she's nice to look at in a pleasingly eccentric way. In fact, I don't just like her, I *admire* her. I admire her athleticism, and even more I admire the commitment she's made, which I'd never make myself, to the daily slog involved in teaching a class of nearly forty nine-year-old children from poor and often illiterate homes where education is not especially valued and the national language not necessarily even spoken, but the fact remains that the compromises, constraints and expectations involved even in ordinary friendship are precisely what I went to all the trouble and expense of coming to this remote little cabin to avoid, so that I could write a book that would be free from—

'Bang!' says Amanda. She's standing in the doorway, with the light behind her, peering into the gloom at my single-

roomed dwelling, with its strewn clothes and books, and its
unmade bed, and she's holding my gun with both hands and
pointing it right at me.

'Jesus Christ, Amanda! *Never* do that! Never point a gun
at another person!'

She lowers her arms but refuses to accept my rebuke.
'Really? I thought you said it was completely safe with the
catch on?'

A car is a kind of body. It has body language. You can see
tentative cars, trying to edge out into traffic but without
sufficient conviction. You can see rude and pushy cars in the
same situation. There are also reckless cars, timid cars and
arrogant cars, and you can read off these qualities from the
demeanour of the car itself, without even seeing the driver.

Cars are bodies. I remember noticing that once and liking
the idea. Of course, I don't see cars at all these days. I *could*
do, but to do that I'd have to drag my own battered vehicle
of flesh and bones off this bed, and into a vertical position,
and across the room to the window, and, being careful not
to lose my balance, get the window open and my crumbly
old body out on to the tiny balcony to lean it over the railing,
taking care not to drop my glasses, and look down into the
street four storeys below – a series of actions that makes me
feel weary just thinking about it. So I don't actually see cars
any more, but I can hear them all the time, lying here, even

in the middle of the night. Cars, buses, trucks, trams; I hear them snapping at each other, braking, crawling forward, grumbling, occasionally flying into rages, once colliding, constantly letting each other know they're there with little parps and peeps, each one with its own particular sound, which is, I imagine, as distinct as the various calls of different kinds of bird, if you only take the trouble to learn them.

I enjoy their presence. Those living metal bodies are company of a sort for me, rather like the company of the other customers of the street cafés where I would sometimes go to work: they don't know you, and make no demands on you, but are still deeply reassuring just by being present.

Funny to think of my former self down there in those streets, sitting outside cafés and bars, climbing on and off trams, driving or being driven in cars. You're looking *around* you all the time, when you're there on the ground. You don't look up because all the things you want are at your level, and so are the things you need to look out for. Once in a while, an aesthetic impulse – a self-conscious impulse I'd trained myself to have – would make me turn my attention briefly upwards to the higher storeys of the buildings around me, like an intelligent fish glancing up at the silvery slither of sky to remind itself that its little pool isn't everything and there is another whole world out there, before it returns to the real business of watching out for pike and hunting for water fleas.

So yes, I occasionally looked upward and, though I can't say I remember it, I surely must sometimes have wondered what went on behind those ranks of windows above the shops and restaurants and bars, but if you'd told me about some elderly person lying on a bed up there, wandering between dreams and ruminations, and trying to avoid thinking about their more or less permanent queasiness, or about the pain that is always either present or creeping back again like a distant discord that they know will in due course be screeching at full volume into their ear, or about the inoperable mass that's drawing them all the time in the direction of the final oblivion that lies, not years away, but weeks or months . . . well, I would have listened politely but it wouldn't have meant much to me, and I would have changed the subject as soon as I could. I knew this was the fate of all of us. Well, of course I did – I'd known that since I was perhaps three or four when, as it happens, I pondered a great deal the dreadful fact that having once been born I had no choice but to die. But by the time I was an adolescent I didn't take it very seriously, and, even now that I've arrived here, it's hard to believe that my turn has finally come.

'On my death bed,' I whisper to myself in order to hear the sound of it. I remember it being a fairly conventional observation that one should do this or that – and perhaps even compile a checklist of thises and thats to be completed while one could – or one would *regret it on one's death bed*. It doesn't really work like that, though. Down there we didn't understand how remote the rest of our lives would seem from this perspective. Those people below me in their cars and trams might not be interested in me up here, but neither am I much interested in them. This is where I am now, and this is where I'd be whatever life I'd led.

She is lying curled up on her right side, with a black halo congealing round her head. I've never seen a dead body before unless you count the Egyptian mummies that were the highlight of our childhood visits to the National Museum, and, in my hyped-up, bruised and trembling state, I weep. Poor Guinevere, poor poor Guinevere, she was so young, and so determined to do good and not to waste her life. She must have been at least ten years younger than me, which helps to explain why actually she was a bit intimidated by me and my . . . well, right now it just seems like cynicism, though I'd prefer to call it realism. She was so young and hopeful. I weep for her, and I weep at the thought of her poor parents, who worked so hard and so long to bring her up. How could I have questioned the authenticity of her feelings, or sneered at her sacrifice, when my own insistence on purity means I never do anything useful at all?

'Because she and her friends fucking *kidnapped* me, you idiot!' I answer myself out loud. 'Because they beat me, and pointed guns at me, and shut me in a cage, and treated me like I was evil, when I only did what most of them would have done – other than maybe St Guinevere here – if they'd happened to be born with the privileges I was lucky enough to have. The bastards wouldn't even do me the kindness of letting me know what was happening.' I pick up her gun and then suddenly the bottled-up resentment erupts inside me from weeks of captivity without knowing where I was, or how long I would be there, or what lay on the other side of it, and I begin to kick silly, priggish, joyless Guinevere as hard as I can, not just once but many times. Her body is already stiffening, and I eventually stop because I realize I'm hurting my foot, already bruised by kicking the frame of my cage. I'm about to wander off when I remember I need the ammunition from her backpack, and kneel down to remove it. I have to force her left arm to get the strap off and the other strap is pinned beneath her, so I have to pull her over, which reveals the fact that most of the right-hand side of her head is missing, so I can see her white brain with its various folds and lobes picked out in dry black blood.

I retch. Around me is jungle. I have no idea where. They stuck a sack over my head. I only know there was a boat journey, and a march, and several hours in the back of a truck, and another march.

I should go back into the cave and see what food there is. I wish I'd thought about that on my way out, but I was too confused by my freedom to think straight, and all I've brought with me is the grubby pack of playing cards that I've kept in my pocket ever since they brought me to this place. I also ought to get away from here. Guinevere might be dead, but there's no sign of Jaco or Rubia or Carlo, or of the various others who came and went, and they may well be alive and coming back soon. In fact, probably the first thing I ought to do is work out how to use this gun.

My hands are trembling. My fingertips are raw. Having broken one of the struts of my cage by repeatedly kicking it, so as to give me a bit of slack, I spent many hours bending bits of wire back and forth, back and forth, back and forth, working one strand until it broke, and then on to the next one a centimetre away, and then the next until I had a hole big enough to crawl through.

If I can find the army, I'll be all right. In spite of the several demos I've been on back in the capital to protest the army's appalling track record of atrocities against poor and indigenous people, I know that, when it comes down to it, they're on my side. I don't even have to think about it. But there's no sign of them. The cave mouth is almost at ground level and they obviously didn't spot it or they wouldn't have moved on elsewhere after the firefight. Quite possibly they came by helicopter, and are already a hundred kilometres away or more. They might not even have been looking for me. It could well be that they just happened to spot Guinevere and the others when passing overhead on the way to somewhere else.

I can't bear to go back in there. But I need food. But that means feeling my way back down that black tunnel, and I could be another half-hour, and the others might come back and I'd be trapped. And what about this gun? Until I know how to load it, it will give me no protection at all. But first I should get away from here. But what am I going to do for food?

I'm paralysed by the need to make a choice. Each alternative seems such a thin and impoverished thing. And Guinevere is no help at all. She lies there vacantly like a doll that's fallen to the floor, her arms still sticking up where I pushed them to get off her pack, her eyes half-closed and just showing a pupil-less strip of white, her head opened up like a diagram in one of my father's instructive biology books.

Perhaps the contents of her pack will help me. With my clumsy, trembling, raw-tipped fingers I fumble it open. There are two spare magazines for the gun, a box of tampons, half a packet of mint sweets, a half-full water bottle, a hunting knife, a small biscuit tin containing a sort of first-aid kit (some sticking plasters, a bandage and a tube of water-sterilizing tablets), a cigarette lighter, half a pack of cigarettes and a mobile phone . . . Oh God, please let there be a signal here, I pray as I try to switch it on, though the chances of that must be pretty much zero, and it turns out that, in any case, the battery is flat . . . There are also four biscuits wrapped in silver foil, and a can of sardines, a pair of nail scissors, and a little photograph in a clear plastic disc, the size of a largish coin, which looks as if it was once part of a keyring, of a middle-aged couple with kind, gentle faces, beaming presumably at Guinevere herself as she took the photo. The woman looks to me as if she might be a social worker or something of that sort in one of the poor neighbourhoods, the man maybe a lecturer in a technical school, and, as decent people with a social conscience, no doubt they brought up Guinevere to be aware of the moral burden of her own privilege, imagining that she would join some sort of helping profession like their own. But she decided that, for all their good intentions and hard work, they were really part of the problem because by doing the jobs they did, they created the impression that something was being done – an idea that was indeed very comforting for people like *my* parents – even though they didn't really change anything at all, since they were failing to address the underlying structural oppression.

Back in the city, people like us found all kinds of stories to tell ourselves, usually involving comparing ourselves with others more obviously reprehensible than ourselves, that would allow us to feel we were really on the side of good and against an oppressive system, even though we ourselves were beneficiaries of that same system. But you had to believe in your own story, at least to some degree, for it to work, and once you saw through it, you had to find another story.

(Question: but why am I thinking about this now, when I'm all alone and lost and in terrible danger? Answer: because thinking about almost anything is preferable to actually accepting that this is where I am, in the middle of a jungle, with no map and almost no food, and enemies out there who'd happily hurt or kill me, who might come back at any time.)

I replace the contents of the pack and sling it on my own shoulders. I'm not going back into the cave. The first thing I'll do is climb the weathered outcrop of rock, shaped like the top ten per cent of a crumbling buried sphere, at whose base the cave lies. Perhaps I will be able to see something in the distance, like mountains, that will help me get a sense of where I am, and if an army helicopter appears, I can wave to it.

I am still holding on to the photograph in its little plastic disc. *They can be my parents now* is, I suppose, what I'm vaguely thinking as I put it in my pocket.

I know that as soon as I start to climb that rock, I'll realize that it was the wrong decision and that I should have done something else. But, whichever option I chose, the same would be true.

I cook Amanda pasta with beans in a tomato sauce. We drink some river-cooled beer. I take her for a little tour of the area around my cabin and she has a few polite puffs on a joint, though it's very obviously not really her thing. She's uneasy, I can tell. She likes me but she's uneasy about what I've made of my life out here. And she's made me feel the same because when she stood in the doorway of my cabin, I saw it through her eyes. I've let it get squalid and, while I've been telling myself that this is good because it means I'm not adhering to small-minded conventions or worrying about what other people might think, I can see, or think I can, that she's wondering what this says about me and my relationship with the world and with myself, and there's a part of me that can't help agreeing with what I imagine to be her conclusion: namely that there's nothing that's really liberating and joyous about all this at all, and actually what's happened here, if not from the beginning then certainly in recent weeks, is that I've sunk into a kind of unproductive stupor, and that what I still like to imagine is a state of calmness and reconciliation with the world has become closer to numbness or indifference.

She talks about her work, about how difficult it is to teach pupils whose parents have never been to school, and have no concept at all of what education is even for. How do you persuade children whose parents rely on a combination of practical experience, superstition and tradition that one can find truths about the world by experiment and reason? How do you get them to see that the roles played by men and women in their particular community are not determined for all time, and can be questioned and overturned? I find myself being awkward and repeatedly challenge her assumptions – in the same kind of way, I suppose, as she challenges the assumptions of her pupils. How do we know that what we educated city people have to offer is better than what indigenous people already have, given that their way of life has evolved over many thousands of years to cope with this environment? 'After all,' I say, 'it's our science and technology, our notion of the human individual as the supreme being, our capitalism, that is laying waste to the world, not their folk knowledge and traditions.'

'Absolutely right,' she answers at once with great seriousness. '*Absolutely* right! There's so much to value about their culture and so much that we can learn from them, *so* much, but there are a lot of problems too. Their marriage customs, for instance, really are quite oppressive, as is the way they police gender roles and traditional norms by socially ostracizing anyone who refuses to conform.'

She's trying to show that she understands my point and agrees with it, but my strong impulse is to go on arguing. It seems to me that she's trying to have it both ways, as we liberal types are prone to do, insisting on our great admiration for the common people (and especially indigenous common people), while at the same expecting the common people to fall in with our idea of what common people ought to be like. But I decide to leave it at that. The truth is I don't trust my own motives. I know that my slight irritation with her fairly conventional stance is not purely based on doubts about its intellectual underpinnings but is driven in part by jealousy, guilt and defensiveness, and that, if I continue, those ugly feelings will become increasingly evident to her as well as me. Also, let's face it, she knows quite a bit about the topic from direct experience, dealing every day as she does with predominantly indigenous children and their parents, while my direct experience is basically zero. I have an uneasy feeling that this uncomfortable fact might be the source of my jealousy.

'Yes, of course,' I say. 'We should respect them but not idealize them.'

'Exactly,' she says, and smiles. 'Oh look, a parrot.'

A small black parrot with a red beak has landed at the railing of my veranda and is watching us with a sharp, interested eye.

'Oh yes, it comes here most days. I've no idea what kind it is.'

She tells me the local name for the species – an indigenous word full of consonants, which I can't get hold of – and adds that these birds are venerated in the mythology of the Upper River. 'It was once a minor god, apparently, but it disobeyed the other gods in order to steal fire from the sun for humankind, and so they turned it into a bird as a punishment, and condemned it to be nothing but a thief until the world ends.'

'It certainly *is* a thief. It's taken food from my table before now when I'm actually sitting there. It seems to be able to tell when I'm sufficiently distracted. It once took a pencil, too. It was red and shiny, so perhaps it liked the colour.'

'Well, if you believe the story, you have to forgive it. It gave us warmth and light.' She looks at her watch. 'I ought to head back now. I guess it'll be quicker going with the flow, but I want to be sure of getting there before dark.'

We part a little awkwardly. I watch her in her boat as she heads off down the river. She sits up very straight, facing forward, determined to meet anything that comes along with her accustomed positivity, but after a while she glances back in my direction, and it seems to me, quite possibly mistakenly, that she does so with a certain reluctance, and that when she sees me watching her and waves and smiles, her undoubted friendliness is qualified by complicated reservations.

But then she's gone and I return to my seat on the veranda to roll myself a smoke. Having flown off on some other errand, perhaps to check some alternative food source that it's also monitoring, the parrot returns and watches me as I light up, its head tipped quizzically on to one side. I feel lonely, which I haven't been conscious of until now, except in the middle of the night. I almost feel glad of the creature's company.

I draw in smoke, hold it for as long as possible, exhale. The parrot observes me. I don't know much about animals, but I'm stronger on cultural history, and I know that the figure of the fire thief appears in various forms in many mythologies, including cultures that have had no contact with each other for a hundred thousand years. Which surely demonstrates that these aren't just stories, they are attempts to describe something that actually exists.

I inhale again. And I decide, admittedly in that rather suspect way that happens when one is stoned and patterns form super-easily and often completely spuriously, that the fire thief is simply a description of life. Life is a fire thief. The law of the universe is that everything runs downhill from complexity to bland disorder, yet life finds a loophole that allows it to flow in the other direction, and become more complex instead of less to the point that it is able to know itself, and eventually to rival in complexity the universe itself: *The man has become one of us, knowing good and evil. He must not be allowed to take also from the tree of life and eat, and live for ever.*

I exhale. Well, okay, that's a different story perhaps.

And then I think, No, actually, it isn't. The serpent is like the parrot, and like the bird it's punished. All of these old stories are part of the same protean mass – or so at least it seems with my tetrahydrocannabinolized brain, which, for some neurological reason that I've never bothered to look into, finds connections in everything.

The bird is still watching me intently. I go inside, find the remains of a packet of biscuits, and empty the crumbs out on the table. It flaps across to gather them up with its beak and its fat grey tongue.

'You're not a god, my friend,' I say to it, standing back politely by the door to let it concentrate on the crumbs, 'you're just a rather smart bird.'

But I do think gods are real. They too are protean, far more so than they're presented as in the various mythologies we've been brought up with, dividing and merging all the time, but they do really exist. They inhabit human minds – and maybe parrot minds too, for all I know, or the minds of pale river creatures – in the same kind of way that minds inhabit flesh.

I will summon them now, I think, relighting the joint and inhaling deeply. They'd be company of a sort.

'So we're agreed on what we're against,' I say. 'But that's the easy part. What exactly are we in favour of?'

I'm sitting at the kitchen table in my apartment, talking politics with my two flatmates, Rémy and Jezebel, and a couple of friends of Jez's who've come to dinner. It's a slightly shabby apartment, but reasonably spacious, conveniently near the university, and – this is my favourite part – it has a balcony that directly overlooks the famous Botanic Gardens, with its shady streams, pools, banks and rocks beneath those enormous rainforest trees that we could, if we chose to look, see right now from our window.

The others start to enumerate things: better pay for workers, nationalization of certain monopolies such as the power industry, legal protections for indigenous people and other minorities, reduction of the size of the armed forces, indictment of certain generals implicated in civil rights abuses in the interior, higher taxes and the closure of tax loopholes, free healthcare, investment in universities, a constitutional guarantee of academic freedom, proper sanitation and electricity supplies in the shanty towns, citizen's councils to oversee the police, closure of certain newspapers that are controlled by and run for the benefit of the oligarch class . . .

'Okay,' I say, 'this is a kind of shopping list of various

demands that have been made over recent years and are familiar to all of us, but we're always talking, aren't we, about the need to change the *structure*, and none of these represent a structural change. What I want to know is: what is the new structure we're going to put in place?'

Jez's friends glance at each other, eyebrows slightly raised. I regret that, because I find one of them rather attractive – his name is Hasdrubal, but Jez just calls him Dru – and had wanted to make a good impression.

'I feel a bit embarrassed about asking the question,' I add. 'I talk all the time to my students about structural change, and yet I don't really know what I mean by it.' I look across at Jez's friend Dru. 'Quite a confession, I know, but there it is. And I wonder if perhaps there's some fundamental thing I've missed that everybody else knows?'

It soon becomes apparent that there *isn't* some fundamental thing that I've missed, because none of them can really answer my question. They speak in generalities, platitudes even – 'we need a society that is run for people and not for profit', 'we need *real* democracy' – but they don't have a blueprint for how it would work, and, when pressed, dismiss as 'state capitalism' the only obvious alternative to the economic system we currently have, knowing as they do that, when tried in practice, it failed to achieve the utopia that had been its objective. It's almost as if we need to keep our destination in soft focus, for fear that it wouldn't stand sharper scrutiny.

Eventually I give up on trying to establish where it is we think we should be headed, and instead ask how we should build the alliance that would be necessary to move things on from where they are. But to this question too the answers are vague and even platitudinous and seem to focus almost entirely on what *other* people should do or not do. In short, my companions don't know any more than I do, and it strikes me that they – we – are oddly uninterested even in the question. The important thing, it seems, is that we believe the right things, not that we do the right things. In theology, I believe, this is known as *sola fide*.

Anyway, pretty soon we've all more or less forgotten my questions and, after returning briefly to the more familiar territory of lamenting the iniquities of the present system, we move on to matters of more personal interest like the appalling state of the institutions for which we work, and various currently fashionable topics in the arts.

Rémy gets up to make some coffee and suggests we adjourn from the table to the soft chairs a few metres away in our smallish but rather comfortable sitting area.

'I'm going to have a quick smoke on the balcony,' I say as we all stand up, 'if anyone cares to join me. It's worth a look at the view if you haven't seen it.'

One of Jez's friends does come out with me, but not the one I was hoping for. This one is called Melita and, while I dare say a perfectly nice person, does not attract me at all, and strikes me as a little prim and self-congratulatory.

'We really don't know, do we?' I say.

She has gone to the railing. The night sounds of the city rise from the streets below: honking horns, the purr of a passing tram, the noisy laughter of a bunch of young men emerging from a bar. The Botanic Gardens are in darkness except for the outer leaves of the trees just inside the fence. 'We really don't know what?'

'We don't really know where we want to get to or how to get there.'

'Speak for yourself,' she says. 'I'm very clear in my own mind.'

And that's the end of that conversation. I often feel that I'm trying to talk with people about the beliefs and priorities of our little tribe as just one of many different ways of making sense of life, one of many little pools of light in the darkness, but that they either don't understand what I mean or refuse to see any validity in this way of looking at things, since they view our tribe's position as simply the truth, or at least the most advanced version of the truth that currently exists, and everyone else's as just plain wrong. I have the impression, in fact, that many people are quite threatened by the idea that they are not standing in the sole true light, but only in one of many different small and dimly lit patches, I suppose because to acknowledge this means also acknowledging the darkness that surrounds us all. It's not even that unusual to hear colleagues and acquaintances expressing the view that certain people should actually be punished for their problematic views, or at any rate prohibited from expressing them. Myself I just can't see how we can be so sure of being right when we are so manifestly unclear of either our goal or the means of getting there. But there is a very ancient school of thought, I know, that says that you can *make* a statement true by forbidding anything that might contradict it. And there's no denying there's something in that. There are, after all, around the world, many millions of very devout believers in various faiths, whose ancestors were converted by force. Our own indigenous people, for instance. And very probably my own forebears, who must have been converted at some point to Christianity from one or another of the old pantheons. I finish rolling my little one-skin joint, light it, and, leaning on the railing beside her, offer Melita first go, which she declines with a polite smile.

I take a puff. 'They lock the gardens at night these days. I always think that it's at its best when you can't get in. I mean, don't get me wrong, I love it in the daytime too, but it gets pretty crowded, and, however hard I try, I can't help noticing that it's really quite a small park that I can walk right across in less than ten minutes. But look at it now! A bit of street light on the outer leaves, but behind that . . . mystery. You would still hear the traffic if you were in there, but it would seem like it was a whole world away. I often come out here at night just to look at it. It's like a portal to another world.'

'I signed the petition against closing the gates. It was an entirely spiteful act by the city government. This was a place where homeless people could sleep in at least comparative safety.'

Irritated, I want to ask her whether she proposes also to open the doors of the National Gallery, where she works as an assistant curator, since that would surely be a much more comfortable place to spend the night, particularly in the rainy season. I may be wrong, given the impossibility of completely separating one's understanding of the motives of others from one's own projections, but it seems to me that what Melita is really doing here is punishing me for my awkward questions earlier by highlighting my shallowness and lack of concern for the marginalized.

But, after all, she is Jez's friend, and I am a co-host of this little party. And what's more, I know that I recognize Melita's ploy (or think I do) precisely because it's one I often use myself. I regularly point out to others the things they've failed to notice because of their position of privilege but which I, with my greater sensitivity, both see and care about. So I grunt something that I hope will sound vaguely like I am accepting her rebuke without my having to actually do so, and take a final puff on the joint before stubbing it out.

'Well, thank you for showing me the view,' Melita says. 'You're quite right, it's really rather special.' And she heads back inside to join the others.

*

It was a mistake to climb to the top of this rock. All I can see from it in every direction are trees stretching to the horizon with the occasional slight rise and fall but no distinctive features at all. The rock itself, smooth and weathered, could be anywhere. It could be an asteroid. It could be on Mars. You could find it in some polar landscape, or in the middle of a desert. It is simply a lump of that particular kind of hard stuff of which the solid parts of the universe are made. And now I've missed my chance to go back into the cave in search of more food, because if it was risky then, it's surely even riskier now when so much more time has elapsed for Carlo and the others to return from wherever they holed up while the army was in the area.

I say the army, and I've been assuming it was the army all this time, but it occurs to me now that the skirmish that killed Guinevere could equally well have been a quarrel within their own faction, or between their faction and one of the rival revolutionary groups, some of which, I know, have become more like organized criminal gangs, or proto-states, perpetuating themselves by demanding tribute in money or in kind from local villagers, and sometimes a certain percentage of their children to serve as a kind of janissary corps, in exchange for 'protection'. In which case, of course, the people who shot Guinevere would be as much a danger to me as Guinevere's comrades. Even the army might turn out to be dangerous if they decided that I was lying and was a terrorist myself. And I've heard that some formations within the army have, to various degrees, gone rogue, and become players in their own right in the game of factions and gangs.

The climbing has distracted me somewhat from the awfulness of my situation. But now I am alone with myself again. My fingers were raw before I started but now are red and excruciatingly painful. I'm beginning to feel hungry. I have no idea which direction to head in. I feel in my pocket for the little plastic disc, and look at Guinevere's gentle parents, trying to absorb some comfort from the warmth of their gaze, though it wasn't meant for me, they don't even know of my existence, and they would no doubt be entirely happy that I should die out here in the jungle, of hunger, or septicaemia, or a bullet wound, if that would restore to them their strong and passionate daughter, who did them the honour not only of absorbing their beliefs but of taking them seriously. I eat one of Guinevere's mint sweets, washed down with a swig of warm and slightly plasticky water, and smoke one of her cigarettes.

I'll head to one of the places where the ground goes down a bit. There should be a stream there, with any luck, where I can at least drink, and perhaps catch a fish. And streams flow downhill towards larger streams, or lakes, or rivers, don't they, though admittedly in this sort of country you can't rule out cliffs and waterfalls, or streams disappearing into sinkholes.

I feel a certain unexpected calmness. I have broken out of my coop. I am back under the open sky, and away from the horror of that broken doll that had once been Guinevere. Now I have a destination as well. Also, having just absorbed some sugar, I am deeply savouring the hit of nicotine as it crosses from my lungs into my bloodstream.

I'll have one cigarette a day, I decide. It'll be my treat, something to look forward to. One's idea of luxury expands and contracts to fit what's available.

'Well,' I say out loud, 'you wanted to be a character in a novel.'

And, to my own surprise, this actually makes me laugh.

It's obvious that before nightfall, I will be in a completely different place, a place of hunger, and sickness quite likely, and certainly pain. In a few days, very possibly, I will be dying or dead. But that will be then, and this is now, so why make myself miserable about it? What help would that be to my future self? And why, in any case, should my future self have precedence over my present one?

The first gods to appear are Jesus and Dionysus, or so I like to call them. Jesus wears sandals, of course, and has the earnest look of the politically aware. 'Every soul is a fragment of the same divine light,' he says. 'This is why happiness is indivisible, and selfishness and egocentrism make no sense. When I call on you to love your neighbour, or offer you my blood, or ask you to turn your cheek, all I'm really doing is asking you to recognize this truth. Suffering must be accepted. Just to shrug your shoulders and let others bear the burden is to deny what you really are.'

Jesus opens his hands, offering his thoughts for me to hear if I have ears to hear them. He isn't really just a single figure, but a multitude, his face constantly flickering from one form to another like a TV set on which someone is constantly changing channels.

Dionysus blows a loud raspberry and laughs. He is a merry, beautiful boy in my imagination, but he's flickering, too, his aspect shifting from cheerful to spaced-out to cruel. 'For Christ's sake, Christ, why can't you lighten up? There's suffering in the world, I grant you that, but you don't make it any easier by banging on and on about it. There's also pleasure and that redeems everything. Happy people don't even need to ask what the point of it all is. It's only when we're sad that we ask that question. So seek pleasure! Seek joy! Seek delight! Why would anyone in their right mind welcome suffering?'

Apollo hovers over the water. His face is severe, though it's too bright to look at for any length of time. 'They're both wrong,' he says. 'Pleasure is trivial. Even the simplest animals know pleasure. And as for Jesus here, with his sentimental nonsense about the equal value of every soul, we all know that's not true. Some people are large and shining, others small and insignificant. Why do you think we have the words "bright" and "dull"? Life is intelligence. The brightest are the best.'

Aphrodite sits on the railing. She isn't like her statues at all, fuller in the figure, and merrier, and much, much sexier. 'Who cares about intelligence?' she says and instantly melts me. No one, whether man or woman, or some other sex entirely, could hear that voice without feeling desire. 'Are you seriously trying to say that what's important in life is being able to solve very difficult maths problems, or have penetrating insights into the cultural significance of modernism in the arts? Give me a fucking break, Ap! Dio is quite right, it's all about pleasure, and pleasure is about the body. And especially it's about bodies together, warm bodies touching other bodies, bodies caressing and stroking other bodies, bodies entering others and being entered. It's about stimulation, and ecstasy, and sweet satiation.'

'Really?' sighs Mother Mary. 'Wouldn't a life that was all about that be like being a horny teenager for ever? Surely you can see how boring that would—'

'Just sit and watch the river,' says another god, whose face I can't see, whose name I don't know, and whose gender I can't tell, but who is very familiar to me all the same. 'Just sit and watch the river. All the rest is—'

'Oh, do give over,' Jesus scoffs. 'There's a reason no one knows your name, my friend, while most of the world knows mine. Whatever followers you have are nobodies. They never amount to anything, they never reach any position of power or responsibility, they achieve nothing.'

'And right there,' says the god whose face I can't see, 'is the reason you've been adopted by rapacious empires for the last two thousand years. You make a drama out of life. You make it into this big pompous story full of noise, and struggle, and suffering, and pathos, and heroism. Heaven forbid that human beings should just quietly enjoy the experience of being alive.'

Dionysus has been following this exchange with amusement but now glances at me. 'You need to choose between us, you know. You can maybe follow two of us, or perhaps even three – life is more fun with a few contradictions – but it makes no sense to try to follow us all.'

'Well, how about that!' Jesus reels back in mock amazement. 'Dio finally says something that I agree with!'

'The rest of them are just sublimations of me,' says Aphrodite. 'The sooner you realize that, the sooner—'

'Oh, for goodness' sake,' Apollo interrupts. 'Just listen to yourself for once. Can you not hear how crassly reductionist that is? And above all, how *infantile*!'

'You have to choose,' Dionysus tells me. And all their various godheads, clustering round me, remind me of a big shiny bunch of balloons, each one a different colour. You can pick whichever one you want, your father tells you as he takes out his wallet, but you know that none of them will look half as good when separated from the bunch, and none of them is the colour you *really* want, because that colour apparently doesn't exist.

But other people choose anyway, I know. Other people make up their minds to believe in one god or another, and dismiss all the others. I've just never learnt how that's done.

'Just fuck off, the lot of you!' I tell them, and they vanish at once like bursting bubbles.

There's only me here, only me by myself on the veranda looking out over the empty river, as the sun begins to sink behind my cabin. There was someone else here earlier who was solid and real. She came a long way, and at some expense, especially to see me, but I spoiled the visit by being cold and unwelcoming, and now I'm here on my own, trying to take solace in the company of beings that only exist inside my head.

I owe Amanda an apology. I'll write to her later, not now when I'm stoned – I'm pretty sure she doesn't really approve of stoned me, and I can't say I blame her – but I'll write tomorrow, or the day after at the latest, and, though it's only two days since my last visit to the town, I'll take my letter downriver as soon as I've written it and post it in the mailbox in the lobby of her apartment building, with its cobwebs and its peeling whitewash, so she finds it when she gets back from work. At the end of the letter I'll tell her I'll wait in our usual café and then I'll go there and spend the time writing until she shows up. I'll have to lay off the weed, which will be good for my concentration, and I'll make a real effort to start a proper novel, with characters, and events, and a beginning, a middle and an end.

A boat appears from upriver. A relatively large one, by local standards, powered by a small outboard motor, with four people inside it, returning perhaps from a hunting trip – I can see a couple of guns – or maybe bringing back some of the latex that local folk persist in illegally tapping from the supposedly protected trees of the national reserve.

A swallow swoops in front of its bows. A momentary whiff of exhaust fumes cuts through the usual smell of green plants and river water, and the stench of stale sweat.

We have moved from the bar to a table by a window, looking out into the street of this bleak southern town, with its austere palette of greys and whites and blues so pale that they are really not much more than greys themselves. Some seagulls are fighting over a discarded slice of pizza. In spite of the latitude the window is only single-glazed, and has a crack running through one of its four panes that lets in little sharp needles of icy air.

I finish my beer, and Ham suggests another, signalling to the barmaid and insisting on paying. I find him strangely fascinating. He is obviously a bright man and in his own way a thoughtful one, and though politically and culturally he seems extraordinarily naive, I can see this is because his intelligence has been focused on entirely different problems from the ones that absorb me and my friends. He tells me that wind turbines are now more than three times the size they were twenty years ago, and that their enormous blades may turn a hundred million times over the lifetime of the machine, meaning the correct choice of materials is absolutely critical to achieve the best possible balance of strength, flexibility and lightness to maximize output during that period with the minimum of disruption. He discusses the challenges of bringing the power to the shore and integrating it into the grid, while minimizing losses during transmission, or during the process of inversion, which, so he explains, turns direct current from the generator into the alternating current used in the grid.

He repeatedly asks me if he's boring me. 'I mean, I'm an engineer, I can happily talk about this stuff all day long, but it doesn't usually interest anyone but other engineers.'

'I'm loving it,' I assure him. 'I won't pretend I understand every single thing you say, but I get the general idea, and there's a real poetry to how you talk about it.'

'Poetry?' he laughs. What lovely brown eyes he has! 'I can honestly say no one's ever said *that* before.'

'And obviously it's great that, you know, you're rolling out this new way of generating power that won't pollute the planet or fill up the air with carbon.'

'I guess.' Oddly, this aspect of his work doesn't seem to capture his imagination at all. It's how things work that lights him up. 'To be honest, I never intended to work in this industry – it's pretty simple stuff in engineering terms – but a job came up ten years ago when I needed the money, and somehow I've stuck with it.' He smiles. 'Are you going to put all this in your next book?'

'Ah. I don't know if there's going to be a next book. I'm bored of the direction I've taken. There's only one novel I really want to write. I've been meaning to write it all my adult life and I've never even found a way of starting it.'

'What's it going to be about?'

'Everything!'

'It must be about *something*.'

'Well, that's my problem, I suppose. I want it to be about everything. I want to write a novel that doesn't have a story, or a beginning, or an end. At least not in the usual sense. Obviously I realize it must have an ending in a literal way. But I want it just to . . . I don't know . . . I want people to be able to open it wherever and it'll . . . I don't even know . . . I have dreams about it sometimes. In my dreams it's amazing. Things happen in it, and they fit together, and they're satisfying, but . . . not in a . . . not in the . . . Ha! You see my problem.'

He laughs again. 'Not really. To be honest, I have no idea what you're talking about. But I'm enjoying listening to you. It has a certain . . . *poetry* to it.'

'Now you're just taking the piss.' I've finished my second beer. 'Do you want another?'

'You are *knocking* them back, aren't you?'

'You're right. I should slow down. It's nice talking to you. I split up with my partner recently – she came down here with me actually, but now she's gone – and so of course I'm feeling a bit lonely. In some ways this is a good place to be lonely in, I think, but it turns out it's a bit *too* good.'

'It's a bit lonely for me, too. I'm from the other side of the mountains. I come down here for four weeks, then I get a week back home, and then I'm back here another four weeks. I mean, I've got colleagues here, of course, and there's no one in particular back home. But still . . .'

'What do you talk about with your workmates here?'

'Good question. We talk about turbines, of course, and inverters, and undersea cables, and electrical distribution systems, and how shit the kit is that we have to work with, and how come we're the ones who have to make this stuff do what it's supposed to do but no one ever listens to us when we tell them that we could cut the maintenance bill by fifty per cent if only they gave us better kit. We talk about oil rigs, too, because a lot of us have been in that industry and, to be honest, it's got a bit more street cred than wind power. And when we're not talking about the machines we work with, we often talk about cars, and whatever other machines we own. Our phones, for instance, we like to talk about our phones. But, apart from that . . . let's see . . . we talk about sport and TV shows. And . . . oh . . . we tease one another about things. We accuse each other of being gay – that's always good for a laugh – or of being shit with money and letting the company walk all over us. We talk about how rubbish the company is, and how it doesn't appreciate us. Sometimes the other blokes talk about their wives back home, or their kids, but not for long because they don't want to seem soft. Actually, they usually *complain* about their wives and kids, and how crap they are. They don't really mean it, I suppose. Oh and – how could I forget? – we talk a lot about money. Who's making the most money. How much money we've got saved up. How to screw the system for a little bit more. It's kind of like . . . you know . . . the *score*, I suppose. Hmmm. I've never thought about it like that before, actually, but that's it: our work is a football match, and money's the score. And most of us are so absorbed in the game, we can hardly be bothered to leave the stadium. It can get a bit dull.'

He smiled at me. 'But I'm enjoying talking to you. What do you talk about with *your* friends, then?'

'Hmmm. Let's see. We talk about politics a lot.'

'Oh, I forgot that. We talk about that, too. As in: you slave your guts out and then the bloody government takes half your money off you to spend on Christ knows what.'

'Well . . . not like that exactly. Though come to think of it, most of my friends *do* complain quite a bit about how badly they're paid. But we don't complain about taxes. When we talk about the government it's usually more about how they're only looking after their own people and don't care about—'

'Oh, we talk about that, too. They just look after their own.'

'And we talk about how terrible the capitalist system is, and about sexism, and racism, and how the army's out of control in the territories—'

'The *army's* out of control? I'd have thought you of all people would think the *terrorists* were out of control.'

I shrug. My friends and I don't even use the word 'terrorist', but I can't be bothered to go into that. 'We talk about inequality, and the way the press and the TV stations are always siding with the rich, and—'

'So you're a bunch of lefties, then?'

'Sort of. We're certainly very much on the side of the poor, and the indigenous people, and the minorities, and so on. Except that we seldom meet any of them. Ha! I used to have a flatmate years ago – Rémy – lovely chap, social science lecturer and a bit of an old-school leftie, he was always going on about forging an alliance with the working class, and how we needed to be guided by the working class. But if there was one thing he couldn't abide it was what he called "tabloid-reading morons".'

'I work with a fair few of them, so I sympathize. And then, of course, there are the ones that don't read at all.'

'Yes, but what I meant was—'

'I know. I get it. He likes the working class but not . . . Yeah, that's funny. So what else do you talk about apart from politics?'

'We talk about culture, and the media, and books and films and TV series. We moan about how the wrong people get the prizes and the acclaim, and the really good people get overlooked because they're too threatening to the system. That old distinction between high and low culture is *way* too hegemonic for us, but we're *very* interested in what's in and what's out. You really don't want to be caught enthusing about something that's out. And most of my friends are in publishing, or are academics, so they talk about the organizations they work for, and how shit they are, and how they don't appreciate us though our work is obviously so vitally important, and about ridiculous workloads and stupid bureaucratic rules, and—'

'So pretty much the same as us, then,' he says.

What a good-looking man he is, with his gentle brown eyes, dark brows and thick dark hair. There's a pleasing modesty about his manner, yet he clearly takes great care of himself. He has a lovely physique that surely must take a lot of time in the gym. And, though there's nothing flashy about his clothes – open-necked white shirt, black chino trousers, navy-blue jacket – they're good quality stuff and fit him beautifully.

'The same as your lot? I'd never have thought so, but now you say it, I can see what you mean. I guess everyone thinks their particular group is underappreciated. Only difference is that in place of your machines, we talk about words and knowledge and ideas. Which actually *are* machines in a way, come to think of it, in that they're structures made by human beings to perform various—'

'Pure poetry!' He laughs. He smells nice, I notice, with just the right amount of aftershave – which can so easily be overpowering – and his cheeks are so smooth that he must have shaved earlier this evening when he changed out of his work clothes. 'I'm enjoying listening, but I have absolutely no idea what you're talking about. Do you fancy getting something to eat?'

He takes me to a place a few streets away that's a bit more lively than the bar we've been in. There are maybe a dozen small groups of people eating steak or chicken with chips at the red plastic tables under harsh white strip lights, with bread in plastic baskets, and music playing that my friends would see as shallow, commercial and manipulative. They're not the sort of people I know at all. Fierce people, I would call them. The men full of latent anger, dressed much like Ham, the better-looking ones sitting tall and straight like soldiers with big broad shoulders. The women are full of another kind of anger, wearing smart sexy dresses and lots of make-up, a kind of hard, wounded beauty in some of them; in others, just hardness. In one of the women, sitting opposite a man who is positively fizzing with anger, there is nothing but defeat. Another signed picture of the president hangs on the wall above them.

'Christ, they really love him round here, don't they?'

Ham glances at the photograph. 'He's a local boy.'

'But what is it about him? I mean, he's harsh, and punitive, and incurious, and—'

Ham laughs. 'Well, look at these people here! How would you describe them?'

'Ha! Harsh, punitive, incurious. Why are people like that in places like this?'

Ham shrugs. 'You kind of have to be like that to live here, I suppose.' He looks around the room. 'I recognize some of these blokes, actually. They're all right, once you get on their wavelength. That guy with the spiky red hair, for instance. There are loads of local guys working out on the windfarm site. Quite a high proportion of them are ex-fishermen. The new quotas have put an end to ninety per cent of that industry, so they're glad of the work. It's pretty good pay, but it's a hard way to make a living, maybe hanging from a structure with a harness, forty metres up, with the icy wind blowing up from the south, and often rain, or hail, or spray. Of course, they're used to that sort of thing from fishing, but I think that kind of job makes you tough and hard.'

'Are you interested in politics?'

'To be honest, no.'

'Hmmm. Well, I have had moments when I think it was easier back in the days when politics were for kings and courtiers, and the rest of the population just got on with life. All my friends are obsessed with politics. We get *so* angry that no one ever listens to us or does the things they ought to do. Angry with politicians. Angry with the people who voted for them. Angry with the media. On and on, every day. Because *they don't do what we want*. I'm honestly not sure why we're so convinced that what we want to happen would actually work. In fact, I'm not even sure if we *know* what we want to happen. But we *do* know they ought to listen to people like us.'

'Ha! Just like engineers, then! *Why don't these idiots listen to us?*'

'Who did you vote for last time?'

He pulls a mock-contrite face, and speaks in a very small, humble voice. 'I voted for the president. I thought, politics is a dirty business, it's not the same as ordinary life, and we need someone tough who can do tough things.'

I throw a bread roll at him. He catches it and threatens to throw it back.

To my surprise, we are having fun.

The decorator has left his ladder in the hallway, which gives me an idea. I persuade Jez to come with me at midnight, when the street is relatively quiet, so she can take the ladder back once I've climbed over the spiked fence of the Botanic Gardens.

I roar and make tiger claws through the bars as she waits to cross the road, and she turns and manages a smile, though she dislikes breaking rules and is anxious to return the ladder to the hallway. I head into the darkness that I've so often coveted from our balcony, pushing through the cool leaves. I've brought a sleeping bag in case it gets cold later, but the night is warm and I want to feel like a wild animal, so I take off all my clothes, and leave them with the sleeping bag beneath a tree. My idea had been to experience a kind of Eden right in the middle of our megacity, but the sad fact is that, now I'm in it, it is, of course, just the same old Botanic Gardens that I've walked through many times during the day, with its familiar asphalt paths, its benches, its wastepaper bins. I graze my shin on a sign giving the name of a fern.

Too late to get out now, though. This is going to be an uncomfortable and boring night. I smoke one of the small pre-rolled joints I've brought with me and prowl sulkily through the trees, failing to be impressed in spite of chemical assistance. Only near the edge of the garden, along the fence that I can't climb over, do I find anything even vaguely approximating to what I was looking for. The street lights outside cast complicated shadows across the ground at my feet, and the street itself has acquired a mystery of its own now that I can't reach it. Even my own apartment building, framed by dark trees, has acquired a certain strangeness, with most of its windows blank, but some still lit and open to the night, and others, more tantalisingly, leaking just a little light from round drawn curtains. From the very top row of windows, two storeys above our flat, I can hear the babble of a party, and someone singing a song in English while strumming a poorly tuned guitar. No one is out on our balcony, and the light in the living room has been turned off.

In a pond just inside next to the fence, its surface barred with light from the street, some kind of miniature duck is drifting quietly on the water while its mate dozes on the bank. An ambulance passes outside at speed, whooping self-importantly and splashing blood-red light over the ducks and their little pool. They take no notice. They are so indifferent to the world outside that it's as if it isn't really there for them at all.

Carlo has gone off somewhere with Jaco. Rubia, I guess, is on sentry duty at the cave mouth: stocky, thuggish Rubia, with her broad face and the wide gap between her two front teeth. Guinevere is reading by the light of their gas lamp, my only source of light, ten metres or so away from me. Lying on my side on my mattress, propped up on one elbow, I watch her. Perhaps wrongly, I sense that what's going on is a performance. It's some worthy text she's reading, some revolutionary bible, but one that she actually finds very dull. Holy texts work better if you don't read them, in my experience. Contained between their closed covers, they have real authority, but study them too closely and you can't help noticing that they're just written by human beings, as flawed and fallible as yourself.

In any case, Guinevere is very aware of me watching her – I feel quite sure of this – and is barely taking in anything at all.

'I could do with some conversation,' I say.

She glances across at me, then turns back to her book and doggedly continues to pretend to read.

'Interesting book?' I ask her.

She looks at me, lips pursed. After a few seconds she makes a decision and, putting down the book, she comes over to stand beside my cage.

'Listen,' she says, and then pauses before suddenly bursting out: 'I thought about what you said. About me being just as middle class as you, and only doing this because it makes me feel good.'

'Well,' I tell her, 'you've got to allow for the fact that you've got me locked up in a chicken coop, Guinevere. It does make a person a bit sour. I dare say—'

'No, you were right. That *is* why I did it, because it makes me feel good. But—'

'But what's the alternative, right? Doing things we think are wrong, just so as no one can accuse us of having questionable motives?'

'Exactly.'

She is very young. She still has the soft skin of a child. She's left her gun over by the lamp and is fiddling nervously with something in her hand, a plastic disc of the kind you sometimes see hanging from the driver's mirror in a taxi, with a picture of St Christopher or Mother Mary.

'Sit down, won't you?' I say. 'You're making me nervous.'

She squats down.

'Tell me something,' I say.

'I can't tell you anything about . . . your case.'

'I know. I didn't mean that. Tell me anything you like.'

She studies my face. 'Okay,' she says. 'I'll tell you what I've found out about power. It turns you into a baby.'

'How do you mean?'

'Powerful people think they're the big grown-up ones, looking down on ordinary folk, like the statues in the government quarter back in the city – all those bearded men with their stern, patriarch faces. But people like that are just grown-up babies. They have people running round doing things for them and making sure they're comfortable, people shielding them from things that upset them, people telling them how great they are, and how brilliant and how important. "Oh, you *clever* boy! Oh, aren't you *strong*! Look how *big* you are on your great big horse!"'

'We want power because it gives us a second chance at being a child? There's something in that. Look at Carlo, for instance.'

'I'm not talking about Carlo. I'm talking about me, and you, and my parents . . .' She glances down at her plastic disc and shoves it back into her pocket. 'And your parents. Your famous dad. All that love he gets from everyone!'

'Ha! He laps it up, it's true. His generosity of spirit! His energy! His ability to communicate! He positively *basks* in it, the old bastard.'

In spite of herself, she smiles, and I smile back encouragingly, because I feel it would do her good to lighten up. The poor girl is so painfully earnest.

'To be honest,' I say, 'the rest of the family find it a bit hard to take, when we know what a crabby old sod he can be at home. So yes, you're right, he is a pampered child in many ways. But I wouldn't call him powerful.'

'Of *course* he's powerful! And so are my parents. You just don't notice the power because you're used to it.'

'Are your parents famous, too? You've kept that quiet!'

'They're not famous at all. Just average middle-class folk. And they *think* they're just ordinary, because that's what they and their friends tell each other. They compare themselves with the rich people in the big houses up on the ridge, and think they're just ordinary downtrodden decent folk standing up to power as best they can. They've got two cars, live in a house with two spare rooms, go on a foreign holiday every year, have a cleaner who comes in once a week, and when they go to the supermarket they buy whatever they feel like buying, but that's how their friends live too, and though they know they're privileged, and like to say they feel badly about it – well, they really *do* feel badly sometimes, I suppose – they don't quite get that this places them among the powerful. I didn't either, not clearly, but I kind of glimpsed it. And then one day I *really* saw it. My phone was affordable because of the shit pay of the people who made it. My foreign holidays were affordable because I went to picturesquely poor places. I was living at the expense of other people, but I was being protected against knowing that fact. And my family's benign stance of being allies of the poor and the oppressed was part of that protective screen. *We were the good guys. It was those others who were greedy and bad.* We told ourselves that was so, even though we actually had enough spare wealth to feed many starving people every year, or cure many blind people, or heal many sick people, and even though we spent the vast majority of that wealth on our own comforts and pleasures – like those sliding glass doors we had put in to make our living room open out into the garden, or that foreign tour we went on – because we knew our hearts were warm, and we worked with people less fortunate than us, and we experienced compassion when we saw the suffering of others.'

She has taken that bit of plastic out again, and is rolling it around almost violently in her hand. I feel that she's close to tears but I'm not sure why.

'And you didn't want to perpetuate that.'

'Exactly. I didn't want to be a baby all my life. I wanted to break out of that cocoon and be with the people on the outside of it. People like Carlo and Rubia and Jaco, who dropped out of school at fourteen, and grew up in one-room shacks, and still had to toil away half the week to pay the rent to a landlord who lived in a ranch with servants and guards, surrounded by electric fences and CCTV. They know how the world really works because they can see it right there in front of them.'

'Hmmm. And yet there are people from that sort of background who make it big – footballers from the slums, pop stars from— Ha! I was about to say from *here*, but I don't know where I am, do I! They flash their money around, they buy big mansions with beautiful swimming pools shaped like hearts, and they have servants, and personal security guards, and chauffeurs in pink livery to drive them around – but poor people adore them! They pin their pictures to the walls of their huts. They pack the streets to catch a glimpse of them. They worship them almost like gods!'

She stops playing with the disc and looks up at me. 'Of course they do,' she snaps, 'because every poor person in this shitty country has been brainwashed from early childhood to dream of winning the lottery and becoming rich, which makes them complicit in wealth because they've admitted to themselves that, if they had money, they'd keep it to themselves as well. And that stops them thinking about the oppression – the *obscene* oppression – that holds them down.'

'Poor people are in a cocoon too, then? So who's left outside to see the world as it really is?'

She squeezes the disc so tightly in her hand that it seems to me, even in the gaslight, I can see her knuckles whiten. 'I'm trying, all right? I'm trying my best.'

'Funnily enough, I believe you.'

She looks at me. 'I'm sorry this means you have to be in a cage,' she says with an effort.

I ache for her, for some reason, I feel protective towards her even, and I feel a bizarre impulse to reassure her that she mustn't worry about my captivity and that I quite understand. But then I remember that what she's actually chosen to do is futile and indulgent, and that her little guerrilla faction has no hope whatsoever of changing anything, so that this is all just theatre, and, what's even worse, it's theatre that barely even has an audience. I remain silent.

She glances down at the disc and then puts it back into her pocket.

'Am I going to get a walk today?' I ask her.

'Not when there's no one but me here. Sorry. Carlo and Jaco should be back in a few hours.'

'Can we talk about something pleasant, then?'

'Like what?'

'I don't know. Places we remember in the city? Places we had fun? What was your favourite outing when you were a child? I used to love the cathedral tower.'

She looks up at me, anguished. Her eyes are pale green, the beautiful skin around them free of any kind of wrinkle or blemish, her pale brown brows sweet and soft. Everything about her is soft and young. It's obvious that she'd absolutely love to answer my question, go back to her childhood for a little while, chat about her favourite places.

But she says, 'I try to put all that behind me. All of it was tainted. All of it was stolen goods. I have no right to look back on it with pleasure.'

'How can anyone ever be happy if we see every pleasure as being stolen from those who are suffering?'

Again she seems close to tears, but there's no chance that she'll let them out. 'I think I'll carry on reading my book now, if you don't mind.'

*

I make a coffee and carry it out on to the veranda. On the far bank of the river, the sun is still rising from behind the trees. A large fish jumps out of the water, and the back of a big pale head appears, then sinks back down into the translucent green. I open one of my notebooks and leaf through my notes and scribbled diagrams till I get to a clean page. I feel fresh and alive after my morning swim.

'Dear Amanda,' I write. 'I just wanted to say I'm sorry that I didn't make you feel more welcome when you very kindly took the trouble to come and see me. I . . .'

No, that sounds too formal. I turn to another page and pause to sip my coffee, mulling over what I want to say to her and how best to put it, so that it won't come across as holding back, but at the same time won't seem to offer something that I'm not sure I want to give. This is a difficult line to walk and I've purposely not rolled myself a joint in order to keep my mind clear, and to stay in the kind of state that (I'm pretty sure) Amanda thinks minds ought to stay in. (I think she's right, at that. I've become over-dependent on the stuff here. It makes me lazy and greedy, and often deceives me into thinking I'm seeing something important when I'm not really seeing anything much at all.) I flip idly back through the pages of the notebook as I think and sip. I find a page where I've done a very rough pencil sketch of a stained-glass window, with notes on the various scenes I might include in its thirteen panels, six down each side and one at the top in the lozenge shape under the window's pointed arch. Stupid idea. Why those thirteen, for one thing? Out of all the things I could include why that meagre, arbitrary thirteen? The truth is that there's no better reason for that particular choice than the fact that they happened to be things that came into my stoned and befuddled mind on that particular day. And the whole window idea was half-arsed anyway, to be honest. It doesn't get you away from plot, and, since you can't cast your eyes over the entire content of a book at once, it doesn't even get you past the limitations of a narrative arranged in a line. Also a window is flat. Two-dimensional, like a cartoon. And reality doesn't feel like that. I need something more dynamic and three-dimensional.

Still there is *something* about those windows, with their bold outlines and bright colours, especially those deep rich reds and blues. In my mind they're connected with a sort of chivalric place that comes from childhood stories: Camelot, Logres, knights searching for the Grail through a mysterious forest, strange encounters in unexpected clearings with unknown foes who refuse even to lift their visors, a wounded king sitting fishing by himself in the middle of a dead and empty marsh, boats gliding across the water with no one in them . . . I do retain a certain grudging and slightly embarrassed attachment to all that – it's very definitely not hip or cool – and sometimes still toy with the idea of my novel drawing on images of that kind.

I did become somewhat disenchanted, though, when I studied history, and learnt that those stories were originally written *for* knights as well as about them. And when I came across the stories in the original, rather than in the sanitized versions written for children, I realized how full of knightly bling they were – golden candlesticks, swords with rubies set into the pommel – and how much they bigged up those wealthy and privileged men as good and noble and Christian and brave, when in fact they belonged to the class that went on crusades and killed and raped and plundered. And then that made me think how modern novels are written to flatter, and now they, too, valorize whatever class of people is their intended audience. Often they let the readers see themselves in a mirror that makes their personal struggles into something heroic. The more 'literary' ones flatter their readers by being clever and 'difficult' and full of allusions, so that it feels rather clever and refined, or maybe 'edgy' and up to date, just to be able to read the book and get the references.

But still there's something in those old stories that I like, and maybe the idea of openings in a forest is the way to ... Oh no, actually, even better, the idea of rooms in an enchanted or haunted castle ... That's just the effect I want because life really is like that, isn't it? We don't experience it whole. Each episode in our lives, each day – even each second in a way – is its own room, and each room is haunted by its own ghosts. Most of the rooms we can't see at all and even the ones we've visited are separated from us by walls and floors, and other rooms. There are stairwells here and there, where we can pause to look down and get a glimpse of doors we once passed through long ago, or look up and see floors whose rooms are still mysterious and unopened. We climb to the next floor and move from room to room. Some are occupied and others empty, some beautifully furnished and others bare, and some, perhaps, contain a strange cup and a spear, which drips continuously with shining red blood that disappears as it strikes the ground. Except not that, obviously, because that's someone else's story and I need to fill my rooms with things that are of my own times and not of theirs, carefully chosen so as not to flatter anyone at all. Not even me.

This is good! In fact, this is more than good. This rush is what I live for! I reach for my packet of grass and my cigarette papers. I know I said I wouldn't but sometimes it just makes sense to loosen the imagination a little and give it its head, and there's really no need to write to Amanda right this minute. It's not like my behaviour was so appalling as to require an apology to be prioritized over everything else. It wasn't even close to being that appalling. I do want to apologize – of course I do, because I know I was a little stiff and unfriendly – but, if need be, tomorrow will be every bit as good as today.

I'll do it tomorrow; that will be fine. I light the joint, draw in smoke, and hold it in my lungs, forcing it to release its chemical magic before I let it go. Dear God, this is a strong one! I can already see those rooms and those stairwells, and all around me, the gods and spirits are stirring.

A series of loud thuds against the back of the cabin makes me jump to my feet, groping for my gun. Holding it out in front of me, the safety catch off, I rush to the back door with my heart pounding.

Three little children are there in the plot where the cannabis plants grow: three sweet little brown-eyed indigenous kids, two of them in nothing but grubby shorts, and the third, the smallest, with a bare bottom and an old T-shirt. They've been throwing clods of earth against my wall. Their parents are doubtless cutting firewood nearby, or doing a bit of freelance rubber harvesting. The oldest can't be more than about five or six, the youngest more like three, and their little faces have been beaming in anticipation of my coming out and laughing with them at their joke, but are now shifting towards dismay because they can see I'm furious, and, although I can already see that my intended reaction to this intrusion is no longer appropriate, it's too late to stop myself.

'What the *hell* are you doing?' I bellow at them, still pointing the gun, my face no doubt blotchy and red-eyed from the dope. 'Get the fuck out of my place!'

Their faces are appalled now. The smallest one gives a little shriek of distress and all three of them run back into the trees.

I'm appalled too. I lower the gun. 'Sorry, kids,' I call after them. 'I didn't mean that! You just gave me a fright. I'll make it up to you! I've got sweets and biscuits. You can come and draw in my notebooks!'

But none of them re-emerges from the trees beyond my plot.

The thing about the real forest is that you can't just walk through it. You're constantly interrupted by shrubs and creepers, some of them spiny or covered in stings, some just tough and wiry, so you have to either cut through them, a job for which Guinevere's hunting knife isn't ideally suited, or find a way round them, which makes progress maddeningly slow. It's horribly hot and steamy, with no breeze to mitigate the heat, and there are biting insects of many kinds that are constantly attacking you, including enormous bluebottle flies that push big blunt hypodermic syringes through your skin to inject an instantly excruciating venom, and caterpillar-type creatures that cling to your skin with rows of little claws so you have to mash them to a pulp to stop them burrowing into you.

Kilometre after kilometre nothing changes, other than in the entirely trivial sense that each individual tree has a different arrangement of branches and any given spot has a different arrangement of the same dozen kinds of tree and creeper and shrub. I'm slimy with sweat and very thirsty, but I know that my half-bottle of water may have to last for many hours, even though the air here is at saturation point and the earth is moist as a warm wet sponge. I'm hungry but my few biscuits, my remaining mints and my single can of sardines, may have to keep me going for several days, so I can't just scoff them down as I want to do. Some kind of monkey or lemur swings down to a branch in front of me and I fire Guinevere's machine gun at it, but it leaps away unharmed, while I check the magazine and realize that I've now used up half of the twelve rounds in there, due to the gun being set on automatic fire. I try eating one of the mashed caterpillar creatures, but its disgusting yellow flesh is so rank that it makes me retch. Ants are slightly easier to swallow. I come across a column of big orange ants, and I stamp on them, snatching a handful and dodging away before too many of their friends have time to crawl up over me. They are crunchy in the mouth and have a sour acid taste, but they don't make me want to throw up.

More trees, more creepers, another shrub with huge leaves, and then the same again, and again, and again. I try to kick a hole in a termite mound but it's too hard and my feet too sore. My fingers are red and inflamed all the way along their length, and their tips are sticky and raw. I try not to think too hard about the fact that the destination I'm slogging my way towards is at best a stream bed in a landscape that's almost certainly identical to this in every other respect, and is, for all I know, a hundred kilometres or more from anything remotely different, such as a human settlement, or a river, or some open country where I might be able to travel at a rate faster than one kilometre an hour. I don't panic only because I can see panic would be entirely pointless, but at the same time I feel no hope. I just keep pushing slowly forward, thirsty, hungry, itching all over, with sharp stabbing pains from all my fingers. I try to remind myself that at least I'm free, I'm no longer in a cage and Carlo and his friends are no longer in control of me, but I also wonder whether I should just have waited for them. I wouldn't have injured my fingers then, and they did at least give me a place to sleep that was away from the worst of the biting insects, and pretty much enough to eat, and very possibly they would in due course have come to some deal that would have resulted in my safe return to the city.

More monkey-like creatures are hooting in the trees above me, peering urgently down at me. They'd provide some meat, but I daren't waste any more bullets. I may need these rounds to protect me against leopards and snakes, even if not human beings. I sit for a rest on a huge fallen tree that's opened up a gap in the canopy above it and allow myself a biscuit, a mint and a swig of water. I debate whether I should open the sardines when I stop tonight. Perhaps I could just drink off the oil – a prospect that seems utterly delicious – and wrap up the fish themselves in the silver foil for later. The ground is very damp. I decide to dig into it with my hands to see if I can find water, but when I try it makes me yelp with pain, so instead I awkwardly poke out a hole with the knife before kneeling down, putting my mouth to the ground and sucking what moisture I can from the spongy peat.

An enormous centipede the length of my arm crawls out

from under the dead tree, and, knowing these things can give a lethal bite, I abandon my rest and continue to shove and hack my way through the vegetation. The huge, sensual flowers and giant leaves would, in the Botanic Gardens, have represented a strange alluring unattainable place where death and desire, horror and beauty, were intoxicatingly entwined as in those famous paintings by that customs officer who never actually saw a jungle, but here in reality they are simply reminders of how nothing around me is changing, and I'm seeing essentially the same thing, over and over again, with the same thorns, the same biting insects, the same constant barriers of creepers and undergrowth to overcome. Perhaps it'll be night before I reach anywhere at all, even a stream, and I'll have to try to lie down right here in this nothing place where all the insects can find me, and wait out the hours of darkness with no sense of being anywhere at all.

I try to think about other things and places. The cabin by the river seems very small and remote, and so does the me sitting outside it, like a figure in the street below seen from the top of a tower. Even myself earlier today, sitting at the summit of that rock, feeling contented and almost cheerful, seems entirely remote and separate from me. *But even then I knew it would be like this*, I remind myself, *and soon this too will be in the past and I'll be in another place again.* Another room, you could say. But there isn't much comfort in this since it seems quite likely that this other room will be exactly the same as the one I'm in now – the same plants, the same insects – except that I'll be delirious and burning up with septicaemia and thirst, and the larger forest creatures will be beginning to discover that, if they fancy tearing off a bite of me, I'm too weak to fight them off.

A flying creature squawks as it alights on a tree above me. It's a pterosaur of some kind, with spiny teeth and a long leathery tail. I think about Amanda. It's been my hope all along that she'll have realized I've gone missing, and will have notified the army or the police so they can search for me, but, even assuming that was true, it would be no use now, since even from a helicopter passing directly overhead, no one could possibly tell that I was here. Perhaps I should light a fire? But I can't keep lighting fires just on the off-chance that someone in an aircraft will see me, given that I haven't heard a single aircraft in the whole time since I came out of the cave and found Guinevere's body, which must have been at least seven hours ago, I think, though it's hard to tell, and if I do hear a plane or helicopter there won't be anything like enough time to make a fire before they've disappeared again. Besides, if an army helicopter saw a fire they might assume it was terrorists and drop napalm on me, or a cluster bomb or something. Everyone knows they're very trigger-happy out here, deliberately goaded as they are by the rebels who lay traps for them such as pits with sharpened stakes at the bottom or foot-sized holes with downward-pointing spikes, which dig deeper and deeper into your flesh the more you try to free yourself.

Oh Christ, I might stumble into one of those, or into one of those rope traps that whisk you off the ground and leave you hanging helplessly until you die.

But as the day starts to fade I can tell the ground is beginning to slope downwards a little and I come at last to a small stream, which in other circumstances might strike me as exquisitely beautiful, with its overhanging ferns and miniature waterfalls, but is now just a resource. I'm about to run down to one of the pools to drink and cool myself and wash my raw burning fingers when I notice a group of ducks down there. Out on the water is what, from his colourful plumage, I take to be the male, while on the far bank is the plump brown mother duck, clucking softly as she encourages her three small ducklings to follow her to a little hollow that she's lined with feathers, and get them to snuggle up safely under her wings as she settles down to sleep. Cluck cluck cluck. *There we are, darlings; Mummy's got you safe, and Daddy will keep a watch out for danger.*

I lift my machine gun, flipping the catch back to automatic, for this is worth a few rounds, and blow the mother duck almost in half with bullets that have clearly been expressly designed to do the maximum internal damage. The male duck rises, flapping and squawking into the air, and I shoot him, too, emptying the magazine. He drops back on to the water and lies shuddering on the surface, while two of the ducklings emerge from beneath their mother's mangled corpse and run squeaking in terror down to the water, and the third flops about helplessly, apparently with one missing leg. In a single swoop I run down the slope and through the pool, snatching up the babies, and then stamping on them and their injured sibling on the far bank.

All five! How about that? I got all five!

I make a fire. I empty the first-aid stuff out of the biscuit tin into my backpack and use it as a kind of frying pan to cook the right leg, half of the breast, and some of the organs of the mother duck, poking the whole thing off the heat with a stick when the meat begins to char. It's exquisite, the most delicious thing I've ever tasted. I allow myself one biscuit for dessert, and then, on the basis that cooked meat probably lasts longer than raw, I pull apart the rest of the mother along with her babies and mate, and fry the whole mess in batches until darkness has fallen and the only light comes from my fire. I shove all the cooked meat into the backpack after removing the spare magazines, the last few mints, the hunting knife, the cigarette lighter, the cigarettes, the tampons, the phone, and stowing them, along with my playing cards, in the various pockets of the filthy shorts that I've been wearing continuously since I was captured. Then I treat myself to a cigarette to celebrate my hunting prowess.

I finally wrote that letter. It took me six days to get around to it but late last night, admittedly not completely drug free but not *too* much off my head, I wrote it. And now it's morning, I carry the outboard motor down to my boat, top it up with fuel, and, bringing my notebook and my playing cards, head off downriver to the town, thinking to spend the whole day there, and allowing myself a single small joint to make the journey a little more interesting, given that it will be many hours before Amanda's working day is over and – as I'm fairly certain she will – she comes to meet me at the designated café, so there's plenty of time to come back down. There's a refreshing coolness over the water, and a patchy mist that you quite often get in the early morning, in some places barely visible but in others quite thick, which makes both banks seem more remote than usual, and therefore pleasantly mysterious.

It occurs to me that I seem very much to like my immediate surroundings to present themselves to me in a way that makes them feel remote and far away, and that I like this because I can then reimagine them as part of an alien and unreachable place like something from a dream. When I think about it, this is quite perverse, but in my defence, it isn't *just* escapism, because these kinds of effects serve to defamiliarize space, by which I mean that, ordinarily, and assuming myself not to be unique in this respect, we don't think very much about the strangeness of there being something called 'here' and something else called 'there', with ourselves always *here* (except in certain odd states, which I have experienced from time to time, when we feel separated even from ourselves) and everything else being to varying degrees *there*, like those trees along the bank, some of which the light-filled mist turns into silhouettes, while others share in that light so that they appear in luminous colour, with the intensified three-dimensionality of a 3D film. And to add to the strangeness, there is also the fact that each individual sentient creature – that fish jumping out of the water ahead of me; those three green parrots, squawking and shrieking to each other as they fly along the right-hand bank – has his, her, their, or its own *here*, from which my *here* is a mysterious and misty *there* like those trees along the bank. People often express surprise at the passing of time – 'I remember it as if it was yesterday,' you hear people say, but also sometimes the exact opposite, 'it was only last week but it seems like a lifetime ago', in both cases expressing the unravellable strangeness of something that was present no longer being so – but it seems to me we rarely notice that space is equally mysterious.

I throw the butt end into the green water. Soon I'm passing my nearest village; as usual, a few people pause by their huts to watch me pass. No one waves, though, even when I wave across at them, and I can't help thinking that perhaps word has got round of my unkind and unnecessary treatment of those three little children, so that now the whole village is angry with me. I'm angry with myself about that incident. I wince with shame every time I think of it – it's a terrible, wicked, devastating thing to crush the optimism of a child – but God knows, the people in the village had plenty of reasons to be angry with me even before that happened.

My airfare alone, from the capital to the provincial town, was more than any of them earn in a year, and that's not to mention the cost of the boat, and all the supplies I consume while sitting there day after day, week after week, doing no useful work at all. On one visit to the village I saw a woman who was completely blinded by cataracts, which – and I happen to know this because my mother had to have it done – could be removed for less than a quarter of the cost of my flight. Such a small thing for me, such a big thing for her, but, though I gave her a few coins, I certainly didn't pay for the operation.

Anyway, I'm past the village now and I can relax and enjoy the morning.

One of those white creatures, those naiads, surfaces with a deep gasp, and I turn quickly away so as not to risk seeing that sad, reproachful face.

When we've finished our steaks, Ham suggests a walk to the harbour. We've got on well, and we've had a fair amount to drink. Although it's ten o'clock at night now, there is still some light because we're so far south. Ham says I should come down here sometime around the New Year, when it never gets dark at all, and even at two at the morning the streets and buildings are eerily lit up by bright cold daylight.

Moored boats creak and rock beside the dock and out along the jetty that divides the harbour in two. There are two tug-like tenders that Ham's company uses to ferry men and equipment back and forth from the construction site and another small ship shaped like an oil tanker, which they use to bring the enormous towers and rotors down the coast from the factory near the capital where they're built, and there's a very specialist boat with an enormous drum at its heart, which is used to lay out cable. Ham explains all this with the boyish enthusiasm that his work seems to awake in him, and which I find for some reason very endearing.

We stand side by side at the end of the jetty, wrapped up in our coats, and watch the red lights along the horizon blinking on and off in the dusk, each with its own slightly different rhythm.

'Do you want another drink?' Ham asks. 'The bars are a bit rough down here, but I know a couple that aren't too bad.'

'It's tempting,' I say, 'but I think I've probably had enough of a skinful.'

'Me too, actually.' He turns towards me. 'Well, it's been an honour meeting a famous person like you. I'm sorry if I've bored you with all my engineering crap.'

'You haven't bored me at all.'

'Oh yes, I was forgetting the poetry of it all.'

'Poetry indeed. It's been a lovely evening, Ham, and so much nicer and less lonely than the evening I expected to have.'

'Same for me. I'm so pleased you enjoyed it. Um, the apartment my company rents for me is pretty near here. I don't suppose . . . I don't mean to be forward, but I don't suppose you'd like to come there with me, and—'

I smile and touch his arm. 'No, I don't think so, Ham, but it's a lovely offer.'

And it really is! It would postpone loneliness and grief and regret, very possibly all the way through to the morning.

Ham is very embarrassed. 'I'm so sorry. You did say your ex was a woman, so I should have . . . But for some reason I felt . . . Well, I was obviously mistaken. I hope I haven't offended you.'

I look him steadily in the eyes. 'You weren't mistaken, Ham, I think you're very attractive, and I'm genuinely tempted. I've never understood those people who treat being gay or straight as if they were like football clubs that once you've picked one, you have to go on supporting it until you die.'

'Ha. Same. It does seem a bit daft, doesn't it?'

I study his face. Admittedly I'm drunk, but I feel I do quite genuinely like him very much. 'We don't have very much in common,' I say, 'but I think we do have *something* in common – something quite deep – and it was lovely to have a chance to find that out. But I'm not sure that you and I—'

He laughs. 'Well, I wasn't proposing marriage.'

'I know. But even so, I feel . . . well, I've just split up with . . . with my partner . . . and I feel it might be awkward in the morning.'

'It might. Though . . . you know . . . sometimes it's good to let tomorrow look after itself, don't you think? Otherwise . . . otherwise you're always—'

'Otherwise you're always missing out on now?'

'Yes, exactly. There you go, look! You're a writer. You know how to find the words.'

I find Amanda's name in a bank of rusty mailboxes, but hesitate before dropping in my letter. I fear that I've been too voluble, allowed myself to get carried away, said things that I might later want to take back. There were times on the journey down when I thought I should tear this one up and write another much shorter and more carefully worded note. But dammit I've spent too much time on this already. I drop the letter into the box where I can no longer recover it.

And that actually feels good, as it turns out. There's only so long you can stare at the chessboard, trying to work out all the possible configurations of the pieces in one, two, three or four moves' time. There has to be a point when you make a move and see what happens.

I head to the café on the promenade where I've said I'll meet her. It's the place we've been for breakfast each time I've stayed over in her apartment. I order a coffee and a pastry, and sit and watch the fountains and the people passing by. After a time I take out my notebook, telling myself that now is as good a time as any to start my novel, but it still won't come, not from lack of ideas or a plan but because of the superfluity of ideas and plans that now fill up several whole notebooks back in the cabin, quite possibly approaching the word count of a novel in themselves.

Never mind. It doesn't work if you try to force it. I feel I'm getting closer, and that's progress. Maybe tomorrow or in a week's time it will finally begin to flow. I like to imagine it bursting out of me like an oil strike, or bubbling and boiling away like that hot pool Amanda and I climbed up to, seething and spitting as it came spurting out of the rock. Wouldn't that be great?

It's good to be away from the cabin and the weed.

'I'm looking forward very much to seeing Amanda,' I write. 'It's funny how I hadn't quite noticed that until now. I mean, I knew I liked her but all the same it felt more like a duty, to write the letter and come to see her. But I wish now I'd done it straight away like I originally planned and not put it off. It would have felt more generous, more committed. It would have been a *real* apology. She would have appreciated that and I would have very much enjoyed her appreciating it. I like her a lot. Unlike me, she actually *is* like a character in a novel in the sense that she does stuff that you could write about and turn into a story. Whereas in my case, well, "Looks at river, rolls joint, has thoughts, makes a coffee, looks at river some more, shoots unsuspecting and blameless river animal for no good reason at all, rolls another joint . . ." What kind of story is that? But Amanda meets people, she interacts with them, she asks things of them – like she did of me – and lets them ask things of her and challenge her – as she allowed

me to do – refusing to be deflected by . . . whatever the name
is of that unpleasant emotion that so often gets in the way
of my relationships with others. What would you call that
feeling? It's a bit like jealousy, yet without actual envy of any
specific thing. It feels grudging but also over-fastidious and
embarrassed. It can easily turn to spite, or to prickliness or
surliness – which I'm afraid it nearly did with me that time
– but I guess it often comes over to others simply as nothing
more than inhibitedness or standoffishness or stiffness. I
guess it *is* jealousy in a way. I think it comes from feeling
required to make compromises, to surrender your own
viewpoint in order to embrace or accommodate the view of
another. Perhaps it's the jealousy a child feels when asked to
share the attention of their parents. But it's also the jealousy
that comes from knowing that, just by being them and not
me, other people are in a place where I can never go.'

I take a bite of my pastry, enjoying the creamy custard
bursting out through its warm and buttery skin. Jesus Christ,
what an unpleasant person I am! I feel that kind of prickly,
poisonous, over-fastidious jealousy *so* often, in *so* many
different situations.

'I'm wrong to sneer at the conventionality of Amanda's
liberal outlook,' I write. 'Any fool can find inconsistencies
and contradictions in someone else's values. But that's just
how it is. Beliefs are never consistent, but either you pick
some of them and use them to give some sort of direction
to your life or you spend your whole life rejecting everyone's

values for not being absolutely pure and true, and never completely untainted by self-interest, and end up doing nothing at all. It's like placebos, I guess. They really work, even though they're not what they claim to be, but you have to allow yourself to believe in them.'

When I've been scribbling away for half an hour, the waitress comes to see if she can get me anything else. I usually come to this café when I'm in the town. It's one of those places that decorate the walls with signed pictures of writers, artists and other cultural figures, and has books you can borrow, and newspapers you can help yourself to, and is a kind of solitary island of bohemian life in this frontier town, which, from a metropolitan point of view, is otherwise a cultural desert. They all know here that my father is the famous TV scientist – in fact, his photo is up there between an actor well known for her left-wing views and a prominent journalist who writes for the second-most liberal of our six 'quality' newspapers – because the absentee owner of this café is an aunt of my mother's, Aunt Xenia, a former Dean of Humanities in our most famous university, and still a formidable woman even now in her old age, who also owns my cabin, where, if the stories are true, she once used to entertain the local tribal chieftains, though she is now too frail to leave the capital. Most of the staff here make a fuss of me, partly I think because they are impressed by the reflected light of my dad, but no doubt also because they're aware that I am related to their own ultimate boss. This particular waitress, though, has always been rather cool and aloof, as if not just unimpressed by these things but wanting me to know that she's unimpressed. Today, however, she is unexpectedly friendly.

'So what are you up to today?' she asks. 'Are you stopping long?'

I tell her I'm planning to do some writing, and then perhaps have a walk around the town, and come back later to meet my friend Amanda. 'You may recognize her, actually. The tall woman who I've come here with a couple of times on Sunday mornings to have breakfast? She quite often comes here on her own, I think.'

'Oh yes, I do know who you mean. That's nice. So you stay over at hers, do you?'

'That's right. Hence the breakfasts here! It's a fair distance back to my cabin, so I usually head off back there in the early afternoon.'

'That's nice. Anyway, what can I get you?'

It's lunchtime now, I decide, so I order a ham-and-cheese sandwich and a small beer. It's good to be enjoying city things again. It's good to be able to take money out of my pocket and buy stuff with it, knowing that when the money runs out, I can just walk to the bank round the corner and it'll give me more. That makes me feel powerful and in control. The only thing that gives me that kind of feeling back at my cabin is my gun.

I decide I'll go shopping when I've had my lunch, not simply for provisions like I normally do, but for fun. There's not a massive amount of choice in a place like this, but still,

I'm sure I can find something a bit smarter to be wearing when Amanda shows up and actually I've got time to get a haircut too. If I don't take too long over it, I could even fit in a quick visit to the public baths to freshen up. And why don't I buy her a present of some kind? A bunch of flowers, perhaps, or a plant in a pot to liven up that damp little apartment of hers?

I look down at my notebook. The tricky thing about placebos, I think, is that you have to believe in them for them to work, and there's no way you can believe in them once you know they're placebos.

But I'm looking forward too much to spending some money to worry now about things like that. I take out my playing cards, shuffle them and start to deal out a row of them for a game of patience: the King of Leaves, the Seven of Coins, the Ace of Swords, the Prince of Cups . . . It's funny how each combination of cards has a different feel. Even the exact same cards seem to tell a different story if dealt in a different sequence.

I find myself wondering how many possible ways the entire pack of forty-eight cards could be dealt out, and spend some time working it out in my notebook, giving up when I realize that the answer will be absolutely astronomically vast.

For some reason, lying here in my bed this morning after one of the foreign women has fed me and cleaned me, I've been thinking about those imaginary forests where I sometimes thought of setting my famous novel. Ha! When I say famous, I mean famous in the rare sense of (a) non-existent and (b) only a handful of people have ever heard of it.

They're the forests from fairy tales, really, aren't they? Forests from the fairy tales of the old countries from which our ancestors came. They take us back to childhood but also to a time when, even in those countries (which these days lecture us, from their deforested landscapes, about the importance of preserving our wilderness), forests could extend for many hundreds of kilometres, and you knew, as you passed through them on rough unsurfaced roads, that behind that bland wall of trees there really were wolves, and bears, and outlaws who would happily kill you for money, and perhaps also – why not? – witches in little cottages made of gingerbread, and dismal caves where giantesses sulked, refusing out of bitterness and jealousy to shed the tears that would release from his tomb the shining god who the whole world loved. Also, there were enchanted castles behind thick barriers of thorns where princesses lay sleeping while, in an upper room, the lance with which Christ himself was pierced continually dripped His precious blood. They all merge together now, those stories, and though it's true that I'm confused as a result of being old and sick, and on my own all the time, and because of the drug they give me for the pain (which, by the way, knocks spots off that stuff I used to smoke back in the day), I'm pretty sure it's also true that they really *are* all just parts of the same story, all just lumps of the same basic substance from which everything is made.

What I used to find compelling about the idea of a forest is that it's divided up – unlike, say, a desert or a prairie – into countless separate and very local and intimate little patches of space by the trees, which prevent you seeing very far. So you can be in one place where life just seems ordinary, but you know that, in other places nearby, someone is grappling with a dangerous enemy, someone else is falling in love, someone else again is being born, and though you can't see what's going on in those other places at the moment, there's no wall between you and them. It's all happening, all at once, in the same place, though we don't experience it that way because of *here* and *there*.

Here and *there*. What *is* that all about?

Time's the same, of course, except that time has two kinds of there, one called yesterday and one called tomorrow. Identity, too. I and you and them: all that's just another kind of here and there. These things strike you when you're very small, and then you get used to them, they seem too obvious to mention – like the fact that an object you let go of falls downward – and you forget that after all there must be a reason for it, and that you don't really understand the reason. I suppose that's why I was so fond of the weed in my younger days. It took me back to that sense of pretty much everything being mysterious and strange.

But now I've come back to the edge again, almost in sight of the nothingness from which I so surprisingly once emerged, and I spend most of my time lying here going from one of those little intimate spaces to another, each one being a memory, a thought, a place I've been, or someone I've known, or something I've read or imagined – and sooner or later they merge together or mutate, as in, for instance, an idea turns into a shape, or a person turns into another person, or a real location acquires the characteristics of an imaginary one, and then I sink into sleep. Even when I'm asleep I know there are certain places to avoid and I can tell when I'm getting near them because of the feelings that radiate out from them, like dread or grief or shame. Sooner or later I forget where I am and stumble into one of those places by mistake, but for quite long periods I manage to keep myself in the pleasanter parts of the forest, wandering about there in my mind while cars and trucks growl and honk and roar in their own separate world below my window, and the leaky tap goes drip-drip-drip in the kitchen I no longer visit.

But all of that's during what you might call the forest phase. As the drug wears off, things close in. There's more pain. It isn't overwhelming yet, but I'm more aware of it and I'm also aware that it's going to get much worse, and so, of course, that alters how I see things, and results in a more pessimistic and fearful view. This is the castle phase. Now even pleasant things have a tendency to turn sour, and instead of open space connecting one place to the next, I have more of a sense of hard stone walls. And at the same time, I'm aware that I'm a prisoner, locked in not by a jailer, but by the sheer crapness of my own crumbling body, which could at best make its way as far as the door or the window, and not even that with any ease. I'm aware of the ceiling above me and the floor below me, and the walls all round, and people doing stuff there, things that I can't see and can't reach and most of the time can't even hear, apart from radios and TVs, though I have occasionally heard shouting matches and things being thrown, and, once, some very noisy fucking, and several times a party going on, and every now and then someone playing a guitar and singing – and the fact that these other people in their own rooms are so near to me, yet completely out of reach, only emphasizes the smallness and meanness of my cell. Everything I turn to in my mind seems stony and hard and difficult to penetrate.

But that's not the end of it, because next comes the dungeon phase, and now the pain is so bad that it becomes the single colour of all my thoughts – a kind of ugly, nauseating redness – so that whoever or whatever else I manage to think of, the thought is always overlaid at once by the sickly redness of pain, and all I really care about is when the fuck is that foreign woman going to come – whichever foreign woman it happens to be this time – and she'd better not be late, or I'll change to another company. I lie here willing her key to rattle in the door. When that doesn't happen, I make myself count to a hundred before I'm allowed to have a second go at willing her to arrive, and, if she still doesn't come, I begin to count again, all the time worrying that perhaps she's forgotten (whichever one of them it is) or been in a car crash or something, or her boss has forgotten about me and told her to do something else, or they've got their rotas mixed up, or my money has run out, and I'll just have to lie here in this dungeon as the demons close in and it becomes more and more like the torture chamber, which, I have imbued just enough religion to vaguely fear, might possibly turn out to be my eternal fate.

But here she is. Here's the sound of the key, and the door opening, and the foreign woman screwing up her nose at the stale air. I know this one. She's called Charity. She comes from one of those little islands – I forget which – and she's always very friendly, so I rather like her, even though she's extremely scatty and often calls me by the wrong name. She laughs cheerfully when I point it out, and assures me it's nothing personal, because not only does she get her many clients mixed up ('my ladies and gentlemen', as she calls us) but she even mixes up her husband with her daughter, or her daughter with her son, and all of them with the dog and the cat, on a pretty much daily basis.

'Hello there, my dear,' Charity says. 'What kind of a day have you been having?'

'Just give me that injection, and it'll get a whole lot better.'

She finds the needle embedded in my arm, attaches the syringe and almost at once the pain . . . well, it doesn't exactly disappear, it's still there at the end of the tunnel if I choose to look for it, but it's far off in the distance and why would I want to look that way?

There's a place I often see in these moments. Nothing happens there, and there's this heavy leaden light. There is something dreary about it, and empty, and yet it's strangely soothing. Hard to believe that it really exists and that I actually saw it with my own eyes.

The same waitress comes up to me again when I return to the café. I've never known her so keen to serve me. 'Oh, you've gone and got changed!'

I suppose she's just a shy person who takes a long time to get used to people.

'Yes, what do you think? I thought I'd make an effort for my friend.' I show her the potted orchid I've bought for Amanda. 'I feel I treated her badly last time I saw her, and I want to make up for it.'

'You look very smart,' she tells me. 'So. You're still planning to stay overnight and then have breakfast here in the morning?'

I laugh. 'I hope so! I think so! But obviously that's up to her. She should be along shortly.'

'A glass of something to keep you going?'

'Just a lemonade, I think. I need to pace myself.'

I look at my watch. (I never even wear it back at the cabin.) It's four. School finishes at three, and it'll take her perhaps half an hour to get home and find my note, and then let's say another hour to freshen up and get changed into evening clothes and walk the very short distance here from her apartment. She should be along before five. I'm sure she will. We parted in a friendly enough way, even if there were uncomfortable undercurrents, and she's absolutely not the type to sulk or bear grudges. She's a very considerate person. Even in the unlikely event that she's got something else on tonight, she'll arrange to meet up later, and maybe give me the key to her flat.

I open my notebook, and attempt to record some thoughts and impressions, but I'm a little agitated, a little nervous. I feel I've entered territory that I normally avoid, though it's hard to say exactly what it is. And oddly, the waitress seems to pick up on my agitation because she's always hovering around, and making comments like 'Still no sign of her then?' or 'What are you going to do if she doesn't show up?' or 'Will you still stay in town, or will you go back up the river tonight?' It's nice, of course, that she's decided to give up her former surliness towards me, and it's definitely something to be encouraged, but she's starting to get on my nerves a little.

'Oh, I'm sure she'll come,' I tell her. 'But I guess I'll go back upriver if not. I've always wanted to experience that whole river journey after dark. You get fireflies over the water at night, and – what do you call them? – those big white creatures . . .'

'Naiads?'

'That's the one. Those naiads come up to doze at the surface in little family groups. You can hear them breathing. And sometimes you can hear the smaller ones squeaking, and the older ones grunting reassuringly. It's all very peaceful.'

She nods, and moves off, not back into the café, but out into the promenade, where I see her in front of the statue of Barca, taking out her phone and making what seems like quite an urgent call, or at least a serious, businesslike one, before coming back to serve another customer.

The air is cooling now, the light is just beginning to fade from the sky and the promenaders are out. Strolling in both directions around the fountains, they greet friends, and maybe stop for an aperitif in one of the cafés, the men wearing suits, the women in smart dresses and fancy hats, and the children out of their school uniforms and in clean and freshly ironed clothes. They are the middle classes of the town, I suppose, but they're not the slightest bit like what my friends and I meant by 'middle class' back in the city, where we used the term to refer self-deprecatingly to our own particular section of society. These are the sort of people, I feel sure, who voted for the president, and go to mass on Sunday, and give their full support to our national army in its war against the terrorist insurgency.

'Still no sign?' the waitress asks. The lights have come on in the fountains – red, gold and blue, the national colours – and small bats are hunting moths around the pretty spherical lamps that line the promenade.

'Nope. Nothing.'

'Have you not texted her?'

'Unfortunately I can't text her in advance when I come down here because there's no signal further up the river, but, yes, I did text her when I arrived in the town.' Being alone for long periods does tend to make you lay out your own trivial thoughts in rather unnecessary detail. 'But she doesn't look at her phone at all when she's at work and it looks as though perhaps something's cropped up and she's still there now.'

'So you'll be going back upriver tonight, then?'

'I guess so. Pretty soon. I'll give her another fifteen minutes.'

'Good plan,' the waitress says and then she walks straight out into the square again to make another call.

'You're busy on the phone tonight,' I say, as she comes back to the café.

'Yeah,' she says, walking past, and then seems to think I am owed an explanation and stops. 'It's . . . it's my boyfriend back home in the city. He's having a rough time.'

Which is odd, because they didn't look like those kinds of calls.

2 THE CITY

The TV is a mass of flags. Dad is standing, as he always does, just a metre from the screen in bathrobe and slippers, his hair still damp and tousled from the shower, munching a large bowl of whole-grain breakfast cereal with yogurt, fruit and honey, and consuming the cereal and the TV news alike with the same . . . What *is* the word? I was going to say innocence, but that would be a very odd way of putting it, and Dad is very much a man of the world, known as both a consummate networker and a tough negotiator, on top of being a brilliant communicator. What I mean is that no one ever seems to have told Dad that appetites can be wrong, or unhealthy, or obsessive, or excessive, or anything other than wholesome. What comes his way he happily consumes – or so in this moment it seems to me – with great enthusiasm, without the slightest feeling or guilt or doubt, and without developing any sort of addictive craving for any particular source of pleasure.

There are still flags on the TV: flags held by children, flags in the shanty towns, flags along the beaches. Noticing me for the first time, Dad waves his spoon at me in humorous greeting. The TV is talking about preparations for the morning's Confederation Day parade of soldiers, brass bands, drum majorettes, veterans in wheelchairs, indigenous folk in traditional costume, which is why the screen is full of our chequerboard flag, whose twenty red and gold squares represent the twenty provinces that came together on this very day a century and a half ago to unite our continent into a single nation – or so it's always said: they were, in fact, intended to represent the twenty articles of a now-defunct constitution written at a time when there were only eighteen provinces – and whose blue border, so we are usually told, represents the sea that surrounds and protects us, though the flag's designer didn't actually have the sea in mind at all, and intended the blue to symbolize the Christian faith that he hoped would bind together those twenty provinces in spite of their disparate origins. People assign all kinds of meanings to the flag. For instance, a now quite fashionable story asserts, inaccurately – for its sole basis is the fact that the novelist, Mago Barca, proposed it retrospectively in his novel *Atlantis Rises*, some forty years after the flag's adoption – that the five columns of the chequerboard pattern specifically represent the five 'civilized nations' from which the founders of the Confederation came, and the four rows the four 'respectable' classes, from landowner to artisan to whom, at the time, the franchise was limited. But anyway, in spite of the lack of agreement about what it represents, there the flag is on the TV – red, yellow, blue – hanging from windows in provincial towns, fluttering from the aerials of vans whose drivers give a cheerful thumbs-up to the camera, and flapping lazily on those white poles that line Confederation Avenue all the way to the Unity Arch, which itself is topped by two rows of little red, yellow and blue flags around the giant statues of Mago Barca and the rest of the national pantheon. Traffic has been shut out of the city centre, and the TV cameras show us metal barriers being assembled to hold back the crowds that are already beginning to gather under the palm trees along the processional route.

'Absolutely *lovely* to have you back safely, my dear!' my father declares warmly, holding out his arms, spoon in one hand, bowl in the other, so I can come and give him a hug. 'Still can't quite believe we've got you all in one piece!'

'Well, more or less,' I tell him.

'I know, I know. Bruised and battered in body and soul. Of course you are, you poor old thing. But mending all the time!'

My beautiful mother sits with me as I eat my breakfast chocolate roll at the kitchen table. (Outside of the glass sliding doors, old Uncle Hector, our gardener, is setting out sprinklers to give our lawns their morning watering.) She wants to know how I am, and how I feel right now about the visit I'll be making in a couple of hours' time, and am I sure

I'm okay about it. 'It does seem terribly early days,' she says. She is as energetic as my father, and with equal appetites, but she likes to demonstrate her sensitivity with displays of deep concern and, quite frequently, guilt, as in 'Of course one does feel terribly guilty about all these wonderful foreign trips', though whether you can really call it guilt when you are proud of feeling it is, I think, an interesting question.

The doorbell chimes, and our maid Natalie shows Amanda into the kitchen. Amanda is wearing a rather lovely pale green linen dress, although her cheerfulness, her unselfconscious athleticism and her mannish height always seem to me, in the most charming way, to subvert her attempts at elegance. My mother greets her warmly with a hug and kisses. That Amanda and my parents became friends during my captivity still seems odd to me because, after all, I'm the link between them, yet I wasn't there when they met and wasn't even aware at the time that they'd done so. Mum calls out to my father, 'Alex! Amanda's here!' and Dad comes shambling amiably through from the living room, large and unshaven, with his abundant grey chest hairs bursting out of the open top of his bathrobe: 'Amanda darling, absolutely *lovely* to see you!'

Presently, I pick up my backpack and Amanda and I emerge into a bright day with a pleasant breeze blowing up from the sea. My parents' house sits right on the edge of the ridge from which the entire city descends to the glittering bay dotted with brightly coloured sails and stitched all over with dazzling sequins of light, each one the reflection of the same single object, the sun, on the surface of a ripple or a wave that happens briefly to be angled towards us. All along the street, with its palm trees and bougainvillea, people are emerging from large white houses, the adults carrying picnics, the children clutching chequerboard flags. From the space below us, church bells are ringing in the city's many towers, while seagulls shriek in the enormous bowl of sunlit air above the sparkling bay. Here and there, little yellow sky-monkeys, with their tiny fierce faces, watch the unusual human activity from the rooftops, assaying the risks and possibilities.

Amanda squeezes my hand. 'Still want to walk?'

'Certainly. Why not? It's a lovely day for it. And it'll give me time to collect my thoughts.'

We descend from the more prosperous suburbs into more modest ones. Down here, red, gold and blue bunting is stretched across the streets and preparations are underway for local events, with stalls and even little makeshift bandstands draped in red, gold and blue flags. Someone has been foolish enough to leave a cake unattended on a table, and a sky-monkey swoops down, steering itself expertly, with its gliding membrane stretched out tight, to alight right next to the cake, and cram into its mouth as much as it can before someone sees it and shouts, and it scampers to safety up a tree.

As the gradient of the slope becomes shallower towards the bottom we reach a street of solid terraced grey-brick houses, which I guess, when they were built a hundred years or so ago, would have housed members of the skilled working class. There are flags here too but not so many, and nearly half of them are not in the national colours, but rather the rainbow colours of the so-called Indigenous Flag, something that became popular, it seems, when I was still living in the Upper River and is now often displayed, not only by folk in indigenous neighbourhoods, but also by people who are not themselves indigenous, partly as a result of that unfounded but widespread belief that the five columns of the chequerboard represent the 'civilized nations' and specifically exclude indigenes, but also to make the more general point that the Confederation we are supposed to be celebrating was in fact built on conquest, expropriation and enslavement, with many documented instances of actual genocidal slaughter. 'A hundred and fifty years of murder, rape and theft should NOT be the cause of rejoicing' someone has written on a large sign displayed in their front window, though in this case, the accompanying flag is neither the national chequerboard nor the Indigenous Flag, but a *third* design – plain white except for a grid of empty squares outlined in black, the idea being that the colours of a new and truly inclusive flag have yet to be decided – which is displayed by a small but significant minority of households along the street, on the basis, I believe (for I'm still not fully up to date with the latest trends), that the use of the Indigenous Flag by non-indigenous people is *itself* an act of appropriation, and indeed of what we academic types like to call 'erasure'.

As we walk along this street, we pass people who look very like my own friends and Amanda's, though ten or twenty years older: professional people, teachers, software developers. They're setting up trestle tables, hanging up bunting in one or other of the various alternative colour schemes, and setting out food, and potted plants, and handmade knitwear to be sold in aid of various local projects and campaigning organizations. Several men are cheerfully engaged in the business of spreading an enormous banner between two houses on opposite sides of the street, which reads 'Party for *Tomorrow*'. For that's a much more positive thing to celebrate, right, than a mythologized and tainted past?

'Babies,' I murmur, and I stop dead in the middle of the street.

'Are you okay?' Amanda asks me.

'Yes, I'm fine,' I tell her, but although it is now some days since my return to the city, there are still moments when I find myself doubting that I'm really here at all. It's as if all this benign, generous, unshowy prosperity, this colourful optimism, is something I'm just imagining, and behind it still lies the forest – the *real* forest, I mean, not the exotic unreachable forest of imagination, but the airless tangled ruthless place where I thought I was going to die.

'Well, when you're ready,' says Amanda, 'this is the house right here, look.'

Confederation Day seems an odd day to have chosen for my visit, with all this jollity going on in the street, and someone even now testing out the sound system with a burst of loud and cheerful, if rather crackly, dance music. But to be honest, when I made the call, and the father asked me eagerly when I'd like to visit, I heard the desperation in his voice and just blurted out, 'Tomorrow, if you like,' without even remembering that it would be our national holiday. And he was just grateful for whatever I felt able to offer.

After a brisk walk along a cold black beach, we're having a lukewarm and rather greasy lunch in a small and almost deserted café. We have been finding it difficult to have fun in this austere place, way down in the south where winds blow up from the Antarctic ice. Even the wine is sour. And conversation, which used to tumble so easily from us, feels like pushing some heavy wheel-less object up a hill. But right now, we are at least enjoying the pleasure of agreeing about something.

Amanda is talking about books she's recently read by currently fashionable writers who don't divide their books up into chapters, or 'parts', or even paragraphs, with some of them also eschewing punctuation marks, or declining to use capital letters, on the basis that (a) these formalities get in the way of authenticity and fail to represent the fluidity of human consciousness, and (b) there is something hierarchical and exclusionary about such conventions, as there is about any set of rules that require the outlay of time and money if they are to be mastered.

'It seems a bit silly,' she says. 'They're just so hard to read.'

'Exactly. Which is far more exclusionary than normally punctuated text. In fact, you have to be very smart and literate to read them, which, of course, is actually the *point*. They're written to admit only those who are worthy.'

'Unlike your famous novel,' Amanda says, glancing up at me with a slightly weary smile, 'which is going to have none of these flaws, right, and yet be nothing like any novel ever written.'

I am stung. 'You see right through me, dear,' I tell her, and a wave of sadness and defeat sweeps over me.

'I'm only teasing,' she says.

'I know, but it's a fair point. I'm sure I'm as bad as everyone else, but I'm going at least to avoid the faux radicalism of gimmicks like unpunctuated and undivided text.'

'Sounds good to me.'

'But there are a couple of things I do want to do,' I say. 'One is to write in the present tense.'

'Not like your other novels, then.'

'No. The trouble with the past tense is that it's a lie. Okay, it's only a conventional lie, because we all know that it's fiction we're reading, but still, it's pretending that these things actually took place somewhere other than in the book itself. The present tense states the actual case, which is that the only place the events are happening is in the mind of whoever is going through the book at that particular moment. I might include imaginary animals from time to time, just as a reminder of that, or set it in a country that can't actually be found on the map.'

'Which also saves on research, I guess.'

'Ha! True.' Again, I feel stung, because, although I know this was only meant as a joke, I can't deny the fact of my own lethargy, which Amanda has seen for herself, and my no doubt narcissistic difficulty with engaging for any length of time with the products of minds other than my own, but would still like to feel that, flawed as it is, there is at least something about my approach that is honest and good. I would very much like Amanda to feel that too.

Why did we come to this dismal place?

'Anyway,' I say, 'what do you think? My latest thoughts on my famous novel! I feel I'm making some progress. What do you reckon?'

She looks at me intently for at least three seconds, and then reaches out to put her hand over mine. 'If you really want the truth, I worry that you're chasing a mirage.'

I think quite a bit about my novel as I make my way very slowly and painfully along that small stream, not with enthusiasm, not with any belief that it is something worthwhile or valuable, or even something that I am ever going to complete, but surprisingly I do still think about it. I'd have assumed that I wouldn't think about such things at all, because I've always had the uneasy feeling that most of the self-important chit-chat that people like me engage in, both inside our heads and between one another, really only happens because of the absence, in comfortable professional metropolitan life, of real existential challenges. We play with symbols, I've always thought, because we need *something* to play with, and our status absolves us from dealing with the material world.

But it turns out that when, metre by metre, you are slowly cutting your way through the material world in the form of thick, tough and sometimes spiny vegetation, you do need something to think about. And what I think about my proposed book is how twee the whole thing is, though I want so badly for it to be deep and wise. It seems to me that what I've really had in mind all this time is a kind of model railway layout, a safe little miniature landscape in which suffering and fear are carefully managed so as not to spoil the essential tranquillity of the overall design, and everything is motionless except for the little train running along its track, over bridges, through stations and (my favourite part) in and out of little tunnels, in order to impart a certain liveliness to an otherwise static scene. I've always been sniffy and superior about books that contrive to wrap everything up neatly, and bring the main protagonists to a happy ending, or to important life lessons at least, and yet my own idea serves essentially the same purpose of prettifying existence, and deflecting attention away from the fact that life has no particular direction and can for long periods be simply grim and meaningless, or even a kind of torture in that you have no control over when or if the suffering will end.

So, I do think about my book as I hack away at twigs and creepers and duck beneath branches and wade through water, and I think too about my life in the world outside, and my friends, my brothers and my parents, and the complicated combinations of feelings that I have about each one of them. They aren't comforting thoughts, they only exist to fill up a vacuum, because whatever I choose to think about is coloured a kind of nauseous yellowy green by my current bodily sensations. I feel slightly sick all the time, and feverish, and continually, maddeningly itchy, as well as chronically in pain from my raw fingers, and the blisters on my feet inside their sodden shoes, and the many scratches and scrapes I've sustained, and the insect bites, as well as the ugly lesions, many of them now infected, that are left behind by the huge brown leeches that I am constantly having to remove from myself. Sometimes rain falls and completely drenches my filthy clothes that are otherwise caked and stiff with blood, pus, sweat, dirt and squashed insects but do confer at least some protection against the numerous creatures that are constantly trying to suck my blood, or lick my sweat, or burrow under my skin. The rest of the time I'm trapped in a stifling treacly heat that feels almost impossible to bear, and perhaps might actually defeat me if I couldn't get a few minutes' respite occasionally by dousing myself in stream water.

In one of those small openings in the forest left by falling trees, four pterosaurs are stalking back and forth around some large dark object. The object twitches and groans. It's the still living body of a fat old ape, which has fallen from a tree and broken its back. One of them jabs at it tentatively and the ape flaps weakly at it with one arm, making the reptile and its three companions squawk and flutter back a metre, before resuming their implacable vigil, watching, without a trace of empathy, for the moment the ape becomes too weak to push them away.

A dying ape, four fierce scavengers left over from the age of dinosaurs . . . You could give this scene a certain dark, exotic glamour if you were telling the story to someone who's never been to a place like this, but in reality there is nothing exotic about it at all. I must try to remember that if I survive this. Real horror is just horror. Only imaginary horror is glamorous.

I approach the ape. Its rheumy eyes look up at me. I fire a single shot and see its head instantaneously split open and its brains spatter out on the ground, while the pterosaurs flap off squawking to the safety of neighbouring trees.

As I continue, wading along the stream now, in spite of leeches, because of the impossible vegetation along the banks, I take the little plastic disc from my pocket and look at the faces of Guinevere's parents.

Later I stop to eat, but what's left of the greasy duck meat is now three days old, and has begun to taste foul, which makes me think it may have caused the diarrhoea that I'm now experiencing, so I scrape it out of my filthy backpack as best I can and fling it into the bushes, where the cooked head of the mother duck looks back at me with one shrivelled eye from beneath a large, round, glossy leaf. I eat one mint. I have tried on three occasions to shoot something fresh. I failed to hit a monkey, and a bird with a long red tail, and while I managed to hit a small deer the size of a spaniel I didn't succeed in killing it, and it limped off into undergrowth too dense for it to be worth my while to follow it, dragging its maimed hind leg. Now I just have a single magazine of bullets, and need to keep it for my own defence.

After another hour I find some large red fruits which I gorge on, but they seem if anything to worsen the condition of my stomach. I'm beginning to feel myself building up, slowly and steadily, towards the ghastly state that precedes convulsive vomiting, and I can imagine a time coming when I will simply be too ill to do anything but lie down on the ground and wait – a terrifying prospect, because I know that pterosaurs, or some other creature, will sooner or later find me as they found that poor ape, and won't even wait for me to die. Yet I can already just about imagine reaching a point where even having my eyes picked out by reptiles will seem marginally more restful that continuing to slog through this endless mass of vegetation. And of course, as I regularly remind myself, I also have the option of doing to myself what I did to that ape, as long as I keep one bullet.

I wonder now if I should have cut the creature up for meat. There would have been a lot of eating there, but just the thought of it is so utterly nauseating that I do finally throw up and afterwards can't get out of my head the idea of biting into one of those hairy hands, or that fat hairy belly.

The stream sinks deeper and deeper into a kind of tree-choked ravine, so now there really is no way forward except the stream itself, and even that is criss-crossed with branches, which I repeatedly have to climb over, or crawl under, or even sometimes dive under, in order to keep moving at all. I am beginning to think that I may have no choice but to abandon altogether the idea of following the stream and retrace my steps, when I realize that the ravine is opening out and that not far ahead of me is more or less uninterrupted daylight.

I emerge into a small valley, formed at the confluence of my stream with another somewhat bigger and steeper one, which has largely been cleared of trees for fields of maize and other crops. As I step out into this new open space, I realize how much I've grown to hate trees. From further down the valley comes the sound of bells – cowbells or goatbells or sheepbells – though I can't see the animals and no human beings are in sight except, maybe sixty or seventy metres away, a woman in a red dress and a blue bowler hat, working a potato patch with a hoe. She looks quite old, though it's difficult to tell the ages of indigenous folk like her who are out in the open air so much of the time. I stand there in filthy clothes to whose mix of disgusting stains I have recently added diarrhoea, with the pack on my back that stinks of duck grease and the machine gun still hanging round my shoulders. 'Please help me,' I croak.

The woman looks up, and immediately turns to run down the valley towards a group of huts, which I now notice behind some trees, shouting all the while in a language that seems to consist almost entirely of intricate clusters of consonants.

They answer the door together. They're older than their photograph, and the enormous weight they're bearing is obvious at once, but both are terribly eager to make me feel welcome, and to assure me they understand the great kindness I'm doing them. 'So grateful,' they say, 'so good of you . . . It must be very hard . . . it would have been perfectly understandable if you hadn't wanted to come at all . . .'

I tell them that it's all absolutely fine, that I needed to do this for myself as well as for them, and that I really appreciate them letting me bring Amanda. I can be quite a nice person, for short periods at least.

They're very nice, too. 'Not a problem at all ... we quite understand . . . wonderful to meet you, Amanda, and, wow, what a good friend you've been . . . We've seen you on the TV, battling away with the government . . . we said to each other, if we were in that position we'd want a friend like you . . .'

'She's been brilliant,' I tell them, and Amanda squeezes my hand. 'She and my parents and my Aunt Xenia. They've all been brilliant.'

My parents I would have expected to fight for me, and Xenia loves a battle of any kind, but the fact that Amanda worked so very hard to keep my case on the national agenda is something I find both touching and somewhat disturbing, because I secretly very much doubt I'd have done the same if the situation had been reversed.

'Oh yes, absolutely,' the two of them agree. 'Your family have been wonderful too, and of course your extraordinary aunt is an inspiration to all of us.'

They have led us through to the living room, which isn't large compared to the one in my parents' house, but is comfortable and homely, made by knocking together two smaller rooms. There's an upright piano with music on it, and a small TV. A whole wall is lined with books – history, sociology, psychology, music – while the wall at the back has been replaced by folding glass doors that open into a tiny but beautifully kept garden full of ferns and orchids, the kind of place that is, I suppose, in part, the basis of the romantic idea of the pristine unspoiled jungle. Both of them are eager, desperate even, for something I have that they long to ask me for, but hold back for fear of seeming selfish or pushy. And it seems to me, too, that each of them secretly longs, in the way that children long for magical impossible things, not just for the meagre something I can actually give, but for something they know I can't give, but which they can't help hoping for anyway.

'I'm very sorry for your loss,' I tell them, moving quickly to close off that cruel impossible hope whose existence seems to me to be confirmed by the tears that spring simultaneously into the eyes of them both. 'If it's any consolation, I honestly don't think she could have suffered very much at all.'

'You mean . . .' begins the father.

'I mean I saw the injury, and I can't believe that she wouldn't have died more or less instantaneously.'

The mother doesn't speak aloud but asks a question that consists simply of her touching, very gently, various parts of her head and abdomen.

I touch the side of my head and she nods and cries.

'Thank you so much,' the father says bravely. 'Such a relief to have that confirmed. Of course, you know they never managed to find her body.'

'I gathered that,' I say, remaining silent on the many reasons, in the form of jackals, vultures, pterosaurs, monitor lizards and even the giant ants that I observed a couple of times dismantling the rotting corpses of birds and monkeys, why there would be no body to find after a day or two.

I glance at Amanda, who squeezes my hand reassuringly, a gesture that I find simultaneously comforting and very slightly smothering. A badly distorted blast of music blares out momentarily in the street outside and falls silent. Several people out there shout and laugh.

'Your daughter was a good person,' I tell her parents.

As happened when we first arrived, they respond to this as a kind of ragged chorus: 'So kind of you to say so . . . after all she put you through . . . not many people would have . . .'

'They *did* put me through hell, she and her friends.' As I speak, I feel an angry impulse like the one that made me kick Guinevere's poor dead body. Why should I swallow this feeling, after all that she and her friends did to me? 'It's pretty terrifying to come back in your boat after dark, heading towards the comforting little blue light that has always meant home and safety and rest, tying up your boat, and stepping into your cabin, only to discover that it's not a safe place at all, and they're waiting for you inside there, and they drag you down and kick you when you try to run, and cover your head with a prickly sack so you can only breathe hot, stale air, and tie you up with ropes that hurt, and drag you away with them, without telling you where they're going or what they plan to do with you, and shouting at you or hitting you when you try to ask.'

'We're so sorry . . . an awful ordeal . . . no one should have to live through that . . . still can't understand how Guinevere got herself involved in anything of that kind because it's really not like her at all . . .'

'That's what made her a good person, though,' I tell them. 'She knew her instincts were flawed. She knew she'd grown up in a little cocoon, as she called it . . . by which she didn't mean your family as such, but mine and Amanda's too, our whole class that creates a kind of fantasy world around itself within which we can feel we are kind and good because we're shielded from the cruelty that we're actually complicit in, and on which our relatively comfortable lifestyle is built.'

'That's exactly what she always said,' her mother exclaims.

'It is,' her father says, grabbing hold of his wife's hand. 'A cocoon. She always used that word.'

'Well, she did her best to break out of that cocoon, and it was brave of her.'

'Thank you,' the mother murmurs. 'It's so generous of you to say that, when she . . . Well, we knew that she *meant* well, but it's so wonderful to be . . .'

'The faction she got in with is barely a political movement at all, and really has no coherent agenda, but I'm absolutely sure she joined them in good faith, and after that tried to be loyal to them, although I'm sure she could see their flaws, by reminding herself of the injustices her comrades had faced.'

'She hated violence,' the mother says. 'She wouldn't even let us kill a wasp.'

'When I first met her,' I tell them, 'I didn't know she was a guerrilla. I just knew her as a waitress.'

'Which is what we thought she was doing,' says her father, 'until . . . you know . . . the police came to talk to us about . . . well . . . about your statement.'

'I met her as a waitress too,' Amanda said. 'She sometimes brought me a coffee.'

'You too!' they exclaim, and I think for a moment it seems to them that, if only a sufficient number of witnesses could report having seen her alive, she might turn out really to *be* alive, for after all only one witness has seen her dead.

'I thought she seemed interesting,' Amanda says. 'There was something about her – a certain intensity. She seemed ... passionate.'

'Oh yes,' exclaims the father, turning in anguish to his wife. 'She was passionate about everything.'

'Anyway, this is her bag,' I tell them, and they crane forward eagerly as I open the backpack, from which I've done my best to clean blood and sweat and rancid duck fat, and take out what I have left of its original contents: the cigarette lighter, the scorched biscuit tin, the knife and the little plastic disc.

'Believe it or not,' I tell them as I hand the little photograph back, 'you were a kind of company for me, during all those days I was wandering on my own.'

This was my old idea of forests, before my captivity: they were places where you could pass again and again from one small world to another. You could pass from here to there, and then be in a new here. And (in this romantic idea of mine) each here is new and engrossing because now you're in a place that previously you only glimpsed – it was *there* but mysteriously it has become *here* – and yet what is best of all about being in this new place is always the new theres it opens up, for you now have glimpses of yet more places ahead of you which hitherto were completely out of sight, but have now come tantalisingly within your reach. And the places you were in before, when you look back at them, are either no longer visible at all or already becoming obscured by trees, and have now acquired almost the same mysterious glamour as the places you have yet to reach.

But I can see now that this notion didn't come from real forests at all, but from city parks. Places like the Botanic Gardens and Temple Park are laid out with the deliberate intention of making a limited area seem large by teasing the eye with glimpses of a seemingly endless succession of spaces beyond the one you are in, while also ensuring that they *are* only glimpses, or you would just see right through the park to the far side.

But in this *real* forest, although the trees do create a screen that prevents me seeing clearly for more than a few metres ahead, and almost completely obscures what may be coming up even as close as ten metres away, there are no proper spaces, other than the spots where trees have fallen and the undergrowth runs rampant, which have no personality of their own. So there is no progression, just more of the same. I suppose in other circumstances, I might draw a good deal of pleasure from the stream, which is a feature of a sort, and which does from time to time widen into pools, or trickle over rocks, or even divide round a miniature island, and would certainly generate a lot of pretty pictures of ferns and so forth if you had a camera, such as you might see in a calendar or in one of my father's programmes about the precious wilderness of our beautiful country of which so much, in spite of the depredations of loggers and mining companies and ranchers, is still almost untouched. But even there the range of permutations is limited, and soon used up.

I wade, I pull off leeches, or I try to avoid leeches by walking along the bank and scratching myself instead on long thorns that seem to carry some kind of toxin because the scratches without exception become infected. I feel sick. All I have left to eat is some of those red fruits that make my diarrhoea worse, plus a single sardine wrapped in foil, which I saved from the tin I devoured last night. I have learnt to eat grasshoppers and preying mantises, picking off their legs and wings and scrunching down their plump abdomens, but I still can't bring myself to eat them uncooked, so I crush the heads of any I can catch and shove them in my now stinking pack to roast when I stop for the night.

My fingers are still raw. The skin tries to grow back but I inevitably do something that rips it off again. Some part of me is always bleeding and my nausea is constant. For some reason I can't stop myself from thinking about that ape, and the idea of eating it. Even though it makes me want to throw up, I keep imagining myself biting through that hairy skin, and chewing on those leathery fingers.

Something silvery glitters among the trees to my left. The stream is already beginning to descend into a ravine, but I feel the need to climb up and see what it is. I find a deflated balloon, silver and pink, tied with a white ribbon, the kind that's released at parties. 'Happy Anniversary' it says. I pick it up and spend a long time looking at it, this fragment of city life that's arrived here from beyond the forest. Sick and hungry and feverish as I am, and increasingly anticipating that maybe tomorrow or the next day, I may take the decision to blow out my brains and close this window on the world for ever, I hold this crinkly little piece of kitschy plastic and grapple with the mystery of its being here, and the way that, just by lying in this spot, it makes this particular configuration of shrubs and trees and creepers, which otherwise would be indistinguishable from the hundreds of thousands of other such configurations I've passed, into something magical and unique, almost like a kind of shrine.

It's taken me a couple of days to relax into this place. At first I was very aware of being alone, and of the cobwebs, the bare wood, the muddy taste of the water, the absence of electric power. And also of the presence, suffusing the whole cabin, of my Great-Aunt Xenia who everyone says is so wonderful but whom, it now suddenly occurs to me, I've never really liked all that much. When I'm in her company, I always feel like I'm dealing with some kind of human steamroller – a bit like my father, I suppose, but more so, and without his innocence and warmth. Xenia doesn't suffer fools or shrinking violets, as people always say of her admiringly, and that's all very fine until you suspect that you belong, in her eyes, in at least one of those categories and probably both.

There were still pictures of hers on the walls when I first arrived, growing mouldy round the edges: her own photographs of various places in the vicinity, and of local characters who she liked to think of as friends. I took the pictures down that first day and stowed them out of sight in a drawer. I made myself a meal on the little gas stove, and smoked some of my cool aunt's weed, but when I climbed into bed, the mattress was damp and sagged in the middle, the air was sticky, and there was a large insect of some sort banging about in the room, even after I'd turned out the gas lamp. I was very much aware of the darkness all around me through which anyone or anything could be creeping towards me, and I thought of all the comforts of the city – air conditioning, electric light, dry sheets, my phone, decent food, my friends, securely locked front doors – and I grieved for them, really achingly *grieved*, even though I knew I would one day have them back, because that was far off in the future, and this was now, and this was all I was going to have for a very long time, and, even though it was my choice, it was a stupid choice based partly on a silly romantic idea of what this place would be like, and perhaps also a little bit on a mistaken desire to impress Aunt Xenia, who I suspect doesn't really like me, though she's always outwardly friendly in the grand manner of my grandparents' generation, and I'm quite sure thinks of me as a bit of a lightweight and a nobody. When she was my age, after all, she already had an international reputation and had worked on three different continents.

The second day I was restless and uneasy. I went for a swim across the river and I won't say I nearly drowned, but I did feel pretty scared for a while on the return trip when the current took me and I felt badly out of control and at one point inhaled some water. But now here I am, sitting on my veranda on day three, all alone and completely at peace, and it turns out that this place is like a new shoe, which feels stiff and unyielding at first, but then you get used to it, and now it feels like the most comfortable thing I've ever worn. I'm looking out over the river, having my evening smoke, and I feel more at home in the world than I can ever remember feeling in my life. I don't have that longing for other places. I don't feel the pull of those pathways disappearing off through the trees, I don't long for a there that's different from here. I am content to be exactly where I am. What more could anyone ask?

Tomorrow perhaps I will start my novel. There's so much in my head, I feel that once I get going, the thing will just pour out of me. But there's no hurry. There's no hurry at all.

'Please don't run away from me!'

But the woman is still running and shouting, so I begin to follow her towards the huts.

Soon I can hear voices. People emerge from the trees. Most of them are men, several of them have guns, and the rest are carrying sticks or hoes or knives. As soon as they see me they draw up in a line, about fifteen of them, and begin to shout at me, but they shout in the local tongue, which sounds oddly dry and papery to my ears, and in which (assuming this is the same one that they spoke in that village along the river) I've only learnt the words for hello, please and thank you.

'Please!' I call out to them in what most probably is not even the right language. There are, I believe, still more than ninety extant indigenous languages, many of them isolates with no known relationship with any other language at all.

They brandish their weapons at me and shout. 'Go away!' they are very obviously saying, though I don't recognize any of the words. 'Leave us alone! We don't want you in our village!'

I point to my mouth. 'Please! I just want something to eat, and some directions.'

One of the men with guns steps forward. He seems to be their leader, and is somewhat taller than most of the others, though still about a head shorter than me.

He gestures towards the forest I've just emerged from. 'Go back,' he says in words of my own language, which I can just about make out. 'No come here, understand? Or we kill.' He points his gun at me. 'Understand? We kill.'

I feel angry. What threat am I? They may be poor, but how could it hurt them to give me, say, a few potatoes, or a bowl of that disgusting maize porridge they eat that tastes like wallpaper paste? Such a small thing to them, and such a big thing to me.

'Just something to eat,' I persist, because, after all, if he shoots me, he'd only be doing what I've already begun to contemplate doing to myself. And I also sense, possibly mistakenly but with some conviction, that this is a decent man who lacks the necessary coldness to actually do it. 'And tell me where I can go.'

The man frowns. He points to the edge of the trees where I emerged. 'Go there. Wait. Understand?'

He gives instructions to one of the three women in the group, and she runs back towards the village. He gestures to me to do as I'm told.

We stop in Temple Park. There are tree ferns here, and little streams, and picturesque rocks, and of course, on the top of its own little hill, there are the ruins of the Temple of Tanit. We find a bench to sit. Normally a place like this would be busy with mothers and young children but, because it's Confederation Day, we have the whole place to ourselves, apart from one little fair-skinned foreign family to whom I suppose the day has no particular significance. They're eating a small mid-morning picnic on the grass, migrant workers, I guess, who probably work in a hotel or a restaurant, making beds or washing dishes for pay and conditions even our shanty dwellers turn up their noses at: two young parents in cheap plasticky clothes, and a little toddler all wrapped up in pink, with ribbons in her wispy blonde hair.

'You've been so supportive, Amanda. It's incredibly kind of you, specially seeing as we . . . well, we were friends I know, but we hadn't really seen all that much of each other. I'm not sure many people would have been so loyal.'

What I mean, but don't say, is that I doubt that *I* would have been so loyal to her.

'I was very touched by your letter. It meant a lot to me.'

She reaches for my hand and of course I let her take it but now suddenly I'm experiencing that emotion that I don't know the name for, and I feel that I've allowed myself to be sucked into something that I don't really want to be part of. I feel that, while I like Amanda, I don't like her quite as much as she seems to think I do and that, while I know she likes me – and God knows she's put in a huge amount of work on my behalf – the me she sees isn't really me at all and it'll only be a matter of time before she finds out.

'You have to bear in mind,' I tell her, trying to be light and jocular but in fact (or so it seems to me) coming over as bottled-up and taut, 'that I'd smoked a fair amount of weed when I wrote it, so a lot of it was probably nonsense.'

She laughs. 'Ha! You warned me in the letter that you'd say that.'

God! So I did. I told her in my letter that the very warm feelings I expressed there were completely real, but that I had this thing inside me – this demon of embarrassment, or jealousy, or fastidiousness, or whatever you want to call it – that would make me want to deny it as soon as I'd said it, just as I'm doing right now.

It's as if I've constructed a siege engine, and given it to Amanda to use against me. Actually, there's no 'as if' about it. That's exactly what I've done, and quite deliberately too, in one of those attempts we make from time to time – I'm assuming it isn't just me – to bind our future selves to the choices we make in the present.

I change the subject. 'It was strange when I went into work yesterday. Everyone felt they needed to be welcoming, and someone had even baked a cake, but in fact almost all of them were noticeably prickly and awkward. It's like—'

The scream of jet engines makes it impossible to continue, and nine shiny blue fighters emerge over the ridge in a tight, perfectly diamond-shaped formation. There can't be more than a few metres between them, and yet they're hurtling along at several hundred kilometres an hour. As they pass directly overhead, five of them simultaneously release trails of smoke – red, gold, blue, gold, red– and then they all turn right together towards the city centre to fly over the Unity Arch and the Presidential Mansion. The mother and father have gathered the little girl up between then, so she is completely surrounded by their arms and bodies, and their three pale faces peer up anxiously at the sky.

'It was like what?'

'Well, I don't know, of course, but my hunch is that they were all very aware I'd had a certain kind of experience that probably none of them will ever have, something they were already slightly uncomfortably conscious of never having had to face. And perhaps they were even a bit ashamed of that fact, rather in the way that young men not quite old enough to fight might feel shamed by the experience of slightly older men who'd been off to war, and fought, and come back knowing things about themselves that the young men fear they'll never have a chance to find out, though they also hope they never will. So it was a kind of jealousy, almost.'

I haven't changed the subject at all, I realize, with a slight feeling of panic, as if I have somehow found myself inside a kind of maze where, whichever direction you head, you always come back to the same place, for I'm actually talking about that same exact emotion that I owned up to in my letter and, to make things worse, Amanda seems to be fully aware of the fact because she's watching me with close attention and obvious sympathy.

'A kind of jealousy,' Amanda repeats. 'Hmmm. You mean, like a child is jealous of a sick brother or sister, for getting all the attention?'

How strange. She really does know what I'm talking about. 'Well, that's in the mix, but it's not only that, there's also—'

'There's also that soldier thing, yes? Their fear that you've grown up in a way, and that they may be doomed always to be innocent children.'

'Yes, that too,' I say, yet oddly with Amanda it's *me* that feels like the innocent. She's a teacher in one of the shanty towns now with a classful of forty kids, some of whose parents, she's told me, can't even point out their own country on a map of the world. I know that I lack the maturity, and the self-assurance, and the ability to set my own needs aside that would be necessary to do a job like that. It would terrify me, and the children would sense that, and they'd gobble me up and spit me out. Yet she handles it without any apparent difficulty at all.

'But my sense is . . .' I go on. 'I could be completely wrong, obviously, and it could just be paranoia, but my sense is that none of them would have been able to own up to either of those kinds of jealousy, even to themselves, and so they had to find another way of explaining their twisty feelings, and came up as a result with something else that, in itself, they must know, is also not really fair but at least they are sort of able to talk about it.'

'You mean that thing you get on social media about how lucky you were to be from a well-to-do and famous family with friends in high places, because you had all this TV coverage, and deputies making speeches in the National Assembly, and—'

'And army generals giving assurances in interviews that they were combing the whole forest area of the Upper River with troops and boats and helicopters, no doubt at vast expense, and even though that same army rounds up peasants from forest villages on a daily basis and holds them without trial, and sometimes even executes them, and the TV remains almost completely silent. All of that. And yet what would they expect folk to do if it was one of them who'd been kidnapped? Are they saying they wouldn't want their people to pull every string they could? If they happened to know someone famous, would they really prefer that person to remain silent? Would they object if, say, the principal of the university weighed in to support them?'

'But you're saying that, at bottom, it wasn't really about that anyway?'

'No. *Really* it was that jealousy thing – or that's what I think – but you can't justify that, can you? Whereas this other thing . . . well . . . one of them couldn't even resist trying to articulate it to me. "It's wonderful to see you, it really is," he said. "We're all terribly relieved you got out okay. But one only wishes that the same public outcry was generated when . . ." Well, you get the idea. His voice was kind of strangled, you know what I mean? It was all choked up because of the emotions he was trying to suppress.'

She's still holding my hand, and she gives it a squeeze.

'I'm afraid I *haven't* really grown up,' I say. 'I think that would take a lot more than spending some time being scared and alone. But it's true that when he said that, I looked at him and I thought, *You baby! You pampered, self-righteous little baby!*'

The little family have now moved over to the pond that is the centrepiece of the park. The father is standing right at the edge of the water, pointing out fishes and ducks. The little girl is taking it all in, her mother squatted protectively beside her to keep her safe, peering into her small proud face to see how she's reacting to this new experience.

'That reminds me,' I say. 'The first night after I escaped, not long before dark, I came across a sweet little family of ducks. The mummy duck was looking after her babies, clucking gently away as she helped them settle down under her feathers. The daddy duck was nearby on the water, watching over them.'

'And that was – what? – a comfort? Or did it make you feel even more lonely?'

'I fucking killed the lot of them, didn't I? I machine gunned the parents and I trampled the babies to death.'

I feel myself trembling. From over towards the centre of town comes the sound of a military band.

She puts her arm round my shoulders. 'Well, they were just ducks, dear. You had to eat. And we eat meat. You and I ate chicken only last night.'

Guinevere passes in my evening bowl of stew. She doesn't meet my eye, she doesn't smile, but she doesn't walk away. The truth is that, though she's tried, she can't quite leave me alone. When Carlo is there, or Rubia, she doesn't talk to me, but when she's on by herself, or if, as now, it's just her there with Jaco, that sweet peasant boy to whom I think she is a kind of goddess of unattainable beauty and sophistication, but whose company she rather obviously finds extremely dull, she just can't help herself in the end from coming to talk with me.

'I used to like going down to Trinity Bay,' she says.

'Sorry?'

'You asked me about the places I liked to go when I was a kid, right? Well, I used to like going down there. We'd spend all day on the beach, me and Mum and Dad, and whatever other kids we happened to meet. Mum would read a book while Dad helped me build huge sandcastles and rivers and dams. And then Mum would come with me to play in the surf. Every day felt like for ever, you know? The beach and the sea stretching away into the distance, the boats on the water with their coloured sails, the sun shining down on everything.'

It's the first time she's ever shared anything personal with me – it's the first time, for instance, that she's told me she's an only child – and I hesitate for several seconds before answering, much as I suppose my father would hesitate if some animal came up close to him for the very first time, and he was trying not to scare it away. Which is odd when you remember that I'm the one in the cage.

'It is a lovely place,' I finally say, 'and so near to the city. We went down there sometimes, too.'

'My parents had one of those cabins behind the dunes, so we went there many times a year.'

'That sounds great.'

She's already retreating, though. 'But I remember one year – I guess I was about eight or nine – we were driving home, and we were on that flyover – you know the one? – that goes straight over the top of the southern shanty towns, and I was looking down at all those rows of shacks with their corrugated iron roofs, and I asked my parents why people built holiday cabins there where there wasn't a beach and there wasn't anything nice anywhere near. And Mum said, "I'm afraid those aren't holiday cabins, Ginny darling, they're people's homes, and I don't suppose they'd live there if they could find somewhere else." And later I found out that they didn't have running water or electricity down in those shacks, and only one room for a whole family. Our cabin never quite seemed the same after that.'

I sigh. It really is rather dreary when people constantly bring the subject back to social justice. 'I think you've got to grow a bit of skin sometimes.'

She shakes her head. 'But it's that skin that makes possible all the bad things in the world.'

'I suppose so, but it's also the thing that makes good things possible, like your blissful days on the sand.'

She doesn't answer me, but she's taken out her little plastic disc and is turning it round and round between her fingers.

'What is that thing?'

'Oh nothing,' she says, and shoves it back into her pocket. She turns away from me, looks up the cave to where the gas lamp is burning. 'Hey, Jaco, do you fancy a game of cards?'

Jaco sits up, excited as a little boy. 'Yeah, sure, Guinevere! That would be really great.'

I sit for a long time where the man said I should wait. The stream trickles over some stones. From behind me I can hear the sounds that have surrounded me for days, the various squawks and hoots and croaks and rattles of the jungle animals, which seemed seductive and alluring when I heard them in the distance from my cabin on the river, but now seem so dull and meaningless as to make me almost physically sick at the thought of being among them once again. From down the valley, a cockerel calls. A goat appears above the bank of the other larger stream across the fields, and looks over at me, before disappearing behind the bank again. So that's where the constant clop-clop-clop of goat bells is coming from: the green and the shade over there beside the stream. I feel slightly trembly and numb, and I have an odd and not completely unpleasant sense that I'm not really here at all. I wonder whether to have a cigarette, though there are only a few left.

Finally, the man reappears. He's still carrying his rifle, but also in his other hand a sack. I have no idea what he asked me to wait here for. Perhaps he intends to execute me, quietly and discreetly, away from the other villagers. For all I know, Carlo may have put a price on my head, and the sack is for the man to put it in when he's shot me and hacked it off. I flip off the safety catch on my own gun.

'Put gun down, please,' he tells me.

'Put yours down then.'

He shrugs, sits down on a log and lays his rifle on the ground in front of him. I still hold on to mine.

'What's in the bag?'

'Bread. Potato. Fruit. Cheese. Chicken. You don't want?' He reaches into the bag, and shows me a round flat loaf of maize bread.

I lay the machine gun down and he flings the bag across to me. There are two whole loaves in there. I devour half of one greedily, pausing from time to time to gnaw at a chunk of hard goat cheese in my other hand. The man watches me.

'You go that way,' he says, pointing not down the valley where I'd been headed, but up, along the course of the other stream.

'No. I want to get back to the river.'

He shrugs. 'River *that* way.' And again points up the valley of the second stream.

'No. I don't want to go uphill.'

Again he shrugs. 'Down there FRENALAT. Understand? FRE-NA-LAT. You like that? Okay, fine.'

FRENALAT is the alliance of guerrilla armies to which Carlo's outfit belongs.

'So you're saying I can reach the river by going up and over the top?'

'Yes. And God people up there.' He makes the sign of the cross. 'God people. Understand? They give food. They show way.'

I remember that cult that Amanda and I talked about, those foreigners and their charismatic leader. This is the first time since I was taken from the cabin that I have any sense at all of where I am, and it feels a bit like seeing, far off in the distance, that little blue light on my veranda.

'I understand,' I tell him. 'They have a holy cup, yes?'

He frowns.

'A mug,' I say, making a gesture of drinking. 'A special Jesus mug.'

He laughs in recognition. 'A Jesus mug. Yes. It's true.'

He takes a bag of tobacco from his pocket, tugs out enough for a cigarette, and offers the bag to me. As I roll up, he watches my hands with their weeping sores. He stands up, walks to a bush nearby and picks off a twig, indicating by gesture that I should rub the leaves on my wounds to soothe them.

'You don't like FRENALAT, then?' I say.

He shrugs, makes the side-to-side gesture of equivocation and then, to my surprise, he launches into a story. It's laboriously slow because of his very limited vocabulary, requiring a lot of guesswork, and gestures, and going back and forth, to establish each element of the narrative, and there are parts of what he says that I have to pretend to understand just so as to move things forward, but the gist is that FRENALAT came to the village some while ago, even though no one *ever* came to their village. The guerrillas ran up their flag, called the whole village together to tell them that they'd been liberated from tyranny, and dispensed various medicines and tools, and bottles of spirits with which to make merry. Several young people were persuaded to join them, and off they went. 'Keep the flag flying!' they told the villagers. 'You're free now. No more tyranny. We'll come back soon with more stuff.'

He looks at me. 'Understand?' he asks, and it occurs to me that it must be quite lonely being the village head up here, with no peers to talk to, and that he's taking the opportunity to get something off his chest.

A few weeks later the army arrived. The rebel flag was still flying and the soldiers were angry. They questioned every single adult, and every child who might just about be old enough to understand, to find out who had welcomed the rebels or cooperated with them. After that they'd called everyone together, and singled out a small group of people including the head man himself and the parents of the children who'd joined the rebels, saying they were terrorist sympathizers and traitors to their country, and would be shot. He'd managed to talk them out of it, and reassure them that he and the others were loyal patriots who'd only acted under duress. In the end, he'd got away with a public beating in front of everyone, and a warning never to do it again. The parents whose children had joined the rebels had their huts destroyed, and their goats and chickens seized. He was told to fly the chequerboard flag in place of the rebel one, and never to take it down.

'Understand?' he says. I assure him I do, and so he carries on to tell me how a few weeks later, FRENALAT came back, found the national flag flying and promptly did exactly the same as the army, interviewing every villager, including the children, to discover who in the village had offered friendship to the oppressor and betrayed the revolution. And, as before, someone must have cracked and told them something, because once again the head man and four or five others were paraded in front of the village and threatened with execution, though again he managed to talk them out of it.

'But no more,' he says and then conveys, mainly in gestures, the discord and distrust that these events have caused in their tiny village, and the constant fear. 'No more army. No more FRENALAT. No more no one. If you come near, we tell you go, or we shoot. We tell everyone go.'

He rolls two more cigarettes, lights them both, and passes one to me as he stands up. He gestures once again at the stream that will lead me to the God people. 'You go see mountain up there,' he says, making a steep cone with his hands. 'Go mountain, and then this way.' He places the imaginary cone away from himself, and draws a path in the air that veers to its left and then drops down. Then he shrugs, absolving himself of further responsibility for what happens to me, and picks up his rifle.

I don't want him to go. 'But I haven't even told you who I am,' I say. 'I'm—'

'I know,' he says. 'Army showed us picture. FRENALAT showed us picture. You trouble, friend. You more trouble even than flags. No come back, understand?' He shakes his gun in warning. 'No. Come. Back.'

I watch him through narrowed eyes. He's not a bad man. He knows how much danger I'm in, and it bothers him to turn his back on me. 'I need a coat,' I tell him flatly. 'Give me your coat. It will be cold up there at night. Give me your coat and your tobacco and I'll go.'

It's all a little awkward. We're sitting at the dining table in my old flat with Jezebel and Rémy and their new flatmate Estela, who has the room that used to be mine. Jez and Rémy seem smaller than I'd remembered them, and I'm reminded of a recurring dream of mine in which I find myself back at school and yet am uneasily aware that I'm far too old for it. Estela, who is a few years younger than the others, seems even smaller. The three of them are not sure whether or not to ask me about my ordeal. It seems obvious that they don't really want to.

But it's not just my recent experience that stands between us, it's also theirs. During the months of my absence, the conversation has moved on – the general conversation, I mean, that takes place both in actual physical gatherings and on the various online platforms to which everyone of our kind subscribes. There have been scandals, and changes in the government, and new laws passed, and various outrageous acts and utterances. There have also been new movies, a TV series that everyone had looked forward to, and enjoyed at first, but is now increasingly seen as shallow, exploitative and politically regressive to the point that there is now a campaign on social media for it to be taken off air. If I wasn't in the room, it would be these events that everyone would come back to for replenishment whenever there was a lull in the conversation, but my presence inhibits them, and Jez and Rémy fall back on talking about old times, like when I got Jez to help me climb into the Botanic Gardens, or Rémy spilled a casserole on the carpet that was meant to last us all a whole week. As they describe these rather trivial events to Estela, and to Amanda who's sitting beside me, I notice how they exaggerate and mythologize them to make them seem more colourful and exciting than they really were. I am supposed to have almost impaled myself on the spikes of the fence, for instance, which wasn't really the case, and the casserole is supposed to have stunk out the flat for several months rather than for the day or two that I actually recall. I guess in the past I would have joined in with that.

And then, too, there is the fact that, although I haven't been part of that general conversation, I have myself been a topic in it, as has Amanda: me as the famous captive in the jungle, Amanda as the loyal friend whose indefatigable campaigning got her interviewed on many occasions on TV and in national newspapers. Rémy, Jez and Estela must be uncomfortably aware that the general conversation included a fair amount of hostility, directed to some extent at myself, as I discovered when I went into work, but also at Amanda, for the jealous emotion is always roused by someone presented in the media as heroic or good.

'It's just a shame we don't see the same kind of campaign when some indigenous person is kidnapped,' Estela is finally unable to stop herself from saying.

The implication is unmistakable, as far as I'm concerned, even though it isn't said out loud: Amanda was at fault in writing all those emails, raising those funds, and starting that nationwide petition, when they were only directed at getting something done for me. But Amanda herself is surprisingly unruffled. 'That's quite true,' she says, somehow avoiding any of the bitterness that would have crept into my voice if it had been me. 'There should be a wider campaign. In fact, you ought to start one, Estela. But I warn you, a thing like that's an awful lot of work.' She touches my arm. 'And we're not even sure it made any difference to what actually happened.'

'I think I'll go and have a smoke,' I say abruptly, standing up. But it's too late; I've already passed the point where I could have kept quiet. 'I'll tell you what's a fucking shame, Estela. It's a shame that people can't just be pleased for me that I escaped from a fucking cage, and that Amanda did her best to help me, without some little prig chipping in to say that someone else deserved the help much more than I did. I mean, Amanda's quite right, what are *you* doing? What are you fucking doing to help *anyone at all*?'

In the stunned silence, I stalk out on to the balcony and light a cigarette. Everything's exactly the same as it was when I used to smoke out here every night. (Well, why wouldn't it be? It was less than a year ago.) The pedestrians pass by below me as before, in pairs and little groups in the warm night. The same old indigenous guy in the same blue cap still sits in his little kiosk on the corner, walled in by cigarettes, and magazines, and cheap plastic toys. The cars still growl and snap at one another. The trees are still dark beyond their spiked fence (which really is *much* less formidable than it sounded in Jez's story), with only the outer leaves and branches catching the street lamps.

It's all the same, but it's no longer possible to play that game I used to play here. As I lean on the railing and draw in smoke, I look across at the trees but, no matter how I try, I can't make them into an imaginative portal to anywhere, least of all to a realm that is wilder, and more dangerous, and more sexy, than our well-lit city. I've been to the place I used to stand here and dream of, and I know that it's just another place. My world is both much larger than it was and much smaller.

Estela comes out on to the balcony. She's pink with embarrassment. 'Listen, I'm so sorry about what I said.' And she turns instantly from the unattractive little prig she'd seemed as I left the room, into a quite likeable, slightly fragile young woman with rather graceful hands and a pleasing freckled nose. 'You were this famous person and I was racking my brains for something interesting to say – you know how it is? – and it just came out before I realized how critical and uncaring it would sound.'

I take her hand. 'Don't worry,' I tell her. 'Really don't worry. Don't think any more about it.'

I'm in a high, flat desert that resembles Mars. I've passed through the upper edge of the forest, where beards of lichen hang from the trees to drink in the warm mist, and into a region of ferns and moss and low shrubs, and then through an ascending series of meadows criss-crossed by little branching streams, where I stopped in the middle of the afternoon to eat some more bread and cheese, outside a solitary shepherd's hut, with nothing inside it but a cold black metal stove made out of an old oil drum, a few planks to sleep on, and a yellowing postcard of the Virgin Mary.

After that I passed several small lakes, and then walked for a while along a dry ravine, climbing all the time, emerging again and again into entirely new landscapes whose presence couldn't even be guessed at from below, and leaving each one behind me in turn, so that it too became just one more layer in a stack of fading memories going all the way down to the village that wouldn't let me in. But that steady succession of worlds is over now because I've reached the top, and the Mars-like desert stretches away into the distance, completely flat, until it reaches a distant volcano, capped with snow, that rises up from the horizon, and is obviously the mountain that the village headman told me about.

The baked red earth is punctuated by nine or ten different kinds of middle-sized plants that are completely unlike any that grew on the slopes or the forest below, some of them with thick, green, almost luminous, stems and fleshy leaves, some with no leaves at all, but simply spines and large white flowers. And there is another kind of plant, taller than the rest and without any kind of external features, just green columns standing a metre or two higher than the rest of the vegetation, almost as if they once supported some kind of roof.

A strange, sharp, but oddly leaden light falls on all of this, both unreal and super-real, terribly dreary in a way and yet also so strange that it's hard to believe it exists at all, turning the entire landscape into a spectacular stage set on which no play will ever be performed. The plants stand motionless, their nine or ten varieties evenly distributed and evenly spaced all the way from here to the horizon in front of that distant peak, each one picked out very clearly and sharply by that slow, grey, dreamlike light.

It's cooler up here. At night it'll be very cold indeed. I pull tight the old jacket that I coaxed off the village headman, and start to walk, as briskly as I think I can sustain, in the direction of the volcano.

*

Two kilometres upstream from my cabin, I turn off the outboard motor and drift. The sudden quietness is wonderful. There's no sound but the soft caresses of the water against my boat, and occasional hoots and squawks from the banks that seem very far away from where I am. Above the river, large, complicated structures of clouds both white and grey are simultaneously assembling and dismantling themselves.

I'm a little sleepy. I was awake for a long time last night, worrying as usual that I was frittering away a unique opportunity to build a new life for myself, but, also as usual, I feel differently now in the daylight, and am stubbornly resistant to the idea that I should subordinate my preferences to the needs of my notional future self. I mean, isn't it middle-aged people who always tell you when you're young to think about your career, and save up for a house, and isn't it the case that what they're really saying is that middle-aged life is more important than young life, which of course they would think because young life is no longer available to them, buried as it is layers and layers beneath them in the distant past? Why is my present age not an equally valid viewpoint, when middle age is still many layers above me, and impossible to see, and quite possibly may never arrive, because after all accidents happen, even to younger adults, and so do fatal illnesses? And, leaving aside this whole generational question, does it make sense at any age to be constantly deferring the present moment for some putative future that may never arrive?

Having finished my single-skinned joint and tossed the butt into the water, I lie back in the boat and look up at the clouds. Would it not be a sufficient achievement for one day to imagine – to make real in my mind, not just as a schoolbook diagram but as an actual fact – the process by which those clouds, as they drift over the mountains of the Western Spine, will release so much water that gravity drags it downhill through the sodden ground until it forms rivulets, and those rivulets come together in streams, and the streams combine into larger streams that, reaching the lower country, merge into tributary rivers that nurture the forest and, combining again many times, and topped up by the rain that the forest itself engenders, eventually become this enormous waterway on which I'm drifting now, that flows all the way to the sea, a thousand kilometres away?

But even with the help of the drug, I can't quite get there. The future is nagging at me. I'm aware that, after all, it's not just middle-aged me that has a stake in this, but even me in a matter of months, to all intents the same age as I am now, who will have to return to a life as a minor academic, which now seems almost unbearably small and narrow, and also somewhat deluded, since it involves pursuing a kind of phantom that can never really be reached, and feels from my present perspective to be almost completely irrelevant to anything important at all.

*

'Hey,' says Rémy, 'why don't we all go down to the Jungle Club?'

We've had quite a bit more to drink as we smoothed things over after my outburst, and in my case the alcohol seems to have rubbed away that edge of jealousy or fastidiousness, which, I now realize, has probably been my problem in these encounters at least as much as anyone else's, though it's impossible, of course, to ever completely separate my own projections from what really comes from those other universes that my mind can't reach. And, from this new and more relaxed position, I can also see that some of the problem, on both sides, has just been a matter of not quite knowing the rules, as in the awkwardness that people with no experience of death often feel about how to approach a recently bereaved person.

'Oh yes, let's!' I exclaim. 'The Jungle Club! Great idea! Have you been there yet, Estela?'

'No I haven't. Jez's been telling me about it. I'd love to go!'

Her eyes are full of smiles for me. We've gone from her apology, to me accepting her apology, to her being grateful that the famous recently returned captive has accepted her apology, to me being flattered by the extent of her gratitude, to her realizing that she's pleased me and seeking to please me more, to me realizing belatedly that actually from the beginning she has been both impressed and daunted by the experience of struggle and danger that I carry inside my head, which is so completely beyond anything she's ever known . . . So now positive regard is fairly bouncing back and forth between us, like the metal ball in one of those old pinball machines that's found the sweet spot where it seems to be able to go on for ever, its momentum recharged by every impact.

I turn to Amanda, realizing that she's quite probably never been to the Jungle Club either, and also, rather guiltily, that I've been neglecting her somewhat for the past half-hour or more. 'You up for that, or are you too tired? It's really nothing special, just a little music club, but it's just round the corner. The three of us used to go down there in the old days, when we wanted to let off steam.'

She smiles. She's had a hard day at school, I know, but she always tries to be up for things. 'Sure. Let's go. It'll be fun.'

We grab coats and bags. All together in the old brass lift, we descend to the street, the electric light, the mild night air wafting warm incense across from the Botanic Gardens, the cars that, after months of my never seeing the things, now seem to me a distinct lifeform, divided into many species, and each individual with its own personality. Rémy and Jez walk in front, hand in hand. Amanda takes my arm. Little Estela walks beside me, enthusing about how great it is to live in this part of the city and wanting to know what had been my other favourite places. We file past the big foreign bouncers in their black suits, descend into a cave of pulsing sound, and Rémy buys a round of drinks while the rest of us rush on to the dancefloor. The DJ is playing the song 'Our

Lost Atlantis', that ecstatic hymn to our vast city, 'with all its darkness and glorious light', described in the past tense as if it has already sunk beneath the waves. It's one of the songs that makes me feel like I'm sixteen again, bursting out of the confines of childhood, and I throw myself at once into the tide of the famous melody that soars so triumphantly above the constant pulsing beat. '*God*, I've missed dancing!' I tell Estela, but she can't hear me so I have to lean forward and yell it into her sweet pink ear. 'Oh I *love* dancing,' she shouts back. 'I could happily dance all night long.'

After the third or fourth song, Amanda takes a break from the dancefloor with Jez and Rémy, but I feel I'm just getting into my stride, and Estela stays dancing with me. That metal ball is still bouncing back and forth between us and it feels as if each time it breaks down another wall or door, so that we are seeing further and further inside one another. I'm quite aware that I'm drunk and allowing the music to carry me away and that this is all just a game, but it feels, at least a little, as if very soon there'll be no doors or walls at all, only a shining highway to a place of magic and delight.

Amanda is on the gallery above the dancefloor, leaning by herself on the banister, watching us. Jez and Rémy beside her are temporarily engrossed in a conversation of their own. Her face is very obviously tired, and I know she was at her school until seven o'clock this evening, dealing with a difficult disciplinary problem raised by one of the children in her class whose parents are constantly undermining her authority, but she smiles at me, and makes a kind of encouraging gesture to say not to worry about her, I should keep going as long as I like, too generous, perhaps, even to notice that glow between myself and Estela, or more likely too generous to worry or sulk about it.

I feel ashamed, but that makes me sulky and defensive. Estela hardly knows me at all, I understand that, and of course I know that whatever she is currently imagining she sees in me isn't really what is actually here, but an illusion created by my recent celebrity. And I'm perfectly aware, too, that, although what I'm seeing in her now includes a certain delicate beauty, that certainly didn't strike me when I first met her, when she seemed a rather ordinary type, not very grown up, not at all an original thinker, and a bit of a herd animal. But I'm enjoying the game we're playing, and I know I'd be free to play it out all the way to whatever disappointing or uncomfortable conclusion it would no doubt ultimately reach, if it wasn't for the fact that returning to the city and finding out how Amanda has fought for me so loyally over all these months has somehow bound me to the friend I made in the Upper River in a way that I didn't plan, and (or so I now feel) wouldn't have sought if I'd been able to think about it in advance.

But still, I *am* bound to her, at least for the present, so I lean forward to Estela, point to Amanda, tell her that my friend has had a hard day and I really ought to be taking her home. Estela looks gratifyingly crestfallen.

'It was great to meet you,' she shouts back into my ear, 'I really hope we'll meet again.'

We fall away from each other laughing, so that we can lie back on our own pillows to enjoy the release and its afterglow. The morning sun streams through the open window, the gauzy white curtains blow in the ocean breeze.

I reach out for her hand. 'This is so lovely. This is exactly what I've always wanted.'

Amanda laughs. 'Well, that's nice to know, because there was a time when I certainly wouldn't have guessed it. You were always so gruff and reserved, and if I tried to hint that we might go this way, you always drew a line so firmly, like in my flat making it clear that you would take the sofa bed before I'd even said anything. I thought perhaps I'd made a mistake in thinking you were into women at all.'

'Hinting? You call that *hinting*? A few minutes after we met, you were suggesting we strip naked.'

Laughing, she covers her face in pretence of shame. 'Oh, don't! I was *so* embarrassed about that afterwards. It was just . . . well, you seemed so unconventional and interesting and bold, with your cabin on the river and your talk about Eden and forgetting the city. I was afraid you'd see me as this dull, dutiful schoolteacher, so I wanted to show you I could be wild and reckless too. And I thought that's how it would be in Eden, before anyone had eaten from the tree. I mean, there was no right or wrong, was there? If you felt like doing a thing, you'd just say so.'

'You would. You were quite right. And . . . well, you out-recklessed me, I have to admit. To be honest, I was very tempted, but . . . you know, I wasn't sure what you meant by it. You seemed so sorted and so wholesome, and of course I didn't know if you were into . . . I mean, I thought maybe you were just thinking about it in a back-to-nature, outdoorsy, naturist sort of way, but I wasn't sure, and I didn't know how to . . .'

'You didn't know how to what?'

'Oh never mind, what does it matter anyway? We're here now. We're naked now. Do you want a coffee?'

'I'd love one.'

The hotel is very beautiful and very comfortable, and it provides in every room one of those coffee machines that work with little metal capsules, which at other times might make me think about all that ore dug up by indigenous miners in dusty stifling tunnels, and then the heat and labour and mechanical work involved in grinding up the ore, and extracting the metal, and blending metals together, and making the resulting alloy into ingots, and beating them out into sheets, and moulding those sheets into these little containers that we use just once and then throw away, to be collected up by men in trucks and taken out to one of those vast tips you see outside cities, where more trucks with spiky wheels crush them down to make room for tomorrow's load, and slum kids search for things to eat or sell . . .

But fuck all that! I don't give a damn. Not one single damn. From now on, nothing is going to disturb my happiness. I make us two delicious little cups of coffee, and crossing the marble floor of our large, white room, with the sea breeze playing with the gossamer curtains, I give one to Amanda with a kiss before returning to my own side of the bed.

'You know what?' I tell her. 'Actually, I *did* know that what you were offering was intimacy. I knew it, but I wasn't ready for it.'

'Well, that's not surprising. We *had* only just met. It was basically, *Hi, what's your name, where to do you come from, what do you do for a living, shall we get naked?* All I can say in my defence is that it seemed a good idea at the time.'

'It *was* a good idea, like all your ideas, and I wish I'd just gone along with it, because I did want to, but . . . but I always have this fear of being trapped, gobbled up. It's silly really. I miss out on so much. I guess that was why I felt myself to be so contented all by myself in my cabin on the river. No complications. No one asking anything of me, no one telling me what I should do or think. I didn't want to spoil that.'

'Well, that was fair enough. You were trying to stick to the project you'd set yourself. Quite right too.'

'My book, eh? My famous book that was going to be my alibi for everything.'

'Oh, come on, it's still in you! You're going to write it one day. I *want* you to write it.'

I lean across to kiss her again. 'I'll finish this book about my captivity. That's my project now. It'll get the whole business off my chest, and let's face it, it looks like making me a ton of money. I mean, I've already made a fair amount before I've even written it – and now they're talking about doing this movie, and . . . well . . . if that happens, we're going to be rich. But that novel, that novel that's not going to have a plot, or a beginning or an end, and isn't going to pretend to be in the real world but is real all the same, and may perhaps take the form of a fairy-tale forest or maybe a stained-glass window . . . I don't know why I keep going on about it, as if it was the whole point of my life. *This* is the point of life. Being happy. I mean, no one even asks what the point is unless they're unhappy, do they? And I'm completely happy now here with you. I honestly don't know why I'd ever want to do anything else but this.'

'That's lovely to hear. But it won't last for ever.'

Her saying this alarms me enough for it to be visible on my face. Amanda laughs. 'I didn't mean you and me! I hope that *does* last. I really do. I meant this, this honeymoon feeling. We know that doesn't go on for ever.'

'I suppose. But, at the same time I can't see why, if we want it to go on, it shouldn't?'

She puts her finger on my lips, as I once did to her, I suddenly remember, back by the lake in the forest. So, although I always think of it as being her, it was actually me that made the first bold intimate move.

'Shush,' she says. 'We're in it now. That's what matters.'

We put down our cups and kiss some more, and then I throw on the white silk robe that the hotel provides, and cross those cool marble tiles again to go out on to the balcony for a cigarette. One of those pretty whitewashed west-coast towns is laid out on the slopes around us, the sky is immaculately blue and, a short way out into the bay, two holidaymakers are playing in a little white dinghy with beautiful rust-red sails. Further out, there's a small island surrounded by sparkling sea, with its own church spire and jetty and a lighthouse painted in stripes of red and white, and, between the island and the dinghy with the rust-coloured sails, a fisherman and his young son are hauling in nets, picking out one by one the silver squirming fish to toss them into the bottom of their tough old boat, while seagulls wheel hopefully around them.

I light up. The world feels so peaceful and benign that it's hard to believe that only a few months ago I was alone, and sick, and being eaten by insects, in that suffocating forest that made every metre of progress a struggle, which is interesting because sometimes, even now, the reverse is true, and it's hard to believe I'm not still there.

I exhale. It occurs to me that if I was one of those fish in the bottom of that boat, this wouldn't be a peaceful moment at all. I'd be literally suffocating. I'd be in a place where I couldn't breathe, but was impossible to escape from and completely beyond my comprehension, thrashing about in terror and pain.

Too bad, I think. It's their turn. And I look instead at the boat with the pretty red sails. A kind of force field surrounds me, thrumming and fizzing as it holds at bay my past and my future, and the suffering of the world, and my many doubts and fears about me and Amanda and life in general, to create this little perfect bubble of happiness.

Amanda has put on her own silk robe to join me. She slips her arm round my waist and pulls me against her so our hips and thighs are touching. I rest my head on her shoulder. She's taller than me, and sometimes I like the feeling that can give me of me being a child and her the grown-up, while at other times I resent it. Right now, it's just that she happens to be taller.

After walking for a while, I feel as if I've been here for ever. In fact, I feel as if there might in reality *be* no other place but this, and that all my recollections of that tangled forest, or the cage, or the river, or the city where I grew up, are nothing more than dreams. It seems so orderly and calm here with these evenly spaced plants in their nine or ten varieties, laid out as if by the landscape-generating function of some computer game whose simple rule is that there must be at least one of each kind in each five-metre square of a grid, and that the gap between any two plants should never be less than one and a half metres, and never more than two. The sun is sinking to my right – it seems I'm walking south – and each plant is throwing out its own long lengthening shadow, in parallel with all the others, neatly and precisely, on the hard, bare ground. You could make a computer program do that too. The only thing that tells me this won't go on for ever, and won't simply be generated in front of me as long as I choose to walk, is that volcano in the distance.

At least it's not difficult to walk here. There's nothing to trip me up, nothing I need to hack my way through, nothing trying to suck my blood or burrow under my skin. But I'm becoming aware that, all the same, there's a threat here more deadly than anything I've yet had to face. I can feel the warmth of the day radiating upwards from the ground beneath me as it pours out from the Earth into that leaden, empty sky, and I know that in a few hours there'll be none of it left.

I hear a woody cracking sound. It comes from behind me but when I look round, there's nothing to see. Then I hear it again to my right. And then in front of me. And then from several directions at once. It comes from the top of those columns that stand out above the other plants, and soon the source of it becomes visible. Feather-like structures are starting to unfurl, two or three of them from the top of each one, very stiffly at first, like the wings of a butterfly just out of the chrysalis, but loosening as they extend to their full three-metre length. And now they begin to move. In a series of slow sweeping motions, like languid oars through water, they reach back, creaking a little and occasionally making a small sharp snapping sound, and then, cupping themselves slightly like a hand, they sweep forward with a soft whoosh. And, though each one has a different rhythm, every single one of them sweeps in the direction of the volcano, as if they are feeding it air. Soon the entire landscape that has been so still and silent is full of their creaking and whooshing sounds, their occasional sharp woody snaps, which merge in the distance into a kind of soft waterfall roar. Wherever I look those same feathery shapes are slowly and steadily raking the air, yet their motion is so regular and constant, and so apparently unresponsive to anything except the fact of the fading light, that it is in itself like a kind of absence, like the ticking of a clock in an empty room.

I'm limping and very tired but I walk quickly because I'm more and more worried about the cold. I have nothing more than the village headman's jacket to keep me warm, and there's nowhere to shelter, and nothing out of which a shelter could be built, at least not without a spade and an axe and many hours of daylight. It's hard to believe that I could ever have minded the heat of the forest, which is so obviously preferable to the freezing cold that lies ahead of me and is already beginning to creep towards my bones, that I can only think of it as comforting and benign. A few stars appear, and the occasional small bat swoops and swerves between the darkening shapes of the plants. I keep walking. Whoosh, whoosh, go the giant feathers above my head. I guess they must bring up moist air from the slopes below that will condense as frost and melt in the morning into dew.

Soon the sky has filled with the brightest firmament I have ever seen, the Milky Way streaming across it all, and while this is certainly extraordinarily beautiful, it's also terrifying because I know just enough about the atmosphere to understand that the shutters of the sky have been flung wide open to the coldness of space, without even a curtain of cloud to hold it at bay. The moving feathers are just shadows now against the stars, steadily working away in the darkness like a clockwork mechanism beneath a blazing universe that itself is a mechanism of wheels, and wheels within wheels, and wheels within wheels within wheels. I wonder if it would be safer to go back, but realize I've left it too late. I'd have to go a long way back down the slope to reach anywhere warmer, and once I got off this plateau I would be attempting to walk on rough and stony ground in almost pitch darkness. I could have stayed in that shepherd's hut with a fire in the stove to keep me warm, and set off again in the morning. It was an obvious, stupid mistake to climb so high when most of the day was already gone, but it's done and I can't undo it. There's no way now that I could hope to find that cosy hut.

'So this may well be the night l die,' I say out loud. It's a lonely thought, not so much because of the absence of companions at the end, but because, if I die, everything that I have experienced since Amanda failed to show up at the café will disappear with me. No one will know about the little family of ducks, or the dying ape, or the ants and grasshoppers

I had to eat. No one will know what I thought about, or what I felt, or how I kept myself going. The only person I've had any sort of conversation with in all that time is Guinevere and she is dead herself, and probably nothing more by now than a few bones scattered over several kilometres of forest. The villagers who drove me away will remember my existence for a while, and the headman will remember how I wheedled the coat off his back, but they know nothing about me, and in any case, no one will ever think to ask them. Carlo, Jaco, Rubia, and the various other guerrillas who came and went, will, if they're still alive, remember a few things I said and did, but they never asked me anything about myself. Carlo just lectured me and, though Jaco would sometimes talk to me, it was only because he liked to hear about the city and about things like the sea, which he'd heard of but never seen. And no one will ask Jaco about me either.

Someone will probably eventually find the notebooks I left in Aunt Xenia's cabin, but everything that's happened since will be a mystery, like some interstellar rock that once passed close enough to Earth to be glimpsed through telescopes but then disappeared again into the darkness beyond the orbit of Pluto.

My teeth are chattering. A large moon rises, and all those even ranks of plants cast long faint shadows over the earth, with a pale flickering between them to show where the moonlight has struck those slowly beating feather-like arms. Whoosh, whoosh, whoosh, they go above my head.

No one will find my body, apart, perhaps, from pterosaurs or whatever other creature fills the scavenger niche up here, and when they're done, the quiet clockwork of the trees and stars will simply carry on.

I walk by myself along the seafront. Amanda has a pile of marking she needs to finish and is working through it in her bathrobe at the desk in our hotel room. Couples are eating pastries in the cafés. Children are playing on the sand. I drop a coin into one of those metal telescopes and look out at the island in the bay. It has its own beach, its own holidaymakers, and even several telescopes like the one I'm looking through now. I watch those telescopes until my time runs out, but I have to drop in two more coins before I finally see someone out there climbing on to the step and inserting a coin of her own so she can look back towards me across the sparkling bay. Here and there – that mystery. She's so far away that I can't even make out her face. And yet to her, the little town on the island is what's all around her, and this place I'm in – the couples in the cafés behind me, the children playing on the beach, the promenade wall already warming in the sun – is remote and far away. It's such an obvious and everyday experience that no one even comments on it, but, really, what could be more strange?

My phone pings. This is another thing that I've had to get used to, this being connected all of the time to everyone I know. I fetch the phone out of my pocket. There's a message from Tan, my literary agent. She knows I'm not looking at social media while on holiday, but she thinks I ought to know that there's a news story doing the rounds about an indigenous rights activist called Amilcar Zero who has just been jailed for vandalizing a satellite relay station in order to draw attention to the structural disadvantages suffered by his people, and unfavourable comparisons are being made between his treatment and the hero's welcome I received after I deliberately damaged that observatory in order to get someone to come and read my note. It's one law for the poor, people are saying, and another for folk like me.

It might be a good idea to comment? Tan says. *Maybe express solidarity with Amilcar? Acknowledge your privilege? Something like that. Happy to help with drafting. It'd be a pity to complicate the film deal!*

I consider this for a few seconds. *I don't want to,* I reply. *I'd like to just leave it. But thanks for letting me know.*

I am irritated by being expected to comply with a judgement made by a mob about a situation I know nothing about, and most of the mob doesn't either. To properly respond, I'd have to give careful thought to the question as to when criminal damage to public property is justified, since presumably no one's saying it's okay just to trash valuable scientific equipment whenever you happen to feel like it, and I'd have to know who Amilcar Zero is, and what precisely were the circumstances in which he acted, in order to determine whether his case was in any way comparable to mine, but I don't feel like doing any of that and don't see why I should.

I turn my attention to the beach and the sea, trying to get past my annoyance, and back to where I was before. If you don't look at social media, I remind myself, it isn't really there. It's a single widthless point in space, inside a matchbox, inside a drawer, which no one has to open and some people never do.

My phone pings again, and now I'm cross. This had better not be Tan again because if she thinks securing a film deal justifies surrendering to a bunch of self-appointed custodians of public morality, hiding behind self-righteousness from their own punitive jealousy, that's up to her, but she has no right to demand the same of me.

But actually the new message isn't from Tan, and feels like a more fundamental threat to my stability. *Hi there,* Estela has written with studied jauntiness. *Just wondered what you were up to, and whether you'd like to hang out some time? Xxx*

We met up several times after the Jungle Club, until I told her we really shouldn't any more. There is no deep connection there. There is only (a) a young woman who enjoyed the reflected light of someone who is the subject of daily abuse on social media, but is also famous in all of the twenty provinces for descending into hell and rising up again like Christ, and (b) myself, who enjoyed her admiration.

What was my excuse for getting involved with her at all, when I'd already become a couple with Amanda? Let's say I was starved, let's say I was traumatized by many months without a single intimate physical contact with anyone . . . It's a bit threadbare, I know, but it's the best I can do. Perhaps transgression itself feels a bit like intimacy, in that they both involve crossing a boundary of some sort, even though the boundary between loyalty and disloyalty, and the boundary between one person and another are two entirely different things? Or perhaps, when even intimacy doesn't seem intimate enough to assuage one's hunger, transgression, with its inherent brutality, its indifference to kindness and civility, seems, at least in that brief intoxicating moment of crossing over, more intimate than intimacy itself? I really don't like Estela all that much, certainly no more than most of the people I know. I don't think she *really* likes me so very much either, whatever she may tell herself. I think what draws her to me is the idea of associating with the famous captive, so frequently discussed on national TV, who made a dramatic escape and is now writing a memoir for which film options are already being sought by several major production companies, and who for all these reasons seems to her to inhabit an exciting and capacious space, hitherto unreachable, into which she longs to be initiated, because then she'd become a real grown-up and could free herself from the stifling bonds of her upbringing, her class, and her own timidity.

Jesus Christ, what is the matter with me? What kind of monster am I? But even now I hesitate, feeling, ridiculous as it seems, a pang of grief. *Hello*, I finally write. *I'm having a lovely time with Amanda in a beautiful hotel on the west coast, a honeymoon almost. Hope you're well. Don't want to meet up, thanks, as we discussed, but no doubt we'll run into each other sometime.*

After I press the send button I feel hollow. I don't know what to do or how to entertain myself. My plan had been to find a café where I could sit at my laptop and do some work on the memoir of my escape from FRENALAT, which I'm hoping is going to make me so much money that it will allow me to escape a lot of other things, like having to work at the university and living in a rented apartment. But I simply can't bear the idea of keeping still.

I look out across the water at the island. I wish I was out there. I wish I was in that other little town, by that other little beach, and that this place I'm in was far away. But I know that wouldn't be enough. What I *really* wish is that I could be there, and yet somehow it would still be *there*, even when I'm in it, and not become here, as every there always does.

It reminds me of a lighthouse not only because it's tall and narrow, and stands on an outcrop above the lake, but also because of those large glass windows at the top, even though the windows have elaborately carved frames and arches.

It brings to mind a fairground helter-skelter, too, though it's made completely of stone. And it also reminds me a little bit of a pagoda. The whole structure is covered with gargoyles and other horizontal shapes, such as coral-like branches, and spirals, and wings, and leaves, which thrust out all over its surface, each one different from all the others, without any obvious pattern or rhythm to their arrangement. A light breeze, passing over all the protrusions, and crevices, draws out faint flute-like vibrations in many different pitches whose harmonics fluctuate second by second.

'Hello?' I call out as I approach it. 'Is there anyone there?' The tower is close enough to the high, bare escarpment for me to hear the echo of my voice from there, but there is also a barely audible echo from the tower itself.

There's an arched doorway, carved with a series of abstract shapes that might perhaps be some kind of hieroglyph. I know I'm not supposed to try the door, but I try it anyway and it isn't locked.

'Hi? Anyone in?' I wait and listen. I can hear a rooster calling in the village at the far end of the lake, but the only sound here is that faint chorus of flutes. I can almost believe it's a chord of some kind, and not just a random selection of sounds, as if the tower's designer had some somehow calculated in advance the notes that each gap and protrusion would generate when a wind blew across or into them.

'Anyone there?' I call again. I step back from the door and look around to see if I'm being observed, but there's no one in sight, not even in the village, which is nearly a kilometre away. Over there the ground is green and fertile. Here around the tower it's red and dry.

I turn my attention back to the door. I've been told that no one in the village goes through it, except on rare and special occasions, and I've been asked not to go through it myself, but, after a few seconds of hesitation, I go through it anyway. It leads into a circular room with a stone floor and a very high ceiling. The room is lit by narrow windows, set into what look like the stoned-up frames of what were originally much larger windows. There's a table in there, with an unlit candle on it, and a bed, and a couple of chairs. Books are stacked up in piles across the floor, and to one side there's a simple wooden staircase, so steep as almost to be more of a ladder. Even though I've been specifically told, by people to whom I owe a great deal, that the stairs are not to be climbed except on those very special occasions, I begin to climb. I mean, having seen the windows of the room at the top, and been told what's in there, how could I come so near without going up? Who turns down the chance of being in the presence of the Holy Grail?

Patterns of varicoloured light and shadow slide down my body, as I emerge into another round, high-ceilinged room on the next level, also lit by small windows, but these windows are filled with coloured glass: red, green, blue, yellow. This room is crammed with carved stone figures of various kinds: men, women, children, animals, angels, packed in there for storage rather than display, as if they are left over from some abandoned project. The bands of coloured light break up their outlines, the boundary between, say, a patch of red and a patch of blue being much sharper than the outline of a statue's arms or face, and I feel as if I myself have become almost invisible, my outline too made inconsequential by these bold bars of colour.

There are more wooden steps going up to the floor above. As I begin to climb, I'm reminded of childhood visits to the Great Cathedral back in the city where I grew up. Climbing the tower was the point of such visits as far as I was concerned. I was never much taken by the tombs of knights or the statues of saints, but when, at six years old, I put my foot on the first step, it felt as if I was stepping right out of the everyday world into a realm of danger and magic.

The next circular room has clear glass windows. There are shelves, and more piles of books, but here there are also paintings, one on an easel, the others stacked against the walls. Many of them depict a naked figure of indeterminate sex, curled in a foetal position inside a small cramped space that's completely surrounded by blackness. In the painting on the easel, rays of light are bursting from the figure's head and seem to be flinging out into the darkness a profusion of animals, plants and tiny human figures. Propped beside the steps that go up to the next floor is a painting in which one of these little figures is fleeing from something through a dark, empty landscape, looking back over its shoulder in fear, and next to it another picture in which an identical figure is running through the same bleak landscape but this time apparently in pursuit of someone who has already disappeared off the edge of the wooden board on which the scene is painted.

I climb the stairs. When the hatchway into the room above is just above my head, I hesitate, aware that even those who helped to build the tower only enter the upper room a few times in their lives.

'Hello?' I call softly, uncertain whether I am more concerned to get myself heard, or worried about disturbing someone's rest. 'Is there anyone there?'

I have a strong desire just to lie down on the ground. I could look up at the universe, listen to the steady sound of those feather-like branches (whoosh, whoosh, whoosh from close-up and that steady waterfall-like sigh from the distance where all the sounds merge together), and give up on the whole idea of trying to get past this place and resuming some kind of life. If one is going to choose a death, it strikes me, this wouldn't be such a bad way to go, though it *is* annoying to think I went to all that trouble to escape from my cage and hack my way through the forest, if it was all just going to end like this, for probably Carlo or someone would have come back at some point if I'd stayed in the cage, and they would have fed me, and it was warm down there, and life would have carried on, and quite likely I would eventually have been released because, after all, I wasn't much use to FRENALAT dead.

It grates with me too that, quite probably, no one will ever know what happened to me, that all of this will simply cease to be and leave no trace at all. But I suppose that was always going to be the case, sooner or later, whatever happens in my life. And, on the plus side, there'd be no pain, no growing old, no more struggling with all the various anxieties with which it's been my particular fate to struggle, not just now, but even when I was an associate lecturer back in the city, and went from day to day without cold or hunger or thoughts of imminent death, but still found plenty to fret about.

A red light blinks in the distance. I think at first it must be a plane – an airliner perhaps – travelling from one coast to the other, but no, sweet Jesus, wise Apollo, blessed Lady Tanit, it isn't moving, and it's not so very far away. That is definitely an electric light blinking on and off somewhere over there, like the lights that the river villages have on the ends of their jetties. Someone's out there! Someone exists in this place apart from me. I hurry forward, and then break into a run, terrified the light might disappear before I reach it. But it blinks away steadily, not shifting from the spot, and as I draw nearer I begin to make out a dark shadow against the stars, as if of a giant plate tipped on its side, and next to it the red light blinking at the top of a column or pole, a jetty sticking out into nothing but empty space.

It's an observatory, I realise, as I approach it. The dark shape is the saucer of a small radio telescope, the pole the antenna through which this place communicates with the outside world. There are a number of other shapes around these two objects, glinting faintly in the moonlight, which turn out to be solar panels, while between them sits a squat, low, bunker-like shape, not even as tall as I am. I rush towards it, searching its metal surface for doors and windows, and shouting out to whoever's inside to let me in. But there's no answer. If there are windows at all, they are hidden behind metal shutters. And the door . . . well, there is a door, a metal door with rounded corners like the bulkhead door on a ship. But if this is an unmanned station, full of valuable equipment, that door will of course be securely locked and there's obviously no point in even hoping that it won't be. Nevertheless, and with that in mind, I try the handle.

The door opens. It's warm inside, there's a faint electric hum and little lights blink below me in the darkness, red and green and blue. This place isn't some empty shed. Even with no one here it's busy and alive. I feel around on the walls next to the door and find a switch. Click! I'm in electric light, as mysterious and as beautiful as an entire sky full of stars. When my eyes have adjusted I see steps descending in front of me into a narrow room no more than eight metres long, that for some reason – possibly to maintain a more constant temperature for the machines – has its floor two metres below ground level. The light that seemed so bright at first is actually soft and intimate, like a jazz club, or an intensive care unit. I guess if it was too bright, it would be harder to read the screens and instruments. There's barely one metre of clear floor space between the wall on the left-hand side and the bank of instruments on the right, with its screens, switches, dials and blinking lights, and in this space are two office chairs, over one of which is draped a blanket. I suppose when people come here, they work at night and need something to keep them warm. At the far end of the room is a cork noticeboard on which are pinned various messages: old weather reports, a reminder to close and lock the door, good wishes left by a departing scientist for the two who will be coming next, a sign written with a red felt-tip pen that says, 'ISHTAR, PLEASE DO *NOT* LEAVE MY BLANKET OUTSIDE THIS TIME,' and messages of a more technical nature that I can't make any sense of at all. Various names recur: Zidon, Alyssa, Juan, Ishtar. A pencil stub dangles on a piece of string.

There must be a phone in here, or some means of communicating with the world. I spend a long time looking for it, but the best I can come up with is a screen on which, after much fiddling with switches and dials, I very briefly manage to conjure up a hissing cloud of static through which I can just make out the image of a family sitting down to eat while a crackly voice extols the unrivalled flavour of

Hannibal's Savoury Sauce. Then the static overwhelms it, and no matter how many knobs I turn, I can get nothing more except random spots and zigzags.

Never mind, I tell myself, and I feel surprisingly calm about the whole thing, the inconvenience of not being able to communicate with the outside world seeming relatively minor when compared with the fact that I am no longer about to die of cold. Realizing that there must be some sleeping quarters nearby, I go back outside and find another low building, but in this case the door is locked as you'd expect, so I return to the room with the instruments, wrap myself in the blanket, and, opening up my bag, dine in luxury on a quarter of a loaf of bread, an apple and a chicken leg, rounded off with a big fat treacly roll-up of the headman's home-grown tobacco that crackles like a bonfire when I inhale. The machines hum and flicker as they process the faint vibrations of the stars.

Treating myself to a second cigarette, I empty out my various possessions on the floor: the box of tampons, the scorched metal tin I used as a frying pan, the plastic disc with the picture of the gentle middle-aged couple . . . My playing cards are still soaked through from my time in the forest. Their bright nursery colours have bled into one another, and are dotted here and there with specks of mould. I spread them out to dry, carefully peeling each one away from the pack and laying them on the warm linoleum in suit order: Coins, Swords, Leaves and Cups, arranged in columns side by side from the ace to the king. Then I turn off the lights and curl up on the floor, and soon the hum of the machines, the little coloured lights and the happy memory of the sauce commercial soothe me into a deep and contented sleep in a kind of miniature city all of my own.

I can try again in the morning to find a way of sending a signal, is my last coherent thought. Failing that, I can write a note on the board saying where I'm headed, and then damage something – throw a rock at the instrument panel, perhaps, or cut through a cable – so that someone will have to come out and fix it.

'So how was your day?' Amanda asks when I rejoin her. She's put away her school books, and has been sitting reading a novel on the balcony in the evening sun in the same swimsuit that she was wearing when I first met her by that warm lake in the forest of the Upper River.

'I hope this doesn't sound too needy,' I tell her, 'but I really missed you. I couldn't quite settle to anything, as if there was some part of me that won't function properly when you're not there. I barely wrote a word. I walked along the promenade. I had a look through one of those telescopes. I bought a couple of coffees and a bit of lunch, but I couldn't bring myself to write. In the end, I went on a boat trip out to the island for something to do.'

'Was that nice?'

I've brought us up two cold bottles of beer from the bar downstairs and I pass her one of them as I sit on the other chair.

'Well, there were flying fish on the way over, and I saw a giant jellyfish just below the surface, and the little town on the island is quite pretty in its way. I'm sure I would have liked it if you'd been there. We could have had a beer in one of the cafés and talked about all the stuff we talk about, and – you know – just enjoyed the feeling of being on an island. But, as it was . . . well . . . I could see it was quite nice, of course I could, but there was a "so what?" quality to it. I couldn't help thinking, What does it really mean anyway when we say a place is nice? Places are just places when it comes down to it, aren't they? Just lumps of matter arranged in a certain way at a certain point in space. But if you'd been there, I'm sure I wouldn't have felt that way.'

'And yet, when I first met you, you were living quite contentedly by yourself in that cabin, not talking to anyone at all.'

'I guess I've had enough solitude recently to last me for quite a while.'

I offer this as a theory, actually, rather than a statement of fact, because I genuinely have no idea if my recent history has anything to do with it, but Amanda is immediately convinced. 'God, yes. That's perfectly understandable.'

'A kind of bleakness creeps in, you know? I suppose it does date back to that time.' As I speak, I'm having doubts as to whether that's really true, but I press on anyway. 'Even when I'm with people I sometimes feel alone.'

'Even when you're with me?'

The beer is relaxing me. I'm enjoying the warm evening sun, and the warmth of her presence. I really can't imagine why I was so thrown by that text from Estela. It's not as if anything of any significance happened between us. We just met a couple of times, and there was a charge between us – well, that was really the whole point of our meetings – so that I didn't feel able to tell Amanda about it afterwards.

'Well . . . you know . . . sometimes . . . But you're the best antidote, and I'm certainly not feeling it now.'

Amanda has her large feet up on the railing. I love the largeness of her, not just the fact that she's tall and muscly, but the way she's entirely at home with being that way. I love her good humour. It's easy to imagine the kids in her class absolutely adoring her.

She raises her bottle. 'Well, that's good, because I'm not going anywhere!'

It's hard to tell where I am exactly on the river after dark. One row of silhouetted trees looks much like another, one right turn in the river is pretty much the same as another right turn, but in a way that makes the anticipation still more pleasurable. Is it going to be this turning? No? Then it'll be the next one, or the one after. I know it can't be far because of the time that's elapsed since I passed the last village.

Meanwhile, I have the fireflies, and the coolness of the water, and the steady rattle of the insects over on the dark banks on either side of me. A naiad snorts in the water maybe twenty metres away from me, just loud enough for me to hear it over the noise of my outboard motor. All I can see of it is a paler patch on the water. What *are* those things anyway? Are they a kind of whale, or are they more like sea cows? Or perhaps that's a silly question. Maybe sea cows *are* a kind of whale. I ought to know this stuff. I need to grow up. It really is rather adolescent of me to remain wilfully ignorant of the natural world just to be different from Dad.

A monkey of some sort lets out a series of shrill hoots in the forest to my left. Several others answer it. Sometimes when I'm out in the boat at night, I like to turn off the motor and just drift for a while, listening to the sounds that emerge from the silence, and smelling the scents that waft around me, when the stink of exhaust fumes has blown away. But I'm too tired for that, tonight – not unhappy at all, but keen to get home.

I roll a cigarette, enjoying the way the tiny orange glow flares up as I draw in smoke. A solitary bird – a cormorant, perhaps? – crosses the river just in front of me, having made a decision for some reason that it wanted to be on the other side. How does that work in a mind that has no language? Does it picture something it wants, or some place that it would rather be? Or is it more of a feeling?

Another turn is coming up. There's still just enough glow from the sky for the river to be paler than the banks. I think this must be the one. In fact, I'm almost certain I recognize that tree over there to the left that's a little taller than the others, standing up against the sky. But even if I'm mistaken, it won't be long before I turn a corner and see my little blue light.

Dru is excited. Over there is one of the stars of a well-known TV series, over here is a prize-winning feminist author, and right behind him – Dru whispers it, though it would be rude to look round again – is an extremely famous fashion model from the sixties who is now an 'ambassador for human rights' around the world. Dru has never been in the presence of so many cool and famous people. Myself, I've grown up with all that – such people were guests at my parents' dinner parties – and I wish he'd calm down. In fact, to be perfectly honest, I wish he hadn't come at all because, sweet and pretty as he is, I've very nearly made up my mind that he won't be a long-term presence in my life and I could do without the mild embarrassment of his excessive enthusiasm.

'Dear God, look over there!' he exclaims. 'Williams, Ithobal and Gil, chatting away like old mates.'

In front of the black marble tomb of some old nobleman from the days of the conquest, are the former liberal prime minister, the principal spokesman of the centrist wing of the Conservative Party and the tall and extremely handsome FRENALAT commander, a member of an old colonial family, who made a deal with the government and became leader of the radicals in the National Assembly. They're laughing together at some shared joke.

I glance across. 'Well, they were all Aunt Xenia's students,' I say, and in that moment, Gil, the former guerrilla, glances across and catches my eye, flinching very slightly as he recognizes me. I turn back to Dru.

'When I came back after my captivity, Xenia kept trying to get me to agree to a meeting with that guy. Apparently he wanted to explain to me in person how he had nothing to do with my kidnapping, and how furious he'd been about it.'

'Wow! A meeting with Gil! Why didn't you agree to it?'

'I never really felt like it. I couldn't help thinking that this was about him and her, and not really about me at all.'

We collect champagne from two fair-haired foreign women, waiting behind a forest of glasses. A second cousin of mine spots me there, so I introduce her. 'I don't think you've met my partner, Dru?' As I feared, Dru starts off at once about all these big names from politics and TV who are all around us, and how overwhelming he's finding it, but luckily my cousin comes from a relatively humble branch of the family, and seems okay with that, so I step back from the conversation and leave them to it.

It's a while since I've been here in the chapter house. We used to come here as kids. Not that my parents were religious, obviously, but they appreciated architecture and they wanted us to learn to like it too. My brothers used to tease me about the gloomy statues with their missing noses, telling me that they were mummified victims of the plague and that I'd better make sure that I didn't get left behind here because the doors were locked at night and the mummies came to life. I didn't believe them even at the time, but I must have half-believed them because the whole place came to evoke slightly queasy feelings in me, and I was always keen to get to the tower, which, although itself somewhat creepy on the way up, led to an open and windy place far above the city that I found quite magical.

Glancing across again, Gil notices I'm on my own now and at once leaves his fellow politicians to come over and grasp my hand. 'Your aunt was a wonderful woman, an absolutely wonderful woman. And she was so proud of you. She was always talking about you, and telling me we should meet. So glad that we finally have, though I wish it could have been in happier circumstances.'

He wants me to like him. He wants a conversation in which he can rehearse the reasons why his wing of FRENALAT had nothing to do with my kidnapping, and absolve himself of any guilt that I might attribute to him. But I point towards the small arched door into the main body of the cathedral as if I had some kind of urgent appointment there, tell him it's nice to meet him and hurry away. The Great Cathedral itself is quiet and almost empty by comparison with the noisy and crowded chapter house, but there are a few people praying, some in the pews out in the nave, others at various shrines, and, of course, as always, a number of tourists are wandering about. They're all being very quiet, but every little sound is amplified and made strange by the huge stone space, as if each small visible human body was accompanied by an invisible giant so tall as to have to stoop to fit in beneath the vaulted ceiling. They say this is the largest church in the world, at least by some measures, and while obviously that's impressive, and makes me think with a certain satisfaction about what a big and important country we live in, the size of it actually takes away something of the mystery that was evoked by the not dissimilar columns and arches in the much smaller cathedral in the town up the river. This place is impressive as an exercise in the display of might, it seems to me, but not so interesting as a work of art.

But oh dear God, there's that picture above the altar! That Last Supper! I'd quite forgotten it was here. The memories it sets off strike me with a force for which I hadn't prepared myself at all. I remember the beautiful little fertile valley as it first appeared below me, more or less circular, with its lake, and the green of the rushes and trees, and the little fields of crops. I remember the neat little whitewashed houses, the church bell ringing, the strange spiky tower all by itself standing on its mound, in the barer ground at the far end of the lake.

Then a familiar voice calls my name. Of course! Why wouldn't she be here? She became a good friend of Xenia's during my captivity, and never understood my complicated reservations about my charming and brilliant great-aunt. I brace myself for a second, then turn to greet her.

'Amanda. Hi.'

Amanda's new partner – a fellow-teacher, as I've been told, who looks as warm and as kind as Amanda – is tactfully standing back by the door of the chapter house, from whence comes the busy hum of many loud and confident people all talking at once.

'I saw you sneaking out here. For a bit of quiet time, I guess, away from your exhausting family and all their distinguished chums?'

'Ha. You know me too well. Look at this picture! It's really quite something, isn't it?'

She picks up the menu. 'Meat,' she announces. 'I need meat.' We're sitting at one of the outside tables of a rather smart restaurant that overlooks the sea and the island. The air is warm. Amanda is wearing a new red dress she's bought specifically for this holiday. She never quite manages elegant, and she's far too good-humoured to be able to carry off cool, but she looks and smells delightful. She knocks back half of her glass of cold white wine. To the left and south of the island, the sun is almost touching the sea.

'Dear God, what a relief to have that bloody marking done,' she says. 'From now on, I'm officially on full-time holiday.

Hmmm. Duck. I *love* duck. Could you bear me eating it?'

'Yes of course, why not?'

'Well, you got quite upset about those ducks in the—'

'Oh, those ducks. Yes, that's weird. Every time I think about them I feel ashamed.'

'And yet you eat meat virtually every day.'

'But I haven't usually watched it settling down for the night with its family.'

'Well, what choice did you have? You could have starved. You had much more reason to eat meat then than we do now.'

'I know. But for some reason, whenever those ducks come to mind, they make me think about the . . . well . . . the limits of kindness, I suppose, the limits of our sense of responsibility towards others, and the lines we draw – the lines we *have* to draw – in order to . . .'

I give up attempting to explain something I don't fully understand myself, and look down at my own menu. It's very expensive – there are plenty of people in this country who earn less in a week than each of us will spend tonight – but it all looks delicious. 'Go on, have the duck,' I tell her. 'I'm going to eat a baby cow.'

The waiter comes with bread and oil to dip it in. He takes our orders and, as he walks away, Amanda rips off a large piece of bread and dunks it straight into the oil. It strikes me, not for the first time, that she understands something about life that I just don't get. She gets on with playing the game while I'm still fretting over the rule book and worrying about the apparent contradictions. The result is that she's much more generous than I am, both to other people *and* to herself. 'Why am I so hungry?' she exclaims happily with her mouth full. 'I must have used up practically zero calories today. I've had no exercise at all. I've hardly even been outside, unless you count the hotel balcony. But I swear I could eat my way through the whole menu.'

She wipes her mouth. I tell her about the annoying message from my agent. She shrugs. 'I think you probably did the right thing. Amilcar Zero became quite prominent while you were away, but he's a divisive figure. A lot of people question his right to speak for indigenous folk when he's only got one indigenous grandparent, and he does seem to be fairly interested in self-promotion.'

'It's making me feel weary even thinking about it. That whole bottomless pit of outrage and counter-outrage.'

'Well, I never even look at social media. I had to when you were away, obviously, but I'm certainly not going to now.'

'Tan is worried that negative publicity might reduce the chances of the film being made.'

'Do you care?'

'Not all that much. I wouldn't mind the money, obviously, but I'm not so keen on the idea of being portrayed on the screen by some ridiculously good-looking actor.'

She laughs. 'Are you kidding? You *are* ridiculously good-looking! I couldn't believe it when you climbed out of the water that first time. Those dark curls, those beautiful eyes!

I felt like I was in a movie myself.'

'Well, thanks. But I'm not good-looking to myself.' She's about to protest, but I hold up my hand. 'I don't mean I think I'm ugly. I know I'm not. I just mean that from my own perspective, I don't have a face at all. Isn't it the same for you? I don't have a face, or a gender, or a nationality, or any of those things. I'm just this thing that looks out at the world.'

We told each other it would be interesting, we agreed that when you've been together a while, it's important to vary the formula a bit, and that we'd had plenty of trips to places that were warm and blue and sunny, but it was a mistake to come to this cold grey southern place. Sunny makes you feel sunny and grey makes you feel grey, and, more dangerous than that, it draws out whatever greyness has been lurking inside you. Sometimes in the evening, when we sit down for a meal in the hotel restaurant, we find it hard to think of anything to talk about.

'I always knew I wouldn't like the film,' I finally say, as plates of fish are laid in front of us.

Her smile is a little strained. 'I remember. You didn't like the idea of a ridiculously good-looking actor playing you.'

'It's not really the looks, though. It's the fact that it just wasn't like that.'

'In what way? I thought you said the details were pretty accurate?'

'The details are very accurate, but that's not the point. I was thinking about it today on the boat trip. The biggest problem with the film is that we're always watching "me".' (I make air quotes.) 'We're always watching "me" fighting my way through the jungle, or breaking out of the cage, or finding the observatory. My facial expressions are sometimes determined and brave, and sometimes weary and hopeless, but we can always see them, while the thing we can't see is my thoughts.'

'Well, it's a movie. That's sort of how movies work. And what are you saying? Are you saying you didn't *have* those expressions on your face?'

'I've no idea what my face was doing. But that's my point. No one was watching me, were they? I didn't really have a face, never mind expressions. I just had this . . . well, this hole, I suppose you'd call it, that we all look out of. On the one hand, there was the world, on the other my thoughts and feelings, and there was nothing in between them. Really it's always like that – it's only other people that have faces – but in this case the situation was particularly extreme because, once I'd escaped from my cage, there were days and days when, not only did I feel faceless to myself, but no one *else* saw my face either. The face you see in the film just didn't exist.'

'So, it shouldn't have been a film at all?'

I shrug. 'This is a problem I think about a lot when it comes to my novel, actually. Should it be first person or third person. I'm always changing my mind.'

She cuts a piece off her fish and puts it in her mouth. I know what she's thinking. She's thinking, *Here we go again.*

'Okay,' I tell her, 'I know my novel bugs you because I'm always talking about it, but I never actually write it. Fair enough. But it's an interesting question in general, don't you think? In a play, or a film, or a third-person novel, you don't get to see that the entire world is experienced by people who don't have faces, looking out at others who apparently do. That's why . . . I don't know if you've noticed this, but if you read a first-person novel, or even an autobiography, and the narrator tells you about some new friendship or new romance, you can see why they like the other person, no problem there, because you can see the other person's face – not literally, obviously, but still, in some way, you can see it – and you can also see the narrator's thoughts. But it's much harder to see why the other person likes the narrator because you can't see *their* thoughts, and you can't see the narrator's face. And the truth is no one falls in love with the absence of a face. We fall in love with faces . . . not looks, necessarily; I don't mean looks, but faces. We fall in love with the way people seem from outside.'

'I'll have to think about that,' she says, taking a sip of her white wine.

I feel like I'm trying my best to have a conversation, but she's refusing to play along.

'This bores you, doesn't it?'

'I wouldn't say it bores me, but . . . you know . . . it's your field and not mine. I guess you might have the same problem if I went on too much about the kids in my class.'

'And anyway, I'm chasing a mirage, aren't I?'

'That came out wrong. I didn't mean to disrespect what you're trying to do. It's just that you seem to expend *so* much energy on it, and yet you've set the bar so high, and made so many rules for yourself, and seem to forbid yourself every possible way of actually going ahead and doing it, that I can't help wondering if it's even possible.'

'It doesn't help that you're constantly needling me with these doubts.'

'*Constantly?* Oh, come on. That's hardly fair.'

'Not out loud, perhaps, but I can see them in your face all the time.'

'I worry for you sometimes, that's all. I worry that you might be missing out on other things you could put your energies into that might turn out to be more satisfying.'

'This is the only thing that matters to me.'

Amanda sighs. We're very close to the big row that we've been building towards throughout this trip. We both know that. And we both know it will be essentially the same row that we've been having over and over for many months, but this time more final, because, without ever actually saying it out loud, we've somehow tacitly agreed that there is a desperate, last-chance, final-throw-of-the-dice quality to this whole holiday. 'So you keep saying,' she says. 'And of course, you also keep reminding me that you couldn't possibly do something like being a teacher because ultimately a job like mine makes no difference to anything at all, which I must admit doesn't make me feel very valued.'

'I've never said my book was the only thing that matters for anyone else, but I wish you'd respect the fact that it matters to me.'

'I do respect that! God knows I listen to you talking about it often enough.'

'But it feels like it's something you have to put up with. Something you have to humour.'

Amanda is always slow to anger and, when she does get angry, it often starts, not with actual crying – she seldom cries – but with tears welling up in her eyes. There are tears there now. 'That's really not true. It's just that you never write the book, and yet it stops you from doing so many other things, and I worry that—'

'Well, maybe if you supported me a bit more. Maybe if you actually made me feel that what I was doing *wasn't* just a waste of time, then perhaps I might make a bit more progress.'

One of her tears has accumulated enough mass to trickle down her cheek. She wipes it away. A woman is glancing furtively across at us from another table. 'I don't see why it should all be *my* fault when you yourself are constantly sabotaging your own project.'

'What in God's name do you mean by that?'

'Surely you must have noticed how you're always making impossible rules and conditions for yourself. It's rather like how you constantly go on about your precious Guinevere back in your cave, and how right she was about the uselessness of pretty well everything that people like us normally value, and yet you're equally scathing about what she chose to do about it, which is *also* useless apparently, just like what I do, and just like what everyone else does, including every novelist who has ever lived. You make it impossible for yourself to actually do anything at all.'

'You and I really shouldn't be together. You're a wonderful person, I'm not denying that, but you don't get me and you never will. The truth is I knew that pretty much from the moment I first met you. In fact, that's the real reason I didn't go for your nudie high jinks in the jungle, and that's why I didn't look very pleased when you came to visit me. It wasn't that I didn't like you – of course I bloody like you: *everyone* likes you! – it was that I could see you weren't going to be the kind of person I needed in my life. The only pity is that I felt so guilty about having those thoughts, and so surprised and grateful that *you* liked *me*, that I didn't have the heart to say no to you.'

Amanda pushes away her plate. She's become very quiet and cold. 'Okay, well, by my reckoning that's about the eighth time in the last few months that you've told me you wish you'd never met me. So I think perhaps it's time I took you at your word, don't you? Especially if I put what you keep saying together with the things you do, like these endless little flirtations with people who apparently give you something

I'm unable to give: Estela, Hugh, Izabel . . . I dare say there are more I don't know about. I've been trying to persuade myself otherwise, but I have to admit it all adds up to a pretty consistent message.' She looks at her watch. 'You know what? If I get a move on, I can probably make the overnight train back to the city.'

I'm not quite sure if she's bluffing, but I very much think that this time she isn't – and that really terrifies me. Yet for some reason I don't fully understand, I've put on a kind of painted mask of bitterness, and even though I know that mask isn't really me, and I know that if I wanted to, I could take it off, and just be myself again – the ordinary self that both of us like – and, even though actually I *want* to take it off because if I did, we could be friends again, perhaps even in a matter of minutes, enjoying our time in a strange and remote part of our country, which a few years ago we would have found quite fascinating, nevertheless for some reason I'm not prepared to do it.

'Okay,' I tell her. 'You go, and tomorrow I'll start writing my novel. My real novel. Not just another of these pieces of crap I've been turning out.'

She stands up. 'Okay. But we both need to understand that this is really it. I'm not just giving you the rest of this week to start your book. I'm freeing you from me completely – and me from you. You went to the Upper River to write your book, you met me, and you've written eight books in the eight years from that day to now, which a lot of people would have been very satisfied with, but apparently none of them matter because you've never even started the one you really wanted to write, and, according to you, that's because of me. Well, who knows? Maybe you're right. Maybe it *is* me that's stifling your inner life and your precious book. There's only one way to find out.'

I long to end this ridiculous hostility. All I need to do is admit I'm in the wrong and that blaming her for my failure to write my book is on a par with the anger I might feel at the idiot who left the brick on the floor on which I stubbed my toe, in the very brief moment before I realize that the idiot was me. But, though I know that's the case, for some reason I don't feel able to say so.

'Okay,' I tell her. 'We're done, then. That's absolutely fine with me.'

3 THE TOWER

I'm walking along the lake. The water is to my right, the steep escarpment to my left, and the village behind me with all its fields and orchards. When I turn and look back, the houses and the church already look very small beneath the volcano from whose flank this entire valley seems to have been scooped out. My legs are weary from my many days of walking, and my progress is slow and a little painful, but it's a relief to be on my own again for a while, and not to have to maintain a face, or to edit the jumble of my thoughts and feelings into some kind of coherent shape in order to let the people here feel they're getting to know me. And it's good to be away from their exhausting kindness and hospitality.

I'm tempted to stop for a rest and a smoke, for there's no longer any urgency about anything. The air is neither too hot nor too cold, my belly is full, and the people in the village will look after me for however long it takes someone to come to the observatory to fix the damage and find the note

I left there. In fact, even if no one does come, the villagers assure me there's nothing to worry about, because they can if necessary take me down to the river themselves. They may have withdrawn from the world but they do occasionally return to it for a variety of reasons, and they'd happily do so to help me out.

So there's nothing I need to do. I could just lie here in the grass and smoke and sleep, leaving the tower and its mason for another day. It's really not far to walk there, it's true, but why walk at all, when my legs are bruised and blistered and weary? Why give myself the challenge of another human encounter, when I could simply doze here until I begin to feel hungry, and then go back to the village and help myself to cheese and bread and beer from the storehouse, which I've been told I'm free to do at any time.

But somehow the tower ahead of me, spiky and hard on its rocky promontory, reproaches my idle inclinations. So much hard work must have gone into it, with so few people to do it, so little in the way of mechanical help – and a strange, prickly intelligence seems to animate it, challenging me not to turn away.

'Can you manage?' asks the taxi driver. She's opened the door for me and is offering her hand. It's the first time that's ever happened, and I wish she'd stayed in her seat, because I can cope perfectly well on my own. But still, she's trying to be kind and the truth is that it *is* a bit of struggle these days to get out of a car, as she'd be able to see for herself if I were to decline her help. So I accept her hand and climb out on to the street. She reaches in for my stick and the little canvas bag I use to carry my sandwiches, my flask of coffee and my notebook.

I ask her to pick me up in two hours' time and, as the taxi moves off, I stare up at the apartment buildings across the road, scanning those familiar walls of brick until I find the balcony of the apartment I used to share with Jezebel and Rémy, back in the days when I was a young assistant lecturer. They say that at regular intervals – it's every year, I believe – every single atom in your body will have been completely replaced, so that the past selves we remember from many years back do not actually contain a single speck of the matter that now makes up our bodies. But bricks aren't like that. If I were to go up to that apartment and walk out on to the balcony, I could touch bricks that had already been there for a century when I lived there, and are still there now, still made of the exact same matter, as they will be for many years to come. It would be the same if I put my hands on the railing. Barring perhaps a few coats of paint, it would be the same metal that I used to lean on when I slipped outside of an evening for a puff of weed.

I haven't smoked that stuff for years. I wonder what it would feel like now. I used to enjoy the way it broke down boundaries between one thought and the next and gave me a sense of all the world as a kind of single vast organic thing, a forest, as I'd sometimes picture it, but a forest in many dimensions, so that it extended up and down as well as around. I used to like that very much.

If I had some weed now, I'd smoke it in the hope it would bring me closer to that old past self. But these days I don't even smoke tobacco.

I turn in the other direction and look through the metal railings of the Botanic Gardens. These railings too, I suppose, are the same ones that were there before, though no doubt also repainted a few times, because pretty much as soon as they apply another coat, the paint seems to bubble and flake. The trees will have grown and no doubt some have been replaced, but my memory isn't good enough to be able to tell how they've changed. The only thing I notice is that the whole place seems surprisingly small.

'Excuse me,' says a young woman who's pushing two children along in a contraption that carries them side by side. I smile at the children and would love to talk to them. They're extraordinarily sweet, and remind me of my nieces and nephews when they were small. I feel a wave of sadness washing over me at the thought that, apart from Christmas and birthday cards, we somehow lost touch. But the woman is looking cross, and I realize I've been blocking a busy pavement.

I move to the side, and continue on my way to the park gate. I move more slowly than I used to but once I get going my limbs loosen up and I really don't need the stick. I carry it more for reassurance than anything because my balance isn't as good as it was and sometimes I feel myself toppling for no apparent reason. It's a strange thing to be old, and to be seen as old by people around me. That young mother, for instance, probably thought to herself that I was a silly confused old fool, standing there grinning at her babies as if I had no idea of the nuisance I was causing.

Yet this is only the beginning, that's the odd part. I can delay things to some extent, I can take exercise, I can eat a good diet, I can get myself checked over regularly by my doctor, but all the same this can only go in one direction. There will be a day, if I live that long, when I look back on my present self as being wonderfully youthful and mobile, in the way that I now look back at my sixty-year-old self, never mind that young thing with curly jet-black hair that used to lean over that balcony there to smoke.

I pass through the gate, and now I'm among the trees that I once liked to imagine as some kind of jungle, back when I'd never actually been in a jungle and thought of them as dangerous and glamorous places, as in the paintings of that chap – what was his name? – that foreign chap who was a tax collector or some such and had never himself been to the tropics at all.

Yes, and why not? After my encounter with the real forest, I used to feel vaguely embarrassed about the naivety of those fantasies, but I really don't see why. The real forest is just a place, after all, but what I'd been reaching for was something else entirely.

Anyway, here I am, so let me just enjoy it: the lavish orchids, the cool green ferns, the trees with their enormous fleshy leaves. And also the mynah birds with their golden crests, the little children running around, the young mothers chatting on the benches, the business people speaking very earnestly into apparently empty air. 'Can you get Tamsin in on this one?' a smart young woman is saying. 'Thanks, that would be great . . . I'm not happy with the quality of it, to be honest . . . I think we should probably make a fuss, don't you? . . . No, and it's not as though it was cheap . . . Get Tamsin on to it, will you, and let me know what she says.'

I walk to the far end of the park and then back again. That's my exercise for the day done, so now I make my way to the small pond next to the fence to sit on the bench there and eat my sandwiches, from time to time throwing a little piece of crust to the miniature ducks that I suppose may perhaps be the great-great-grandchildren of the ones I watched that night when the whole park was empty except for me – the great-great-grandchildren and *their* children, I should say, for, as well as the two adults, there are two charming little ducklings covered in fluffy yellow down.

When I've finished eating and dusted off the crumbs, I open my flask, pour myself a cup of strong dark coffee and take out my notebook, but I don't immediately begin to write. I take my time over things these days, even more than I used to, and even though I'm increasingly aware that I'm going to have to crack on with it if there's to be any chance at all of my ever writing the novel that hovers there tantalisingly at the edge of my field of vision.

Nothing much will happen in it, that's how I feel about it now. Most books are crammed with things happening, but all that busy stuff is just a distraction in my opinion, in books as it is in life. All these busy people throughout history, invading countries, building cities, inventing alphabets, imposing new and more enlightened religions, cutting down forests, discovering things – but then replanting forests again, and discarding those same religions, and telling everyone to get up to date and follow instead the latest new ideas that one day will be discarded too . . . And where has all this busyness got us? They say that by the end of the century everything will have gone to pot. And okay, I'm sure that old people have *always* said that, but these days the young people are saying it even more than us old ones, because it's not a question of manners or mores any more, it's about the material conditions of life itself, and it's them that are going to have to deal with it.

Our Lost Atlantis. It won't really be like that, I know, but I used to love that song. Even when the busy, pulsing city was all around us and we were at an age where we could roam all over it and experience its delights as the fancy took us, it still seemed much more vivid and magical when the song imagined it for us as if it was already beneath the waves, as they say the lower parts really will be, in less than a century's time, including the National Assembly building and Temple Park. That song allowed you to feel nostalgia for something that still existed, which is perhaps as close as you can get to being 'there' at the same time as being 'here'. Nostalgia for something that's still here: these days I have that feeling a lot, and I don't even need songs to help me.

I open up my notebook. I leaf through the pages in which I've already written sketches and notes for the latest iteration of my novel. I have dozens of these notebooks back in my flat and in a way they did become books, because all of the books I've written have been off-shoots from this process. But I know inside myself that each one resulted from an act of betrayal and only got written when I turned away from my original objective and headed off in a completely different direction to the one I'd intended. Like revolutions and religions, they only succeeded by surrendering to the very forces that they were supposed to transcend. But I keep trying. I am reasonably well for my age, apart from the arthritis. The heavy smoking of my youth has so far not caught up with me. I could easily have another ten years in me before I reach my dotage, and that surely is plenty of time.

I turn to a blank page and begin to write.

'If a story consists of a number of scenes or elements, one might think that a tragic story was one in which most of those elements were painful, and only a few happy, while a happy story was one in which only a few were painful and most were cheerful. But that isn't actually how it works. A story in which the main character is wretched for most of it but finds resolution at the end is a happy story. A story in which the main character is happy for most of it, but is then undone in some way in the final pages is tragic, even though the sum total of happiness is greater in this second story than in the first, and the sum of sorrow is less. So in fact it's the order in which the elements occur that's important rather than the relative weight of tragic and cheerful episodes. So, for instance . . .'

One of the adult ducks quacks softly to the other and I pause to watch them. Now that I've finished feeding them, they've all climbed out on to the bank opposite me, and just in front of the fence, through which I can see the busy street and the row of apartment buildings where I once lived, getting on for half a century ago. The mother is settled comfortably on the ground with the ducklings around her. The father is standing on one leg, having one last look around, before tucking his head under his wing to take a nap. Although I've tried to become a little less ignorant about these matters, I still couldn't say what kind of duck these are, or what habits they have, or where in the world they originally came from, but I do like watching them and remembering that inside each of those small heads is another whole universe, completely inaccessible to me, but nevertheless as real as my own.

A car honks, very loudly and suddenly, just beyond the fence. It gives me an unpleasant jolt, but the ducks seem not even to notice it. I turn back to my notebook, but I don't immediately start to write. I'm thinking about the fact that I feel sad if I review my life in date order, because I see wasted opportunities, again and again, and now very few opportunities are left at all, only a steady narrowing of the field of possibilities, and a gradual increase in sources of discomfort, fear and humiliation.

But who says I have to look at it in such a linear way? If the story of a life were broken down into its different elements, and each one written on a separate card, one could select cards from the pack in different combinations, and every combination of cards could be arranged in different sequences, as I used to do with those old playing cards I had with me in the jungle, with their old-fashioned suits of Coins, Cups, Swords and Leaves. I still have them somewhere in a drawer. Some sequences would undoubtedly meet the criteria for sad stories, and even tragic ones, but others, even if constructed with the exact same cards, could be optimistic tales that left the reader cheered and hopeful when they put down the book at the end.

I smile. This takes me back to that idea I used to play with of a story presented like a stained-glass window. A story can't literally do that, obviously, because it's a line and not a surface, but it can act like the viewer of such a window, who doesn't look at each element of the story in time order, but glances back and forth between them and extracts from that process an overall effect.

Someone has come out on to my balcony to smoke. Or what was my balcony. I can't see from here if it's a man or a woman, but whoever it is has dark hair and is leaning comfortably on the railings, using one bare foot to rub the calf of the other leg.

When I wake up he's in the kitchen, singing along happily to some crappy pop song. He's frying bacon and brewing coffee – I can smell them, and I can hear the crackle of the fat and the gurgle of the coffee machine. Soon he's going to bring me my breakfast as a treat, and expect me to be pleased and maybe have sex with him one last time before he has to go off, as he mentioned last night, to a meeting somewhere at nine o'clock. I get out of bed, and, grabbing my coat to cover my nakedness, I open the glass door that leads out on to a tiny balcony. The icy air blasts in. I'm ten floors up. The sky is a pale grey that's almost white. To my right is a building site where a gigantic construction crane is lowering a girder on to a structure that will soon become a tower just like the one I'm in. It's well below freezing out here, and the balcony's floor is numbingly cold against my bare feet. Beyond the harbour wall, long lines of grey waves are rolling in, one after another after another.

'Let *all* the warm air out, why don't you?' Ham says as he arrives with the tray. Back in the kitchen, one of those local-radio DJs is witlessly babbling about nothing in what he seems to imagine is a humorous and sexy voice.

I come back into the room, closing the doors behind me. 'That looks nice,' I manage to say, though I don't feel like eating at all.

'Well, it's not every day I get to wake up with a famous—'

'Oh for Christ's sake, leave it, will you?'

'Sorry.'

'And don't you *dare* make another joke about "poetry".'

'You've woken up in a grumpy mood!'

I can't bear him. I can't bear the thought that I'm here with him and that last night we were naked and all over each other. I know it's not fair. I know that in fact he's a nice man, and in his own way a thoughtful one, who just happens not to have been socialized into the same kind of milieu as me and my friends, but there it is, I can't bear him.

'I'm sorry,' I say with an effort. 'There was no call for that.'

'This was a mistake, you're thinking?'

'Yes. My fault. I knew it would be and went ahead anyway, so it's my fault entirely. I suppose I was dreading a night alone. But, I mean, it was only two days ago that I last woke up beside Amanda. A bit too soon for . . .'

I sit on the bed, and look down at the spread he's arranged for me on a tray: a plate of bacon and those seaweed-flavoured potato cakes that are the local speciality, a cup of coffee, and a glass of orange juice, along with a single plastic rose in a tiny vase, which I suppose he thought I would appreciate as a gesture of tenderness. Perhaps he keeps it in a drawer for these occasions.

'I'm afraid I don't think I can eat this.'

'Never mind. I should have asked you.'

I place the tray on the floor and reach out to him. 'Have you got time to . . .?'

'Well . . . yes, if you're sure, but is that a good idea if, you know . . .?'

'It's a terrible idea, but it puts off the moment when I'll be able to see that.'

'That doesn't make a lot of sense.'

'Ha. No it doesn't. But you must admit there's a certain po—'

'Hey! If I'm not allowed to make that joke, then nor are you. Why don't you drink the coffee, and eat whatever you can manage, and then we can both get dressed, and say goodbye.'

I'm thinking of making a journey. It's not without its dangers. There's a real chance of serious injury and even death. But sometimes you have to take risks. And if I'm going to do it, I feel I should do it now and by myself, though I could quite easily wait for someone else to do it for me. A quest isn't a quest unless you yourself climb the perilous tower.

There's a fair amount of planning involved, though it's important not to spend too long over it because the window of opportunity is narrow. I need to work out, first of all, the best way of levering myself into a sitting position. There are a number of possible strategies, and I must choose carefully in order to put myself in the optimal position for initiating the next move, which involves getting both feet on the floor. After that, the big question is how best to stand up (something I haven't attempted on my own for many months), while minimizing the risk of losing my balance before I'm able to get my hands on my walking frame. This will be the most dangerous moment by far, at least until I reach my destination, because I wouldn't be able to get myself up from the floor, and, more to the point, I'm almost certain to break something. My bones are extremely brittle these days, and it's no fun lying for several hours on the floor with a broken bone, as I've already had occasion to find out. This mission of mine is like driving along a bumpy road in a car that's made of glass and has seriously defective brakes.

But I'm not quite ready to stop doing anything at all. These rails next to my bed should help. My arms aren't too bad, actually, or better than the rest of me, anyway, and I can make them do most of the work. It's going to hurt, not just in my joints, but inside me where the worst pain always is, and where the thing is slowly growing that I know will kill me, but I'm going to press ahead in any case.

Honk honk. Peep peep. Parp parp. Four storeys down, the afternoon traffic is muttering and squabbling. How far away all of that is! How remote from me! No one knows I'm up here. And no one down there, I'm pretty sure, has ever embarked on a journey such as this, or has any real conception of what it would be like.

It's not just that I'm far above them, either, because I'm also in the past. Things have changed down there in ways that I no longer understand. Manners are different, mores are different, politics are different. Things that we thought were the final truth have turned out to be foolish errors. Things that we didn't even imagine have become part of everyday life. For instance, when the foreign women come to wash me and change my diaper, they sometimes have to speak to their head office, but when they do they don't take a phone out of their pocket as we would have done, they just narrow their eyes and speak into the air in front of them. I've no idea how that works, but they seem completely at home with it, just as we were with our phones, because they're already inhabiting tomorrow, while I'm still stuck in today. Not that they'd see it that way, of course. This is today as far as they're concerned, and I'm far behind in yesterday.

Enough prevarication. I must concentrate. It's time to put my feet on the floor.

The bats are heading out to hunt. Carlo is keeping watch at the mouth of the cave. He's smoking and brooding out there, as I imagine it, pondering his next move in the complex multiplayer game that, from what I've overheard, carries on constantly between the various FRENALAT factions. Rubia,

Jaco and Guinevere have been playing cards but have begun to bicker, Rubia and Jaco amusing themselves for a while by mocking the posh city accent that Guinevere has worked so hard to suppress.

Then Jaco comes up with a new game. A while ago he brought some long sticks down the cave with the view to whittling them into spears, a project he soon grew tired of, but now he has the idea of using them to swipe at the bats. Rubia joins in and soon the two of them are shouting and laughing as they leap and lash about. Guinevere pointedly declines to join in, picking up one of her books and pretending to lose herself in it, as she so often does.

Most of the bats are too high up to reach, but eventually Jaco manages to knock down one of them that foolishly flew too low, and he and Rubia begin a new game of tormenting the animal by yelling abuse at it and prodding it with their sticks as it flops about on the ground, unable to get away. I suppose one of its wings is broken, or possibly the creatures are just unable to take off from the ground. My father would know. All I have to go on is that I don't recall ever hearing of a bat that could walk.

Guinevere continues to pretend to read, frowning as if with intense concentration, and huddling closer to the book all the time as if she was trying to disappear into its pages completely. But eventually she's unable to contain herself and flings it to the ground.

'What's it ever done to you, you cruel bastards?' she says,

and interestingly her voice has lost all traces of the Upper River way of speaking she's been trying to acquire, and has all the authority and privilege of our class.

The two of them do stop, though with poor grace. 'We're only having a bit of fun,' mutters Jaco.

'It's just an animal, for Christ's sake,' grumbles Rubia. 'It's just a dirty little sky rat.'

Guinevere stands and goes over to the creature, which is no longer flopping about, but is still alive and trembling. She squats down to inspect it, and then stands up and, after what looks like a brief struggle with herself, she stamps down hard on its head, inspects it again to ensure that it's dead, and then returns without a word to her book.

'Jesus Christ,' says Rubia. 'Talk about taking the hump.'

Jaco looks a little more guilty – it's because he hates the idea that he's disappointed Guinevere, I think, rather than any remorse about the animal itself – but he puts a good face on it.

'God, I'm bored,' he says. 'I'm going to go and see what Carlo's doing.'

'Good idea,' says Rubia. 'Old misery here can stew by herself.'

'Yeah,' says Jaco, jerking a thumb in my direction. 'Or maybe go and chat to her best buddy there in the cage.'

Rubia laughs loudly, Jaco glances uncomfortably at both Guinevere and me, and then Rubia switches on a torch and the two of them head off towards the cave mouth.

'At least take the bat with you then,' Guinevere calls after them. 'We don't want it rotting down here.'

'Bury it, if it bothers you,' Rubia calls back, and Jaco looks back uneasily but doesn't stop.

Guinevere continues to pretend to read until I speak to her. 'They're pretty heartless, your friends, aren't they?'

She looks up. 'They're hard because they have to be. We're soft because we grew up letting other people do all the nasty things for us. It's nothing to feel smug about.'

'No, I agree. But those are the people you want to put in charge. Those are the people you claim are going to usher in a kinder, fairer world.'

She glances towards the cave mouth to check that the others are out of sight, and them comes over to squat down next to my cage.

'Why are you so determined to prove that nothing can make any difference? Are you *really* so happy with the world as it is?'

'No, of course not. But the way I see it, there is kindness and there is generosity, but there's also cruelty and selfishness, and I can't help thinking there always will be, whether I like it or not. There isn't some kind of sunlit tomorrow where those things have ceased to exist.

'Hello? Anyone there?'

No answer. I grasp the handle and push. The door creaks

open. The upper room of the tower is full of complicated light. Of the large windows that completely surround it, half are filled with clear glass, and the other half with coloured designs. There is a patterned carpet on the floor, overlaid by the brighter patterns projected through the glass, and straight in front of me there's a tomb, such as the ones in the chapter house of the cathedral back in the city, with a statue of some dead knight, or bishop, or wealthy merchant, lying prone along the top of it, except that in this case the rich fabrics with which the tomb is draped appear to be real, and not just carved out of stone and then painted.

And then, just like in the stories my brothers used to tell to frighten me, the dead knight moves. He turns his great head. He opens his bruised-looking, cavernous eyes, and he looks straight at me.

'Who are you, and what are you doing here?' he says, speaking in the odd foreign-sounding accent that I've already heard in the village. With a grunt of pain and effort, he levers himself stiffly into a sitting position. He must be in his mid-seventies at least, but his eyes are sharp and full of energy. He reaches for a walking stick that's propped at the end of his couch, and brings it in front of him so he can rest his hands on its pommel. He's wearing a kind of robe.

I tell him who I am, and how I came to be here in his valley, and how the people in the village have been very kind to me.

'Didn't they tell you that the tower was private and holy?'

'Yes, they did. They told me I was welcome to come and have a look at it, but I shouldn't go inside. I'm afraid I—'

'You're afraid you decided to ignore that?'

'I'm very sorry, but they told me that this was where you kept the Holy Grail, and curiosity got the better of me.'

To my surprise, because he looks to me like the kind of Old Testament patriarch who would happily smite down his foes, he simply shrugs. 'Well, that's understandable. And in your case almost justified. The rule was made for the people who live here, and was for their benefit. Because holiness is soon worn away by familiarity. I know that from my own experience, unfortunately.' He sniffs. 'The less they see of the cup the more precious it remains.'

'So you're the Mason?'

'That's what they call me.'

'And you built this tower.'

'Yes, with help from the others, of course. It was a single-storey building at first, but I felt it should stand out more, given its role in our community, so I added another storey, and then another and, as you see, now another again. I'm climbing towards the heavens, like they did in Babel. Ha! Perhaps God will send a thunderbolt and strike me down. I had plans to fill in these windows too and build a fifth storey, a sixth, a seventh, but I may not bother now. Sometimes you must settle for what you have. And it's peaceful up here. It's very peaceful. I've reached an age where I'm content to be detached from the world. My only problem is the stairs. It's a long way up and a long way down for an arthritic old man like me. Another reason not to build any higher.'

'You're no longer very involved in the life of the village, from what I gather.'

'There's nothing particularly new about that. I figured out pretty quickly that I wasn't cut out to be part of a community. I make things, I tell stories, but I'm not much good with latrine-cleaning rotas, or organizing activities for children, or settling disputes. And I also realized pretty early on that I needed to preserve distance if I was going to carry on playing my particular role.' He chuckles wheezily. 'I'm like the cup. The less they see of me, the more useful to them I am.'

'You send across words of wisdom, I gather.'

'Wisdom?' He smiles, and watches me for a couple of seconds before answering. 'Hmmm. I'm afraid you're making fun of me. I write a few pages for them every week, so that the Preacher has something for her Sunday gatherings. I leave it to her to decide what to do with them.'

'Thoughts on the Bible, I suppose?'

'I don't often bother with that these days. It was a rich seam for many years – old stories have a resonance, don't you agree, that new ones really can't match? – but, well, I'm sure you know how it is, any story is limiting after a while. It's like always looking at one face of the moon. Sooner or later you wonder about the other side. So lately I've started writing my own stories, though I sometimes use biblical metaphors to make us feel at home. Jonah in the belly of the whale, for instance – that's a current favourite. I mean, imagine it! You're inside a whale's stomach, deep within its body, and it's under the sea, and it's far away from the shore. You couldn't get much more trapped than—' He breaks off. 'I do apologise. That was thoughtless of me, when you've just told me you were shut in a cage for many months.'

'Don't worry.'

He examines my face, his eyes slightly narrowed. 'I'd be extremely interested to know what that was like, if you felt like telling me.'

'Well, when you actually face it, it's unbearable, so you learn to find ways of distracting yourself. But sometimes distraction doesn't work and then you're in the truly awful position of being somewhere that's unbearable and yet must be borne.'

He leans forward, nodding emphatically, his deep eyes fixed on my face. 'That's very interesting. I find myself thinking about that a lot lately. Things that are unbearable and yet must be borne.'

He's very much enjoying this conversation, it strikes me, as if he's been starved of this kind of talk for a very long time. I suppose if you're a prophet, you don't often get a chance to talk things over with people, because your whole job is to know things, and not to have any doubts.

They're all over me. These kind, old-fashioned people with their foreign speech came running out to greet me as I limped into the village, and now they're very energetically looking after me.

It's all rather overwhelming. I'd prefer to have a bit of time just to look around, acclimatize myself to human company, and get some sort of sense of the village itself. But they're absolutely determined to care for me. They heat up water and fill up one of a row of old tin tubs in the village bathhouse, where apparently they all bathe and wash their clothes together, and several women clean my various sores and wounds, patting them carefully dry and applying ointments and bandages, while other villagers kill and roast a calf for me and serve it up under the beautiful wooden beams of the village dining hall, with potatoes and white cabbage and hard brown bread, along with spring water to wash it down, and a kind of potent mead. The entire population of the village is there in that one room, a hundred people or so, all talking animatedly in that odd singsong accent. I recognize and understand the words when people speak to me, but still have a sense that I'm listening to a different, northern, tongue. The clothes they wear are a century out of fashion, especially the women's long dresses and head scarves.

All of them watch me – and particularly the children, in that sly, knowing, slightly mocking way that children have – but they know they shouldn't crowd me, and so only the small group of adults who share my table attempt to talk to me. These include Helga, with her straw-coloured hair and her fierce grey eyes, who calls herself the Preacher and seems to be the one in charge.

I haven't drunk alcohol in a long while, I'm very tired, and darkness is falling. Earlier today, I spent four hours trudging across that high desert, wondering whether it was a mistake to leave the observatory at all, and whether I should go back there and wait, and then, with a much lighter heart, but much wearier legs, several more hours clambering down the steep and crumbly slope into the circular valley next to the volcano.

'I think I need to sleep now,' I tell Helga.

'Of course, of course!' They lead me out of the tiny hall into the village's single street of bare impacted earth.

Helga and her husband Peter insist on my taking their bed, which is built into the wall of their one-room house, a few metres away from the other large bed from which a selection of their grandchildren sit watching me in the candlelight. Helga and Peter are not young – in their sixties, I would guess – but they insist on sleeping on a rug on the floor, and in this they are backed up by the six or seven other villagers who've followed us into the house to ensure that I have everything I need.

'Of course you must have their bed!' they all tell me. 'You mustn't worry about them at all!'

I fall asleep almost as soon as I lie down, but in the middle of the night I wake with a full bladder and go outside. The stars are as bright as they were up on the plateau. The village is silent and dark, but at the far end of the lake, the windows at the top of the tower are still glowing.

I'm on my way now. I'm moving under my own power. It will be slow but, as long as I keep going and don't stop altogether, I have plenty of time. In fact, I'm somewhat tempted to make a diversion to the balcony. It would be nice to look down at the cars and the people once more, but that would use up time and energy, and is certainly not without its risks, especially during the door-opening process, when I'd have to transfer some of my weight from the frame to the handle, and during that difficult transition over the ridge between the interior and the exterior floors, when I'd have to relinquish the frame entirely and reach for the railing.

I would like to see the cars, though, two lanes of them in each direction, and the people going in and out of the shops and cafés, and that line of big squat palm trees that grow down the middle of the road, like enormous, plump pineapples. I used to enjoy looking down on all that, and it would be reassuring to see it all still there, even though it's tomorrow down there, and I'm still in yesterday. But I remind myself I could easily get one of the foreign women to wheel me out there sometime. All I'd need to do is pay for a bit of extra time and, let's face it, the one thing I'm not especially short of is money. Several of them have offered to do it, actually, but a kind of stubbornness has prevented me from accepting. Spiting myself has always been a hobby of mine.

Anyway, I forgo the balcony and the open air, and content myself with a glance through the window at the other large apartment blocks across the street before I return my attention to the task in hand. Galahad didn't turn away from the Grail, I suppose, in order to do a spot of sightseeing. I myself wouldn't have taken a detour when I was struggling along that stream in the forest.

Well, not a major detour like this, anyway; though, come to think of it, I did take a small detour to put that poor animal out of its misery when the pterosaurs were trying to pick out her eyes, and also, more pleasantly, to go to . . . oh, my memory is so bad now, what *was* that place? I often dream about it and, whatever unpleasant scenarios my unconscious mind has been laying on for me, it always comes as such a balm. But somehow I can't quite picture it. All I can think is that it was a kind of shrine with some kind of precious object inside it, pink and silver, *very* precious, which seemed to come from an entirely different world.

But never mind that now. On a mission such as this, distractions can easily kill. Get my toe caught on a bump in the carpet and this whole wobbly clapped-out vehicle with its absurdly slow reaction times and its ridiculous glass bones could topple forward and I'd break my arm, or my jaw, or Christ knows what else. I need to keep my attention on the path ahead. My one job now is get me safely to my goal and

I'm attempting to do that in a spacecraft whose responses are slow and clumsy and always overshoot, no matter how careful I try to be.

What was that place, though? What was that beautiful shining pink thing that was so comforting because it reminded me there was a world outside?

I realize I'm starting to feel faint. It's my old blood pressure problem, which I'd almost forgotten about because it doesn't intrude much when I'm lying down. But now it's happening in the most dangerous place it *could* happen, halfway to the moon, with nothing within reach to hold on to. I lean forward on my walking frame in the hope that, if I do pass out, myself and the frame might form some sort of tripod.

It takes about ten minutes before I leave the town's lights behind me. There will still be occasional lights between here and my cabin. There are four villages along the way, and from time to time I'll pass fisherman with gas lamps in their boats, but right now there are just the fireflies, flashing their tiny green lanterns over the river's soft skin.

I'm worrying now about the note I left her. I was a fool to write it when I was stoned. (And I wasn't just stoned, to be honest, I'd had a few beers as well.) It was *far* too fulsome. Amanda is a lovely person, of course, but she was only looking for friendship, not some sort of declaration of love. Now I've probably scared her off.

It wasn't just the dope and the booze that made me misjudge it, though. As much as anything it was solitude. I was okay on my own – I *am* okay, I'm absolutely fine – but when you've gone without something for a while, of course it has more power than usual when it comes your way, even if you were quite happy without it. Company and companionship have become unfamiliar to me. They've become intense and complicated. The drug and the beer just unlocked all that.

Her situation is completely different. She's living in a town, she works with people all week, goes out regularly for drinks in the evenings, and has conversations with her friends and family back in the city every day via one app or another on her phone or her laptop. All I was to her was one of a number of friendships she made in this part of the country, which she was happy to foster by reciprocating my visits to her apartment by making the journey up to my cabin. Like most people, she was probably mildly curious about me because of my famous dad and my great-aunt. I doubt she was really much put out by my coolness when she came to visit. We all put up with other people's minor foibles and moods, after all, and she knew I came here specifically to be alone. She probably just concluded that she'd picked a bad time to visit. In fact, if anything about me put her off on that occasion, it was more likely to have been the rather sordid state of the cabin and the fact that I was so obviously stoned. But I doubt if even those things were that big a deal for her.

But now I've left her this letter, this ridiculous gushing letter, saying – what was it? – 'I'm afraid I may have given you completely the wrong impression, because I think you are perfectly lovely and right now I can't imagine anything I'd like more in the world than to have you with me on the veranda here, sitting and watching the river go by while we talk.' And after that the self-exposure, the bit about how 'something always makes me shrink away from people, and perhaps especially the people I'm most drawn to'. Holy God, she didn't need that! She just wanted someone to meet for a chat, and to share our impressions as two city folk having an adventure in the backwoods of the Upper River. But following on from that was something even worse, because now came that stuff about how the whole thing would probably happen again when we next met, and she might well feel me shrinking back like I didn't want to be with her at all, but if so, she should take no notice because those weren't my real feelings, my real feelings were very warm and tender and entirely appreciative.

Oh God, how could I!

A fat beetle buzzes by, momentarily sharing with me the small intimate space around the boat, and then disappearing from my universe for good. A fish jumps. Birds call out to each other from the trees on either side of the soft dim water, though I can only just hear them over the throaty roar of my outboard motor.

I imagine her opening my letter. I imagine her embarrassment at the assumptions I make in it. I imagine her wincing at the fantasies I have apparently projected on to our relationship, and the expectations they seem to imply. I imagine her pitying me a little for my loneliness, but wishing she didn't have to, and wondering how to tactfully let me know that she really doesn't think of me in that way. She mentioned once that the most tiring thing about teaching is that you have to act a part for six whole hours at a stretch and how, while everyone plays a role of course – we all monitor our tone of voice, our facial expressions and so on to be sure of giving the right impression – there was something uniquely exhausting about doing so continuously in the ruthless gaze of forty nine-year-old kids from homes that valued toughness much more than kindness, and so she liked to have a quiet hour afterwards by herself before she was ready for company again. You wouldn't want a note like mine to come home to after a day like that, let alone want to rush straight out again to meet the person who wrote it.

God, how embarrassing. I'd better write her another note, apologizing for the first one. I could come right back this way tomorrow and leave it for her. In fact, seeing as tomorrow is Saturday, I could probably catch her in person and apologize to her face for my clumsiness, my lack of lightness, which to be honest has always been a fault of mine, but has certainly been aggravated by solitude, as I can explain to her, and then she'll—

But no, actually. On second thoughts, it would *not* be a good idea to come back tomorrow. I mustn't let my eagerness to clear this up make me *compound* my offence.

I've reached the first of the four villages between the town and my cabin. There are about twenty huts there, but the only electric light, apart from the little red beacon that blinks at the end of the jetty, is a single lamp on a pole by the water's edge. About twelve people are squatting in its light, some of them talking, others just sitting and smoking or playing with those strings of beads that most Upper River folk seem to carry around. A small radio is playing the old hit song 'That Distant Land', and one old man is amusing a couple of his friends by wriggling his hips in imitation of that pretty young singer they've seen on TV.

I'm on their side of the river but still at the very far edge of the light cast out by their lamp, so I can't be much more than a shadow to them. They watch me pass, but I don't intrude on their consciousness enough to interrupt their conversation.

And now they're behind me and I'm back in the dark again, with just the reflected starlight to show me where the water ends, and where the forest begins.

I can't see it now, but lying at the bottom of the boat is a smart blue plastic bag containing the new clothes I bought just to meet her in. I changed out of them before I set off, thinking to protect them from river water. Dear God, I even dressed up for her!

I find the bag and fling it out into the darkness. I mean, what was I thinking?

*

'It's a very striking picture,' Amanda says.

'So much going on,' I say. 'All those people, each with their own story, each with their own understanding of the world, each with their own quite different trajectory, but all momentarily finding themselves together in this one particular point in space and time. Even the following day, no two of them will remember these events in the same way, yet it just so happens that this is a moment that will be celebrated and re-enacted for thousands of years, including right here in this church. They don't know that, though. One or two seem dimly aware they're in the middle of a kind of . . . a kind of explosion, I guess, which is flinging out consequences so far into the future that angels have arrived to watch it happen. But look at the waiters! They haven't noticed anything. They're just getting on with their jobs. To them it's just an ordinary Wednesday night.'

'No. They obviously can't see those angels.'

'They had a copy of this picture in the little church up there in that village. I'm sure I told you about it. That funny little community where I was staying when the army came for me. '

'The Grail place? Of course you told me about it! You even brought me right here once, just to tell me about them. Do you not remember that? We came here specially to look at this painting!'

'Did we really? I'd completely forgotten.'

'It was after the Temple of Tanit.'

'Oh. The Temple.'

'Yes. Right after the Temple. You suddenly wanted to show it to me, remember? It summed up something you wanted to share with me. We came on foot, and we had to go a very long way round because of all the streets being closed in the city centre, because of the marching bands and the crowds and the flags. Oh, by the way, this is Chris.'

Her friend comes over to shake my hand. A nice, warm, open face. 'So sorry about your aunt. A wonderful woman. You must be very proud of her.'

Dru puts his head round the door of the chapter house, wondering where I've got to.

'I'll tell you what,' I suggest to all three of them, 'why don't we go up the tower?'

Now that he's sitting on it, dangling his long legs, I can see that what the Mason has been lying on is not a tomb but an altar, though there's nothing on it but himself.

'Stories,' he says. 'That's my job. I come up with stories. Of course, they're all about me really . . . well, I'm all I know . . . but I like to think others will find things in them that they recognize. Every month or two I come up with a new one and then Helga makes of it whatever she wants to make.'

'So each story supersedes the last?'

'I wouldn't say that. It's hard to hold them all in your head but I wouldn't say they cancel each other out. My current story began with a nightmare that woke me up clammy with fear. But I don't suppose you want to hear it, do you? I would have thought you've had enough of nightmares for the—'

'I'd like to hear it.'

He shrugs. 'Okay, well imagine this, then. Imagine a solid that was *really* solid – solid all the way through, I mean, not made of grains or atoms, but solid at every level of magnification, so that it's impossible to crack, or chip into, or burrow through. And imagine that this is what nothingness is, and not empty space as we usually imagine. Space is still a thing, after all. You can move through space. It's somewhere where things can be and things can happen. But through real nothingness, any kind of movement is impossible. And there's nothing beyond it, so even if you could drill through it – which you obviously can't – there would be no destination to get to.'

He pauses to examine my face. 'Got it so far? Well, now imagine – and this was my nightmare – that, in an infinity of solid nothingness, there is a single tiny flaw. A bubble, if you like, like the bubbles you get in glass. And trapped inside that bubble is a solitary living being, who is the only living being in existence. Well, that's God. God is all alone and always has been, with nowhere to go but where he is. He's Christ nailed to a cross, if you like, but it's a cross where he can never die, and from which he can never descend, because there's no possibility whatever of him being anywhere other than where he is. Ha! Just like you said, it's unbearable but he has to bear it.'

The Mason has been looking at his hands as they grasp the knob of his stick, but now he glances up at me beneath his bristly Old Testament brows, and seems to hesitate, as if he's read some sort of rebuke in my face. 'Or *she* has to bear it, if you prefer,' he says. 'Why not? In fact, I think I'll call her "she" from now on.'

'It sounds a very strange story to live by.'

'Well, my approach is to attempt to tell the truth, and then deal with the consequences. And my idea was that God came up with a sort of solution. She imagined a world. In her imagination, she came up with a thing called space and another thing called time, and then she split herself into tiny pieces, and spread herself out across this imagined thing called space and this other imagined thing called time. And, as a result of that splitting, we think there are things and places and days and nights, and each of us believes that we are just one individual among many, one sentient being among many sentient beings, even though, when you really think about it, our actual *experience* is quite the opposite and there is only ever one. Do you see what I mean? There is only ever one. It feels itself to be looking out at a world of things and faces, but *it* has no face and it itself is the only thing it actually *knows*. And that's where it all comes from: God by herself in her tiny cave, surrounded by nothingness.'

'That *is* a nightmare.' I'm really quite shaken. Just as the Mason warned me, this is all rather too close to my recent experience.

He nods. 'There are consolations, though. The terrible truth is always there in the background, it doesn't go away, but all the same it's just the beginning, and there are lots of other stories that flow out from it. For instance, let us for simplicity imagine that God started off by splitting herself into just two parts. You could see the two as a man and a woman if you wanted – Adam and Eve, why not? – or two men, or two women, or even two animals, if you prefer. The key point is that the two of them are essentially one and the same, but God must do her best to forget that, in order that they can seem to themselves to be two entirely separate beings. The trouble is that being separate is also lonely, itself a reminder of the loneliness that the entire universe was created to avoid, so they long to be close together, yet when they get too close, they stop being two separate people and become more like one again, and that too reminds them of the loneliness of God. So then one of them backs away. But that creates distance between them, so the other one feels abandoned and moves towards the first one. But that makes the first one afraid of being gobbled up and waking up alone in the cave in the rock, and so she hastily moves further away. And they end up chasing each other round and round, and back and forth, trying to be close and trying to stay apart, both at the same time.'

The Mason looks at me and shrugs. I wish he hadn't told me any of this.

'But what on earth's the point of an idea like that? I thought your stories were supposed to provide guidance and help people to live a good life. How does that story help anyone? What can we possibly learn from it?'

He laughs. 'Well, that's Helga's job. That's why I'm up here and she's over there in the village. She has that trick of knowing what to do. Stories never really tell you that. In fact, the truer the story, the less useful it is. I'd go as far as to say that, if it were possible to sum up the entire world in a single story, that story would give no guidance whatever, because it would be an account of why things have to be exactly as they are, and why everything that happens, and every choice that's made, is as necessary and inevitable as every other.'

'So why tell these stories at all, then?'

'Ha! Good question! It's hard to say. For some reason it just happens to be what I need to do. And Helga assures me she finds them useful. To be perfectly honest with you, she's the one with the difficult job so I try to help her out by coming up with a few principles or axioms that she might draw out. For instance, from the story I've just told we might derive something like, "Be close but not too close," or "Look after others, but look after yourself as well."'

'But . . . but those are just . . .'

The Mason barks with laughter. 'I know, I know! They're just platitudes. Anyone could come up with them, without going to all the bother of a story.'

'I guess so, but . . .'

'Ha! You *know* so! And platitudes always miss out the hard part, don't they? I mean, any fool can say, "Look after others, but look after yourself as well." It obviously makes sense. The difficulty lies in knowing where the balance should be struck.'

'That's the part I find difficult, certainly.'

'Well, that's Helga's job. She makes the world *work*. I just build the tower and provide the stories. I don't know why but she assures me she finds that helpful.'

He smiles, and shrugs again.

'May I ask your real name? They just call you the Mason in the village.'

'Of course. My name is Stein Pedersen.'

'What did you do, back in your own country, before you came out here?'

'I was a mason there, too: a stonemason like my father. It was pretty routine work, most of it. No one would have asked me to build a tower like this.'

'Have you always been alone?'

'No. I had a wife when I came here. Unfortunately she died. I'm afraid it wasn't the easiest of marriages. She couldn't see why certain things are just . . . well . . . *necessary* for me . . . you know? She couldn't understand my point of view.'

'Nor you hers, I guess?'

His expression suggests that this thought has much less hold on his imagination – I notice he hasn't asked me about my name, my background, my occupation – but, in a spirit of fairness, he concedes the point. 'I'm sure that was also the case.'

He contemplates what he's just said for several seconds, and then repeats himself, this time with something rather closer to actual regret. 'I'm sure that was the case. You're quite right. I'm not an easy person to share life with.'

I'm being shown round a utopia.

'So this is where we store all our grain,' I'm being told, as we emerge into a stone-paved village square with a large and beautiful plane tree as its focal point. 'Of course, anyone can help themselves to it whenever they want, but most of it we use to make bread in the village bakery here, where everyone takes a turn.'

'We meet every Wednesday to solve problems and allocate tasks,' someone else explains, as I stop to look around me at the harmonious sight of the various buildings of stone and wood that surround the square, and at the high scarp beyond the rooftops, against the cool blue sky. 'And Sunday gatherings are to remind us what brought us here in the first place.'

'Here is where we make glass and work metal,' yet another villager tells me, and smilingly holds up for my inspection hands that have been scarred by fire. 'A few of us are specially good at such things and are excused from work on the land.'

I have slept all night in a warm soft bed, with the comforting sniffs and grunts of other sleepers in the room beside me. My stomach is full of bread and fruit and meat and my battered body is tingling with the warm baths it has soaked in, and the ointments and salves that have been applied to it.

'We try to ensure,' Helga tells me as we head towards the church that forms the centrepiece of the village, 'that disagreements are not allowed to fester. If two people can't sort things out between themselves, each can choose an advocate, and the village as a whole chooses a mediator, and then they all stay in the meeting hall to talk and pray until, one way or another, the matter is resolved.'

'Of course,' says her husband Peter, 'there's less to argue about here than you have in the world outside, since we hold everything in common, and none of us is either rich or poor.'

For some reason I find myself thinking about those gods that my lazy, drug-addled imagination used to conjure up for me back in my days by the river, and I imagine them hovering round me now. Jesus is tense and ill at ease, as he usually is around Christians, like an anxious parent watching a clumsy child stepping out on to a stage. Apollo is scathing about the mediocrity of this miniature society, the lack of opportunity for real achievement, whether artistic or scientific, the lack of any encouragement for brilliance. 'And don't get me started,' he says, 'on the slavish reliance on superstition.' Aphrodite, meanwhile, thinks that everyone is sexually repressed, and Dionysus finds the whole place dull and stifling. Where is the passion, he wants to know? Where is the ecstasy? Where are the joys of destruction and creation? And then Tanit appears, in her capacity as goddess of war, to sneer at the softness of it all. 'They only survive at all because of their isolation,' she says. 'It would only take two or three soldiers of fortune to arrive with guns, and they'd all become slaves.'

It's all very pretty, and if I visited a place like this as a tourist in some foreign country, I'm sure I'd take many photos, but I can't help myself from wondering how on earth these people can bear to confine themselves, for their entire lives, in something as small and parochial as this little village.

'And think of all the meetings they must have to go to,' mutters the river god, the one that has no name, 'all the strokes they must have to constantly give one another, all the petty arguments that have to be defused, all the nosiness and the gossip. Surely anyone who has the slightest imagination must feel like screaming sometimes, or running amok just for the sake of variety, and crave for a place where no one knows them, and no one expects anything of them at all, and they can be whatever they choose.'

I keep looking across at the strange, spiky tower that stands on its own small prominence at the far end of the lake.

'That's very striking. I'd love to have a closer look at it.'

Helga smiles. 'We can go there whenever you feel ready.'

'I wonder if I could go there on my own? I don't mean to seem rude or ungrateful, but I've been so long by myself that it's quite challenging being surrounded by people all the time. I think I'm going to need to give myself a bit of space at some point.'

'Of course, of course,' says Peter. 'We mustn't crowd you. By all means have a walk along the lake. But I'm afraid you can only look at the tower from the outside. It's our holy place, you see. We don't go inside ourselves except on special occasions. You'd have to get the Mason's permission to go in, and he might very well not grant it.'

Helga opens the church door. It's actually quite beautiful inside in a modest, austere kind of way: these rough stone arches, these plain windows of knobbly glass, and what appears to be the lesson for the week, written in chalk on a blackboard: *Look after others, but look after yourself as well.*

'No cross,' I observe.

'No, we've never had a cross,' Helga says. 'As the Mason used to say, if we're going to follow Jesus Christ, we should have a symbol that represents what he said when he was alive, not a story that others told about his death.'

'And that cup there . . . Is this what you believe to be the Holy Grail?'

They both laugh. 'Not the Grail,' Helga says. 'That's just a fairy tale! This represents the Holy Chalice, the real cup that Christ himself used at the Last Supper.'

'But of course this is just a cup,' Peter says. 'It *represents* the Chalice. It's not the Chalice itself.'

I'm simultaneously slightly relieved and a little disappointed. The relief comes from learning that they're not quite such a bunch of cranks as I'd been led to believe, the disappointment because it turns out that, in spite of my scepticism, I have imbued enough of those old stories in my childhood to have been looking forward to being in the presence of something that might just really be the Grail. (And Grail is what I still call it in my mind, whatever their objections to the word.)

'I apologize,' I say. 'It did seem rather far-fetched. It's just I'd understood that—'

'The real Chalice is in the tower.'

So they *are* a bunch of cranks. Oh dear. I find that almost embarrassing, even as the tower acquires a new and magical allure in my mind.

'It's important not to be greedy, we feel,' Helga says, 'in spiritual matters as in everything else.'

'Oh look!' I exclaim. 'That painting! I know that painting. It hangs in the cathedral in . . .'

The cathedral I mean is the one back in the city, which was a regular outing in my childhood, a place where we took the families of Dad's many foreign visitors. For me as a child, the highlight of the place was always the tower, and the rest of it was just something to get over with as soon as possible, so I never gave more than a passing glance to the painting that hung above the altar. But now the familiarity of it, in such a strange and unfamiliar place, gives it an extraordinary power, and has the effect of making me really look at it in a way I've never done before: those dark shadows across the table, the sharp, stormy light that cuts through the glass carafes, the waiter in the foreground, for whom this is just another private party, asking a customer if everything's all right, and, deep inside the picture, Christ giving bread to the disciple next to him.

As we emerge from the church, the tower is still in full sunlight, but the escarpment behind it is in shadow. Of course I don't believe any of this nonsense, but it is staggering even just to imagine the possibility that the cup used in that very scene could be just over there across the lake, behind those lonely windows.

I didn't pass out. That's one blessing. I had to stand like that for quite a while, leaning over my frame, while the waves of dizziness moved through me, but eventually they faded and I was able to move forward again. It's been a long hard journey and there were moments when I was sure I wasn't going to make it, but I've reached my destination – the chest of drawers – and now comes one of the hardest and most dangerous parts of my quest, because I need to open a drawer, and I happen to know that it's a stiff one that requires a fair amount of force, and is therefore likely to resist at first and then come out with a jerk. The one thing you don't need, when you have slow reactions and bones made of glass, is to find yourself suddenly thrown outwards into space in a direction where there's nothing to grab hold of.

So, before attempting to open the drawer, I need somehow to get a grip on the chest itself with one hand, sufficiently firmly that I can rely on that single hold to keep me upright. And then I need to push my frame to one side in such a way that it won't get in the way of me pulling out the drawer, but will still be near enough for me to make the transfer back to it when it's time for my return journey. My body is the landing vehicle, the frame the orbiting module with which I must dock if I'm to have any chance of getting back to Earth. I feel quite afraid. I feel that I've been a stubborn fool to embark on this journey at all, considering that I have people visiting me three times a day who could easily have done it for me, and it doesn't help that right now I can feel the pain coming back. In fact, it's happening much earlier than it would have done if I'd remained on my bed, for my own treacherous internal organs, hijacked and swollen by disease, have been pulled and yanked about by my shuffling progress across the room, and they feel like lumps of red-hot lead.

But I've come this far and I can't give up now. If I can just complete this manoeuvre successfully, find what I need, and transfer it to the canvas bag that's attached for this sort of purpose to the front of the frame, I actually don't even need to make it back as far as the bed, because there's an armchair between here and there, which is, if anything, slightly easier to transfer to, and is one of those electric ones with a little handset that allows you to move the footrest up and down. To sit up in a chair for a while would make a pleasant change and I'm not sure why I haven't used it lately. They're always suggesting it, those foreign women. They're always offering to help me there. I am *very* stubborn, I'm afraid. That jealous, spiteful feeling rises up inside me, and I end up refusing offers of help that would actually be to my own benefit. The stupid part is that it makes no difference to them at all whether I say yes or no. They aren't the slightest bit offended when I refuse. They just shrug and say, 'Well, if you're sure,' and then give me my meds, wash and change me on the bed, and head off to wherever it is they go in that mysterious world out there where it's already tomorrow, so that the only person I've spited is myself. I'm a fool like that, and always have been, but sometimes the little comforts and consolations that people kindly offer me seem so small and so trivial compared with what I've lost, that they almost feel insulting.

Anyway, never mind that. Stay focused, that's the thing. Get this procedure wrong and I could end up lying on the floor with my smashed bones sticking out through my skin. So first of all, I need to let go of the frame on one side like this. It all feels very precarious with only one hand to hold me up, especially when you consider that the frame itself isn't rock solid, isn't attached to the floor, and can itself fall over, but that's what I'm doing. And now, having managed that, I need somehow to reach across the chest so I can hook my fingers over the edge of it, and give myself a degree of resistance to any sudden movement backward. This is hard. This feels very unsteady and unsafe, but I manage it. The next stage is, with my other hand, to push the frame sideways out of my way, but not out of my reach, and without snagging it on the carpet or toppling over. When I've done that, I can tackle the drawer.

Honk honk. Parp parp. The curtains waft about round the half-open window. Strange to think that there's a street full of people down there who think nothing of walking about without any kind of support at all. But I must stay focused. There! Well done me! Skilfully manoeuvred! The frame is out of the way of the drawer but is still, at least in principle, within my reach. I put my hand on the drawer and cautiously test it. I do *not* want to end up on the floor with the whole thing on top of me. But it comes out more smoothly than I'd feared. Even better, my memory hasn't let me down, and the things I want are actually there.

I take them out, lay them on top of the chest, and push the drawer closed. Still holding on with one hand, I reach with the other for the frame. It's hard to drag it sideways when its two little wheels are meant for going backwards and forwards. Ouch! Sweet Jesus, that hurt! But I've managed it and the frame is in front of me. I transfer my acquisitions to the canvas bag. I release my grip on the chest in readiness for putting this vehicle of mine through a difficult three-point turn.

To six-year-old me this was a real adventure. Like proper adventures, it took time, and there were stages to it, and you had to pass through several different realms, each with its own distinct character. First you went through a small arched door and climbed a tight spiral staircase. You might think that this was going to take you all the way to the top, but no, it only took you to the huge, dim, empty loft that lies between the stone vaulting of the nave and its outer roof. This had a very distinctive, gloomy, woody smell, and you had to cross it, before climbing a dozen wooden stairs to a small door that opened on to a part of the rooftop, over which sheets of lead had been moulded, like pastry over a pie. You could see the old stone statues of saints around you, looking down into the Cathedral Square below, but you were too far from the edge of the roof to see what they could see. (One time, I remember, when we came here with some foreign friends of Dad's, there were three little sky-monkeys up there, only a few yards away from us, gathered around a carton of potato chips.)

There was a short walk then along a path of lead until you came to another little arched door that you had to open, beyond which was another stone staircase. At this point, for the first time, you were inside the tower itself, though I'm not sure I conceptualized it in that way when I was small. (In fact, I don't think I had a mental map at all: it was all about sensory impressions back then.) The tower steps were daunting because they carried on relentlessly for the equivalent of three storeys and were very steep and not designed at all for the short legs of a child, and, though you could hold on to the rope in the middle, you sometimes had to relinquish it to people coming the other way (foreign tourists, typically, speaking some exotic northern tongue). To make it worse, those uncomfortably high and steep steps had been worn down by several centuries of feet into deep saddle shapes from which it would be very easy to slip backwards. Arrow slits let in a small amount of light and several times you reached what looked like it was going to be the top, but turned out just to be a kind of landing the width of a couple of steps, which gave access to the rooms inside the tower, in one of which, behind a kind of cage, and fixed to a kind of machinery made of wood, there were enormous bells – each one could easily have held four or five children my size. The worn stone, and the feeling of precariousness that came from the treacherous sloping steps, combined with my six-year-old sense of the dreadful antiquity of this building, created a very particular mood, oppressive and sinister, which added considerably to the glamour of the whole experience. As a child, when people spoke of the Holy Ghost, and how he was everywhere, I imagined being surrounded by this ancient, tomblike stone.

When you finally reached the top, you stepped out through another little arched door, on to a narrow gallery that led right round the tower, and from which you could look down at the old city, and out over the sea, and across at the towers of the business district, and back at the new city climbing up the hill, all the way up to our house, which, when I was little, Dad would help me find through his big binoculars. This was the culmination of the whole trip, and the highlight of it was the sight of the tiny figures moving about in the square below, where we ourselves had been not long before, taking photos with tiny cameras, and feeding the miniature mynah birds and tiny sky-monkeys.

I haven't been up here for many years now and of course the climb no longer has the epic quest-like quality it once possessed. I can see that it's not really particularly long or difficult or dangerous, and, after many plane journeys – they too were once also an exciting adventure – and many visits to mountains and skyscrapers, I find I'm no longer particularly enthralled by the experience of looking on the world from above, or struck by the illusion of smallness that comes with distance.

Dru emerges after me. Amazingly, though he's lived in the city all his life, he says he's never been up here before. Amanda and Chris follow him through the little door. 'Wow!' says Amanda. 'I'd forgotten what an incredible view it is!' But, if I'm not mistaken, she's having to force her enthusiasm, and would much rather not have been taken away from the memorial party in the chapter house, and the company of all those interesting people who she wouldn't normally have a chance to meet, for that, after all, was what she and Chris came here for, and not to help an ex-partner re-enact a childhood treat that can't, in any case, be replicated.

The problem with the island, when I'm actually on it, is that it feels fake. What looked from a distance to be a charming little fishing village has long since ceased to be a village at all. I suppose a few people still live here, but the place is essentially a small theme park. The pretty white fishermen's houses are all second homes or holiday lets, the church is a shop selling souvenirs, and the choice of eating places consists, at the lower end of the price range, of a kind of industrial unit, inside the shell of an old building, which is designed to deliver microwaved versions of local dishes to as many visitors as possible, and, at the upper end, of a couple of chic little 'artisanal' places, which try to persuade the better-off visitor that they're not like that other place and that the food they serve is in some sense 'authentic' and 'real'.

'Artisanal', it occurs to me, as I eat a light lunch in one of these restaurants, has come to mean 'place where nice middle-class people perform formerly working-class jobs'. Even the waiters in a place like this are slightly arch, and have degrees in literature or the performing arts. And that thought suddenly makes me think of poor Guinevere, who saw through the world, and, unlike most of us, tried to act on what she'd seen. People say that, in prisons, everyone hates the paedophiles, even the rapists and the murderers, but Guinevere was like the one prisoner who realizes that, just because someone else's crime is viler, it doesn't mean your own crime is anything other than vile.

I leave my food unfinished and wander along the waterfront. Out here, I can see, beyond the headlands that enclose the bay, more islands in both directions that can't be seen from the mainland, each one as inviting as this one seemed when I looked out at it from the shore.

I go to one of the telescopes, drop in a coin and, after a bit of searching, I find our hotel. Amanda is out on the balcony. Even through a telescope, she's too far away for me to make out her face, but something about the long, loose curve of her body is unmistakable as she sits on one chair with her feet on the other, a coffee cup on a small table beside her, looking down at what I assume is the schoolwork of one of her pupils.

For some reason I feel an ache of loss and longing, as if she wasn't just on the other side of the water, but far off in a past I can no longer reach.

After a short rest, I fumble in the bag attached to the frame. I take out a notebook, some reading glasses and a pen. I've made it to safety. I'm in my chair and here I can remain until my next carer arrives.

There is a small crisis when I drop the pen, and a long and uncomfortable episode ensues as, by trial and error, I work out a way of leaning sideways and downwards to retrieve it. This manoeuvre sets off a long bout of coughing, after which I wipe the greenish blood-streaked phlegm on my sleeve and allow myself another rest with my eyes closed, the notebook on my lap and the pen grasped firmly in my hand. My pain would be beginning to nag at me by now in any case, but it has been greatly aggravated by all this moving about.

Someone upstairs is playing a radio. I hear only the insistent thumping of the bass, but whoever lives up there likes the old stuff, and I recognize the song. Outside in the street, the cars, as ever, are snapping and grumbling at one another as they pass on either side of those big squat palm trees that resemble giant pineapples.

When my body seems to have settled down somewhat, I open my eyes again and look down at the notebook. It dates back to my last attempt to get my famous novel off the ground, famous in the sense that . . .

But I've made that weak joke too many times.

There's a date on the cover and below that several different titles, each one of them crossed out. With my clumsy fingers I make my way through a forest of scrawled black marks on white paper, like winter trees in snow. There are page after page of notes and plans and little diagrams, all inscribed there many years after I'd last actually published a book. Here, for instance, is a page I remember writing in the Botanic Gardens about ten years ago, sitting on a bench in front of that duck pond beside the fence. I'm looking down at the words that my past self wrote, in handwriting that's already a little wobbly but is far more fluent than anything I can manage now, and I'm thinking how strange it is to know that what I'm looking at isn't just a replica of the notebook I wrote in then, but is the exact same one I held in my hands ten years ago, marked with the exact same ink that flowed at the time from my pen. I had brought coffee in a flask, I remember, and I had just eaten some tuna and cucumber sandwiches. And I remember that I looked up at the building opposite, where I once lived at an even earlier time – long, long ago – in that apartment I shared with Jezebel and that fellow with the rather old-fashioned left-wing views, and that as I looked up it, I had the exact same thought I'm having now about the way that physical things endure, and how they pass like time machines from one epoch to the next.

This is not that much of a coincidence, actually, because it's a thought I often used to have. It doesn't strike me so frequently now, because I seldom encounter things from the past and am therefore not often confronted with the strangeness of material objects still being here when they come from a far-off there.

I leaf through more pages. A lot of the ideas are pretty half-baked, to be honest, and hovering over them all the time is the knowledge that, even back then, I'd left it far too late. I must have known perfectly well, really, as I sat there on that bench, that the project for which I was making notes would never actually be realized. Apart from anything else, my last book had done so badly that no one was likely to want to publish another.

Halfway through the notebook, the words and scribbles stop and I reach the empty pages I've been looking for. It's not that I abandoned my project at that point, for there were other notebooks after this. It's just that from time to time, I would toss aside one notebook and start a new one, because there was something hopeful about a pristine cover in a different colour and clean and empty pages that made me feel that, perhaps this time, I really would come up with a viable plan.

I fold the notebook back so that it will lie open for me on my lap. I apply the ballpoint to the page. Straight away it skitters about, making a scratchy pattern on the paper, as if this was a séance and some impish spirit was trying to take control. Holding it firmly against the page, I draw the pen upwards. A very wobbly line appears, which I force with difficulty into a shape that just about functions as a letter of the alphabet. I'm going to have to print this in capitals, I can see, if there's to be any chance of anyone being able to read it.

I transfer the pen to a spot to the right of the circle, and lower it to the page again, where it makes another small skittery pattern. Making a concerted effort to resist the imp, I commence work on another letter, lift the pen again, transfer it to the right. Soon I've written a whole word.

I take a pause to celebrate. The cars grumble outside the window. I embark on a second word and then a third.

OUR LOST ATLANTIS. That's what I've written.

I lift the pen, and move it over the page with the slow,

slightly jerky deliberation of a construction crane over a building site. Then I lower the pen and begin a new line with another flourish of random wiggles. It's not going to be tidy, that's for sure, but it's pleasant to know all the same that, even now, I can still send something out into the world.

We ride down together in the aluminium cube of the lift. He looks very smart in his work suit and his neat brown coat. I ask him about the meeting he's going to. He explains it's to discuss progress with a firm of specialist diving contractors, which has the job of checking the steel hawsers that anchor the turbines to the seabed. I didn't know they floated, I tell him. I thought they stood on the bottom.

He laughs. 'I thought you looked a bit glazed over during that part of the conversation.'

The laugh is strained. I've hurt him, I can see, but not really because of my failure to grasp the finer points of windfarm construction. What did it was the cold flash of contempt that I subjected him to when he came in with my breakfast on a tray. I know what that feels like. It's like an icy wind blasting through your soul. You have to be an exceptionally confident person not to be shaken by the contempt of others.

'I didn't glaze over, I promise, but you went into such detail that sometimes I was still busy trying to picture one thing when you moved on to the next.'

I meant that to sound friendly, but it came across as

defensive and forced. The lift stops at the third floor, and a burly man in overalls steps in, an electrician perhaps, here on a contract like Ham's divers, carrying a tin box of tools.

'Ground floor,' says the lift, and we follow the burly man out into the clean, anonymous lobby. There's one of those bland civic murals on one wall, made of beige-coloured tiles, that depicts a scene in the lives of the tribespeople who were the original inhabitants of this part of the southern coast. I stop to look at the caption beneath it, which explains that the name of this building meant 'Hope' in those people's now-extinct language, but also meant 'East' and 'Sunrise'. You never see them in the streets, of course – there are only a few of them left – but the sign explains that the name of the town itself also comes from their language. Apparently it means 'Place of Many Octopuses'.

Ham has stopped with me, because we haven't yet said goodbye, and I realize that I'm deliberately delaying that moment, which is odd, because up in his flat a few minutes ago, I couldn't wait to get away.

'Funny, isn't it?' I say. 'We drive out all the people who live in a place, yet we still like to keep the name they gave it. It seems we always want to keep something from the past, even if we ourselves have destroyed it. It's like a hand to hold on to, I suppose, when you're reaching forward into the dark.'

Ham smiles. 'I know I'm just a thick engineer,' he says, 'but I have absolutely no idea what you're talking about.'

We head towards the sliding glass doors through which

the burly electrician has already passed and emerge into watery sunlight and icy air. At the top of the eight steps that lead down to the street, I grab Ham's hand to make him stop.

'You're not thick at all, Ham, and I like you very much.'

Already at the foot of the steps and heading for the building site next door, the electrician looks round with a frown as I kiss Ham on the cheek.

I can almost see the burden lifting from his shoulders.

'I like you too,' he says. 'You take care of yourself.'

We go down the steps, and then with a momentary touch of my hand, he turns right towards the harbour and I turn left and up the hill that leads back into the oddly desolate streets of the town centre.

Guinevere has been silent for several seconds.

'All right,' she says, 'so you're saying that the world can't really get any better than it already is, and, however shitty and unfair, this is just the way things are?'

The last of the bats has left the cave now, and there's almost no sound except for our breathing and the hissing of the gas lamp a few metres away.

'I'm afraid I do tend to think that.'

'I don't agree, but let's suppose you're right, and everything is just the way it has to be and everything that happens is just what needs to happen.'

'Okay, and . . .?'

'That would mean, wouldn't it, that what I'm doing is just as important as what anyone else does? The insurrection is necessary. It's a part of the way things have to be as well.'

I'm about to answer her, but a series of loud, thunder-like noises come echoing down the cave. They're so distorted that at first I don't recognize them at all, but Guinevere clearly does because she jumps up straight away to grab her gun.

'See you,' she calls back as she runs towards the cave mouth to help fight off the attack.

'You're being very frank with me,' I say, 'considering that we've only just met.'

The Mason shrugs, legs dangling from his altar. 'I'm frank with everyone. I never pretend to be more than I actually am, or to know more than I really know.'

'Really? Even about—'

'Ha! About this, you mean?' He reaches behind himself for something and tosses it across to me.

Taken by surprise, I fumble the catch and nearly drop whatever it is he's thrown at me. It's conical in shape, quite small, but heavy, made of what looks like pewter. At the pointed bottom end, there are three small prongs to allow it to be set down on a table.

The Mason laughs at my surprise and shock. 'If you'd made an appointment, I could have put on a show for you. I would have told you to come after dark. The stairs would have been lit with candles, and, when you opened the door to this room, that cup would be on the altar, with only a single small candle next to it to show it off. But I'm afraid if you will just barge in when I'm taking a nap, you only get the unadorned version.'

I turn the cup in my hand. 'And this is the thing you've told them all is the Holy Grail?'

'The Holy Chalice. Yes. Why do you look so surprised? What sort of cup did you think they'd have two thousand years ago in a rented room above a pub? Some gold monstrosity studded with diamonds?'

'From what I've read, you persuaded all these people to give up their old lives in the northern countries and come out here on the basis that this is the cup that was used at the Last Supper?'

'I thought it would be a focal point. I've never liked the cross.'

'But your people back there across the lake, they don't just see this as a symbol, they see it as the actual—'

'Well, I believe it is! No one can be certain of anything, of course, but I think there's reasonable evidence for it. It would be boring to tell you the whole story of how I got hold of it, but it had been passed down through a family who themselves assumed it was a fake. It was inside a leather bag that had dried hard around it, and when I cut it open there was a folded piece of papyrus inside with an inscription in first-century Aramaic. I had it translated and it read, *This is the cup my master Yeshua had us share, that last time we ate together.* I cut off a piece of the leather and a piece of the papyrus and had them tested in a lab. I didn't say what they came from, obviously – the last thing that thing needs is to be the centre of a media frenzy – but I was told the leather, the papyrus and the ink were all about two thousand years old. You can't do a carbon test on metal, I'm afraid, but I took the cup to a very famous museum, without mentioning the story that was told about it, and the people there said it was a drinking vessel of a type you find in the period and in the part of the world that the story claimed for it. Put all that together. What would you think, if it was you?'

I remember the painting in the village church: that epochal moment, like an explosion caught in its first few nanoseconds, when the blast wave has barely begun to radiate outward, and I feel light-headed, almost as if I'm about to faint. 'Jesus!' I mutter.

The Mason laughs, watching me with amusement from under his patriarch brows. 'That's the man! He once drank from that very cup you're holding. Think about it for a moment. Put aside any doubts you may have, just for a minute, and tell me how it makes you feel?'

'It feels . . . I don't know. It feels magical.'

'Of course it does. It's a relic. Relics are powerful. Back in medieval times they couldn't get enough of them: real physical objects right here in the present that come from the story-world of the past.'

He's still watching me closely as I feel the weight of the cup in my hands, this clever, energetic, desperately lonely man, who is slowly retreating towards the sky. It's not that the people in the village aren't allowed to argue with him, I realize, it's more that they don't want to. Sensible people that they are, they're happy to leave him to it, wrestling on their behalf with meaning and doubt.

'Mind you,' he says, and he's clearly very used to arguing with himself, 'all this is predicated on the assumption that something magical really did happen in the past. If you take the view that the Last Supper was simply an office party, which it very probably was, the value of that thing there begins to fall.'

I take the cup across to him and place it carefully in his hands, uncomfortable with holding it any longer.

'I don't know about that,' I tell him. 'I was struck by your story about the two people who need to stay apart even though they also need to be together. I suppose anything is magical that makes you feel like it's possible to have here and there at the same time.'

'Do you really think so?' he says.

And he smiles as he looks down at his precious cup, apparently genuinely relieved by what I said.

Now this really *is* the tree. I was mistaken about the last tree, and about the one before, but this is *definitely* that tall tree on the final bend, the one that leans a little to the left. I can only just make it out against the sky, but all the same I've got no doubt at all that I'm right. One more corner and there will be the little blue light of my cabin to welcome me home.

I've been through a lot of stages on this journey. I began in a state of shame, convinced that Amanda was made so uncomfortable by my note that she chose not to come and meet me in the café. But as I continued up the river, the less likely that seemed to be.

At the second village, there were a few people sitting by the riverbank. They didn't have electric light, but they had a little fire going where they were cooking something fatty and pungent, and I could see a dozen grown-ups squatting round it, smoking and talking in its light, while a group of kids played what looked like a board game of some kind. I waved, but no one bothered to wave back. They must have heard my outboard motor, but they perhaps couldn't see me at all.

Whatever her feelings about the note, I decided, Amanda would have come to meet me if she'd known I was waiting for her, or phoned me at the very least. She wasn't the sort to let someone down just to avoid feeling uncomfortable. And, after all, however clumsy and florid, the note was an apology, and a declaration of how much I liked her. She might have been embarrassed by it, but it was a compliment to her, and you really couldn't say there was anything unpleasant about it. In fact, the more I thought about it, the more I became convinced that the reason she didn't turn up must have been something completely unrelated to my note. A problem might have cropped up at school, for instance – some disciplinary problem that had to be sorted out, perhaps, or a staff meeting, or even a parents' evening if they had such things – and she just hadn't got home yet by the time I gave up waiting.

I came to the third village. There was no sign of any life there at all, other than little slivers of yellow gaslight showing through cracks in some of the huts, and the blinking red light at the end of the jetty that all the villages had to prevent boats from crashing in the dark. Half a kilometre on, I passed a boat with one of those big gas lamps the locals used at night to attract certain kinds of fish. There were three people in the boat, two men and a small boy. They had an outboard motor, but they were just drifting on the water with their net trailing behind. They peered at me as I passed through the outer edge of their little patch of light, and the boy shouted something that made the two men laugh, though I couldn't make out what he said above the sound of my motor, and it was probably in one of the local languages.

She might have arranged to meet a friend at the cinema, I thought, and gone there straight from school. She'd once mentioned that was something she did from time to time. She didn't answer my text, it's true, but it was entirely possible that she ran out of charge, or simply forgot to turn on her phone again at the end of the school day.

This scenario seemed a lot more plausible than the idea that I'd embarrassed her so much that she couldn't bring herself to meet me, and I felt so reassured by this thought that I was able to think about other things until the fourth and final village, where there were a few people sitting by the water, next to a gas lamp. Still rather ashamed of having frightened those little children, I made sure to steer towards the middle of the river where they wouldn't be able to see who I was. But I didn't worry too much about that either. Those children gave me a fright, that was all, and it's not as if I hurt them. I began to relax into the night, enjoying the cool air, and the feeling of being far out on the quiet cool water with nothing and no one to bother me.

And now here I am, after several times feeling certain that I've spotted the tall tree that marks the final bend, knowing without any doubt that this time it really is the one.

Perhaps when she finds the note, she'll be pleased, I think. That surely is at least possible? That was my original intention, after all: to please her, and to reassure her that my prickliness was not in any way a judgement on her, because she's every bit as lovable as her name suggests. And she seems to like me well enough – she went to all the trouble of hiring a boat, didn't she, and travelled twelve kilometres just to see me? So why on earth would she object to my telling her I liked her? If anything, I should be worried that she might read *too* much into my note, and imagine . . .

But I'm turning the corner now. My blue light appears in the distance on the right-hand bank, showing me my way home.

From the Freedom Fortress a couple of kilometres away comes the sound of a twenty-one-gun salute, one explosion for each of the twenty provinces and one for the Federation itself. Seconds later, a number of rockets go off, even though it's the middle of a sunny morning, and splatter the sky with patriotic colours: yellow, red and blue. We can hear the cheering of the crowd over there that's gathered to watch the pageantry.

We've been here half an hour. The foreign couple with the little girl headed off some time ago and, as far as we can see, we have the whole park to ourselves.

'Let's go up to the temple,' I say.

Since the indigenous people never, to our knowledge, constructed anything in stone, the Temple of Tanit is the oldest masonry structure on our entire continent, built, as the information boards are keen to tell us, a millennium and a half before the next wave of settlers arrived from across the sea. There isn't much of the temple left, apart from the foundations, the stumps of a few columns, and the artificial hill on which it stands, and it's never really caught my imagination. Over the years I've laid my hands many times on the remains of those columns and tried to enthuse myself with the idea that these very stones could have been touched all those years ago by the priests and priestesses of the moon goddess, yet for some reason they've always stubbornly insisted on just being stones. But it's a pleasant spot from which to view the rest of the park, with its artful landscaping, its miniature gorge full of jungle plants that delighted me as a child, and its various statues and fountains.

Of course, the centrepiece of the temple is the large and ornate tomb of the novelist Mago Barca. It has all the usual columns and weeping cherubim and other gewgaws that are so characteristic of the heavy 'Punic' style of the late nineteenth century, including the inevitable personifications in stone of the Five Civilized Nations, and, on the top of this whole elaborate confection, Barca himself reclines on a black obsidian slab. He is twice his natural size, carved in white marble in the imagined garb of one of the virile Carthaginian adventurers he believed to be the founders of our civilization, and gazing sternly out into a future where he fondly imagines he will always be seen as a kind of giant. The marble is somewhat tarnished now by soot and lichen, and by the carved initials of scores of visitors.

'Have you ever read anything he wrote?' Amanda asks.

'Only for research purposes, and only as an artefact of the Punic Revival. No one reads his stuff for pleasure, do they? It's almost unreadable. He thought he saying such profound and important things, but it's just his prejudices and fantasies, dressed up in a lot of pompous nineteenth-century waffle as if they were eternal verities.'

We look up at him reclining complacently there, above that great fancy pile of symbols.

'He reminds me of the Mason,' I say, 'resting on his altar at the top of his spiky tower.'

'Up there by the volcano with the God people?'

'That's the one. He was so different from the rest of them. They were so determinedly jolly and positive, and he was so complicated and full of doubt, and yet he'd brought them there, and somehow it was his job to sustain them.'

'From what you've said, they'll do perfectly well when he's gone.'

'I don't know. I think they do need him in a way. He adds another dimension to their tiny world, makes it more spacious, perhaps, maybe even makes it bearable.'

'Maybe he can carry on doing that when he's dead.'

'True. Dead prophets are sometimes preferable to live ones, aren't they? And his stories *were* taking a very dark turn. Poor Helga must really struggle to extract something positive from them.'

We're still looking up at Barca as if he were the man we're talking about, and I start to tell Amanda about the nothingness that's more solid than rock, and the solitary being trapped in that tiny bubble from which there's no possibility of escape. I suppose this sets off all the fears from the period of my captivity, and in the jungle, and up on that high desert where I thought I would freeze to death, because, although I began telling the story in a purely factual way, I rapidly find myself becoming quite distressed by it.

'It's the reality behind everything,' I tell her. 'That's what he said. We only imagine there's a world out there, beyond the wall of our single self. But really there's only one self in existence, all alone for ever, not even able to die, and there's nothing beyond the wall at all.'

I walk away from the monument, to the edge of the flattened top of the artificial hill on which the moon goddess's temple was built. Amanda follows me.

'But that's just silly!' she says, slipping her arm round my waist. 'If we're going to buy the idea that everything we're looking at doesn't really exist, even though we can see it and feel it and touch it, then why on earth should we take seriously the fantasy of a lonely and narcissistic old man, far far away from here, and all by himself at the top of a tower he's built to hide in?'

I laugh, and then, while still laughing, I begin to weep. I had no idea up to this moment how much I'd been haunted by that story, but I feel she's freed me from it. I turn towards her and, for the first time, we really kiss.

I'm at the top of the escarpment. I've been walking for many hours since the first light of day, and I'm looking down from a desert into a small but fertile valley where at one end of a lake, a little village clusters around a church, surrounded by green fields. I notice the tower, on its own bare promontory at the far end of the lake where the ground is stony and uncultivated. It's a strange structure, and rather striking, with its spikes and its lighthouse-like windows, and I think to myself that maybe that's where they keep the Holy Grail. But of course it's the village I aim for as I begin to descend the slope.

Charity finds me in my chair and tells me off. 'Why didn't you ask me to help you? You've been very silly and I'm very cross. You could have fallen and broken your leg! You could have been lying there for hours.'

'I know, but it did feel good.'

'Well, I don't want to come in here and find you dead on the floor.'

She gives me my drugs though the needle in my arm, and changes me, and feeds me, and helps me back to my bed.

'If you want to sit in your chair again, or go out on the balcony, that's absolutely fine,' she tells me, 'but for goodness' sake, do it when one of us is here to help you.'

'I've got a favour to ask you. I've written a letter. It's in the bag on my frame. I just tore some pages out of my notebook, so it's not very neat, but I'd like you to post it. It's to an old friend. I don't think she's as decrepit as I am, and I'd very much like her to come and see me.'

'I'll do that for you certainly. I'll do it tonight on my way home.'

'You won't forget, will you? You know what you're like.'

I meant this to be a gentle tease about her self-confessed scattiness, but I can tell straight away that I've offended her. 'You know I don't forget things like that,' she says a little stiffly. 'Now, is there anything else you need before I go?'

'No, that'll do. I'm starting to feel sleepy already.'

'Okay,' she says. 'Sleep well then, Katerina, and I'll see you tomorrow.'

ACKNOWLEDGEMENTS

This book began during the COVID-19 lockdown in 2020, after a long period of not writing at all. I said to my wife Maggie one evening, 'Enough prevarication; tomorrow I'm going to begin my novel,' and she observed that 'Tomorrow I'm going to begin my novel' wouldn't be a bad opening line. I took her advice, sat down to write the next day with no particular plan, and completed the whole first draft in six weeks. So that is yet another thing for which I must be grateful to Maggie. There are so many. I am so very lucky to be with her.

A first draft is one thing, a finished book is another. I'm not sure if many readers understand how important the role of the editor is in steering a book from its raw beginnings to its final form. Editing someone else's book is a difficult and subtle art. I've been very lucky with all the editors who have worked with me, and my new editor for this book, Sarah Hodgson, is no exception. She's been great.

The copy editor also plays an underrated role in making a writer's prose look smoother and more accomplished than it otherwise would, and I am very grateful to Alison Tulett for once again undertaking this task.

I would also like to thank my friend Sarah Brown who read the first draft and gave me very helpful feedback. Sarah is writing a book about Shakespeare and science fiction. It's quite a feat, and I recommend it.

Many thanks, too, to my fellow Corvus authors, Liz Gifford, Kate London and Vanessa Tait, who read what I'd written in the first week, and encouraged me to carry on.

Finally, I'd like to give my special thanks to Richard Evans, not only for the cover design of this book, but for all the current covers of my Corvus novels. I really love what he's done for them.

The painting of the Last Supper hangs, in the real world, in the church of San Giorgio Maggiore in Venice, just across the water from the Doge's palace, and was made by Tintoretto in the final decade of the sixteenth century. There is an excellent reproduction of it on Wikipedia and it's well worth looking at. (Make the image as big as you can on your screen: there's so much going on in it.) I'm not sure I've ever come across a painting that had such an impact on me.

DON'T MISS THE EDEN TRILOGY FROM CHRIS BECKETT

WINNER OF THE
ARTHUR C. CLARKE AWARD

Chris Beckett is a former university lecturer and social worker. He is the winner of the Edge Hill Short Fiction Award, 2009, for *The Turing Test*, the prestigious Arthur C. Clarke Award, 2013, for *Dark Eden*, and was shortlisted for the British Science Fiction Association best novel award for *Mother of Eden* in 2015 and for *Daughter of Eden* in 2016. *Tomorrow* is his ninth novel.